Lady Louisa Wentworth knows she will never marry well—her family's impoverished estate has ensured as much. Resigned to spinsterhood, the proud beauty has agreed to chaperone a young American heiress who seeks a titled husband through the turbulent waters of London society.

The dashing Duke of Hawkhurst *must* marry wealth for the sake of his family. This well-heeled young American, Miss Jenny Rose, would do quite nicely. But the girl's infuriating chaperone seems determined to keep them apart. And worse still, Hawk finds himself far more attracted to the intoxicating Lady Louisa than to her innocent charge!

A romantic subterfuge is called for—as desperate Hawk plots to draw the heiress into a compromising position, making marriage a necessity. But when it's lovely Louisa instead who falls into his sensuous web, this game of hearts takes a passionate and most unexpected turn . . .

Lorraine Heath

A Duke of Her Own

An Avon Romantic Treasure

AVON BOOKS
An Imprint of HarperCollinsPublishers

This is a work of fiction. Names, characters, places, and incidents are products of the author's imagination or are used fictitiously and are not to be construed as real. Any resemblance to actual events, locales, organizations, or persons, living or dead, is entirely coincidental.

AVON BOOKS
An Imprint of HarperCollins*Publishers*
10 East 53rd Street
New York, New York 10022-5299

Copyright © 2006 by Jan Nowasky
ISBN-13: 978-0-06-112963-6
ISBN-10: 0-06-112963-1
www.avonromance.com

First Avon Books paperback printing: November 2006

Avon Trademark Reg. U.S. Pat. Off. and in Other Countries, Marca Registrada, Hecho en U.S.A.
HarperCollins® is a registered trademark of HarperCollins Publishers Inc.

Printed in the U.S.A.

10 9 8 7 6 5 4 3

For my realist
From your dreamer
With love, always

Chapter 1

London
1888

Gentlewoman of noble birth offers to chaperone
genteel American lady in need of social guidance. References provided. Send inquiry to the
attention of Lady Louisa Wentworth, in care of
this publication.

The Lady's Quarterly Review

"What in the devil is this?"

Lady Louisa Wentworth jerked her
head back slightly to avoid having her nose bruised
by the publication her brother was flapping furi-
ously in front of her face. She'd been enjoying her

1

usual breakfast of porridge laced with butter, milk, and an abundance of sugar before he'd come storming into the morning dining room as though he were some avenging angel. Delicately pressing her linen napkin to each corner of her mouth, she summoned up every ounce of fortitude within her in order to confront his belligerence with serenity.

"It appears to be a magazine," she said.

"Not *this*!" he shouted, frantically jerking the periodical up and down, before slamming it on the table. He pressed a blunt-tipped finger beneath a particular block of words. "This!"

Glancing at the familiar phrasing, she took a calming breath. "My advert."

"Your advert," he repeated with an unnatural calm that caused a frisson of unease to travel the length of her spine. Then he quite simply erupted in anger. "Your advert! You're advertising for a position as a chaperone?"

"Yes, and I have an interview later this morning, so I would appreciate it if you'd cease your shouting so my digestion is not unduly upset."

"You are *not* taking a position as a chaperone. I absolutely forbid it."

Her stomach tightened into a painful knot. Having made her decision after much agonizing, carefully scrutinizing her options, weighing the benefits against the disadvantages, and accepting the enormous consequences that would ensue after effectively changing the direction of her life, she wasn't about to allow him—or anyone else for that matter—to deter or forbid her from seeing her plan through to the finish.

"I'm twenty-six years old, Alex, old enough to do as I please. Serving as a chaperone is a respectable position for the daughter of a peer—"

"Unmarried ladies younger than thirty require a chaperone. How in God's name can you *be* a chaperone when you *need* a chaperone?"

Shoving back the chair, she came to her feet, tossed the linen napkin into her bowl of porridge, and steadfastly met her brother's blistering blue glare. She wondered if her blue eyes darkened as much as his did when challenged.

"A lady requires that her reputation remain pristine when there is some chance in hell that a gentleman will seek her hand in marriage. No gentleman is going to ask for my hand, and you damned well know it." His jaw had dropped at her first bit of profanity; his eyes had bulged at her second. "I have no dowry at all. It is time that I face reality, that *you* face reality. We have nothing of value—"

"We have ourselves."

"Then allow me to rephrase and be perfectly clear. You have value; you have a blasted title. I have nothing. No dowry, no property, no hope of ever enticing a man into looking past my impoverished state—"

"Somewhere a man of rare intelligence exists who can see your true worth."

She laughed bitterly. "Dear brother, how long shall I wait? I've never been courted. Oh, a few men have dallied with me here and there, but it was more for sport than any serious consideration. No one sends me bouquets of flowers. No one sits beside me in the parlor, chatting aimlessly. No one dreads running the formidable gauntlet of asking you for my hand. I'm not seriously sought after—not at all. The reality is that I never shall be. Not as a wife anyway, and I will not stoop to becoming some man's mistress—"

"I would kill any man who even entertained the notion of using you thusly."

Yet she knew he had no compunction whatsoever about keeping a mistress for himself. Men were such odd creatures. Still, she thought it sweet that he would jump to her defense so quickly.

"Alex, I'm weary of being without funds, of not being in charge of my life or my destiny, of waiting in vain for some man to decide I'm worthy of his affections or his attentions when I come with nothing."

Alex looked down at his shoes, slightly worn, a sight that tore at her heart, because he'd always taken such pride in his appearance. Their situation was becoming very sad indeed when he went so long without replacing his shoes.

"You are worthy of a great deal more, Louisa," he said quietly. He lifted his gaze to hers, and she could see how he suffered because the truth of their lives was not as either of them would wish it to be. "But to take a position, to be seen as someone's servant—"

"A chaperone is not considered a servant."

"Semantics. You will serve at their pleasure."

"I shall have pin money." Making light of the situation was the only way that she could avoid weeping every moment of every hour of every day. She was no happier with her decision than Alex was, but honestly, what choice did she have? She was well past her prime, and now that American heiresses had descended on London like ravenous vultures and were taking the choicest among the lords, she had no desire to settle for the scraps—not that any had ever been tossed her way. But still she had to allow for the possibility that it might happen, that some aging lord might see her as a last resort.

But not the young and virile ones. No, they were taking advantage of the wealthy Americans, marrying their daughters when they could come to terms on a generous settlement. Why shouldn't the British ladies take advantage as well? Why should only the men benefit from this madness of Americans wanting to elevate their status by becoming titled?

"Louisa—"

"Alex, I'm quite determined to see this through. Please don't make it any more difficult than it already is." Giving him a gamin smile, she returned to her chair. "I hadn't expected you to hear of my plan. I didn't realize you read ladies' magazines."

Pulling out a chair, he sat as well, his anger effectively doused. It always burned so brightly it could seldom burn for long. "I don't, for God's sake. My mistress showed it to me. She had quite a chuckle over it, I can tell you that."

They were well ensconced in poverty, yet he still managed to keep a mistress, had no qualms whatsoever about asking merchants to extend his credit so he might continue to enjoy all the benefits life had to offer. Louisa detested that particular habit, but it was one all merchants seemed to expect of the nobility—allow them to purchase items in haste and pay in leisure, usually not until the end of the year, if then. And if not this year, then the next.

She, however, believed one should live within one's means. Their problem was that their father, upon his untimely death three years earlier— ironically he'd been reviewing the latest figures for debts owed when his heart quite simply had ceased to beat—had left them with no means whatsoever, and Alex had not accepted that fact yet. Although the state of his shoes indicated he might be on the cusp of facing the unfortunate reality of their situation.

"Your mistress can read?" Louisa asked smugly. "Fancy that. I had no idea you'd chosen a woman based on her intellect."

As fair of complexion as she, Alex had difficulty hiding the fact he was embarrassed. Crimson crept over his chin and high onto his cheeks. He cleared his throat as though hoping to distract her attention from his brilliant coloring. "So what do you know about this position for which you'll be interviewing?"

"It's with the Rose family. They have two daughters—"

"Of New York?"

"You know them?"

"Not personally, of course, but I have heard the rumors. James Rose is a banker, from what I understand, and extremely well-off."

She nodded, acknowledging the rumors he'd heard to be true. "I'll know more once I've spoken with him and his wife. I suspect they are hoping to land each of their daughters a titled husband."

A mischievous smile crossed her brother's handsome face. "You don't say? I've heard these Americans are more than generous when it comes to arranging a marriage settlement." Leaning forward, he whispered conspiratorially, "I'm talking thousands. And here I'll have someone in a position to put in a good word for me."

"Would you want to marry an American heiress?"

"Much less work than serving as her chaperone."

She laughed. "Gentlemen don't serve as chaperones."

Reaching out, he took her hand, all teasing gone from his face. "I'm truly sorry, Louisa, that you've had to resort to actually *working*. I feel as though I've let you down."

"I don't blame you, Alex. You're not the reason

we have so little, although I will admit I do get cross when I think of your mistress living in what would be the dower house if Mama were alive and you ever did marry."

"Thank God, she's not."

She tugged her hand free of his. Their mother had succumbed to death shortly after their father's passing. The physician had identified the cause as pneumonia, brought on by the damp weather, but Louisa had always believed it to be a broken heart. Her mother's rather lengthy list of shortcomings did not include an absence of love for her husband.

"I'm sorry, Louisa. It would only be more difficult if she was alive, and well you know it. Her insatiable appetite for spending went a long way toward putting us where we are today."

"A habit you seem to have embraced."

He grimaced at her chastisement, but he could not deny the truth of her words. "A man must have his distractions; otherwise, his responsibilities will overwhelm him, and he'll be of little use to anyone."

She rolled her eyes at that ludicrous statement while her stomach rumbled. She did wish she hadn't tossed her napkin into her porridge. *Rather bad planning that.*

"And to whom might I attribute that ridiculous sentiment: Hawkhurst or Falconridge?"

"I fail to understand why you think so poorly of my friends."

"They are a bad influence. Neither has bothered

to take a wife and see to the business of his title."

"Neither have I for that matter."

"My point exactly."

"Well, perhaps this year will be the one when we'll each take a wife. A pity the Roses weren't blessed with three daughters. You could steer them all toward us."

"I'd steer them away from you is what I'd do."

"Have pity—"

"On them I shall. *If* I'm offered the position. I have to endure the interview first and leave them with a favorable impression."

"I daresay you shall charm them."

"Can you guarantee that my daughters will marry a man with an impressive title and lineage?"

Louisa fought not to stare at the behemoth who called herself Mrs. Rose. She in no way resembled the delicate buds for which her family was named. Rather she sat in the massive yellow floral-print chair across from Louisa giving the impression that she was queen and failure to provide the right answer would result in her shouting, "Off with her head!"

Louisa darted a glance at the two young ladies sitting on either side of their mother. Jenny's deep green eyes reflected amusement at her mother's question. Louisa had no idea what Kate might be thinking. Her gaze was focused on the novel she was reading, as though she truly couldn't be bothered with this nonsense of finding a husband.

Clearing her throat, Louisa met Mrs. Rose's gaze, a gaze as green as her elder daughter's. Her hair, however, was another matter. She'd passed her vibrant red hair on to her younger daughter, Kate, while Jenny's was a muted shade, more like mahogany.

"I would do my best—"

"And if your best was not good enough?"

Louisa could sense she was on the verge of losing this position. Mrs. Rose seemed dissatisfied with every answer she'd given. Louisa's father had been only an earl. With a haughty sniff, Mrs. Rose had stated she'd hoped for a duke's daughter to serve as chaperone. Louisa suspected in truth she'd hoped for more than that: the daughter of a prince or king.

Mrs. Rose thought Louisa dressed dowdily. Well, not every lady could afford to hop across the Channel to Paris and have Charles Worth design her gowns.

Louisa spoke too quietly. The quiet-spoken Louisa had refrained from explaining that she spoke with refinement, something with which the American mother was obviously not familiar.

Louisa's stomach rumbled. Damnation, it always did when she was tense. Mrs. Rose arched a brow as though the low growl emphasized whatever point she'd been attempting to make.

Louisa fisted her gloved hands in her lap. "I'm well acquainted with the lords. I'm familiar with their character, their heritage, their family scandals, and their family triumphs. I know the value of their titles. I know of their dalliances. I recognize who is suitable and who is not. I would seek a husband for your daughters as I would seek one for myself. One who is kind—"

"I care nothing at all if he is kind. I care only that he is well placed among the aristocracy. Can you guarantee me his position will be such that other American mothers will look upon me with jealousy and unbridled envy because my girls have done so well for themselves?"

With resignation, Louisa shook her head. "I can't guarantee that, no. I would strive to ensure that your daughters would make a good match, but I can't guarantee that others would be envious. In all honesty, I'm not certain any chaperone could meet such exceedingly high expectations. We can only guarantee our own actions, not those of others."

"At least you appear to be honest."

"I *am* honest," Louisa quickly countered. She might desperately need this position, but she could swallow only so much pride without strangling, and she'd reached her limit. "I'm striving not to present a false impression or create false expectations."

Louisa thought she detected one corner of Mrs. Rose's mouth twitching, as though she were more amused than annoyed at Louisa's sudden show of nerve.

Mrs. Rose tapped a neatly manicured finger on

the lace doily covering the arm of the chair. "Were you in a more favorable position, which lord would you select for yourself?"

Louisa's stomach tightened at such a personal and intimate question. It was a test. She was certain the nasty woman was giving her some sort of *test*. She angled her chin only enough to show she wasn't intimidated without appearing haughty. "Having never been in a more favorable position, I've never given the matter a great deal of thought."

"Oh, come, come. Every woman fantasizes. Who would be your ideal mate?"

"Oh, Mama, surely you are aware that the man a woman fantasizes about is not necessarily the one who would make an ideal mate," Jenny said.

Louisa was stunned that the young lady had spoken exactly what she had been thinking. An image of Hawkhurst—dark, roguish, dangerous— flashed unexpectedly through her mind. An odd thing really, as he was neither fantasy nor ideal . . . well, perhaps he was a bit of fantasy, if she was honest with herself, and hadn't she just claimed to be honest?

Adding to that honesty was the admittance that he was partly responsible for her present situation. Whenever he visited her brother, he ignored her as easily as any other man. If she couldn't even snag the attention of her brother's most trusted friend, then what hope was left to her? None.

"Why, Lady Louisa, you're blushing," Jenny said.

"I'm simply not accustomed to being bombarded with such personal inquiries. We English are a bit more circumspect when it comes to hiring someone to do a specific job. Who would be ideal for me, Mrs. Rose, has no bearing upon who might be ideal for your daughters. If it is your fear that I will offer some competition, I assure you I will not." A painful admission, but again a truthful one. "All my efforts and energy shall go toward fulfilling your expectations."

"I admit I have not found your answers satisfactory—"

Louisa's stomach knotted as disappointment swelled through her. Did she graciously accept defeat or did she make one last, valiant effort—

"Were you to hire me to serve as a social chaperone for your daughters, I shall do all in my power to see that you are not disappointed in the outcome of our association. We would all benefit, and is that not the measure of a successful partnership?"

"Do you often interrupt your elders?" Mrs. Rose asked.

"No, I hardly ever interrupt anyone, and I apologize for my rudeness. I simply wished to make my final"—plea made her sound as though she were begging, and she refused to stoop that low and acknowledge that was exactly what she was doing—"to address what I consider strong points in my favor before you said anything we might both wish you hadn't."

"What I'd planned to say was that I've grown

quite weary of our going in circles, but have decided you will do. You're hired." She came to her feet, with a rush of movement that had her skirts rustling. "My husband will work out the vulgar details of payment with you. You may move in tomorrow. A room will be readied near my daughters so you are available to them at all times. Don't disappoint me, Lady Louisa. I'm not someone you want to disappoint. I can make your life miserable—"

"Yes, yes, I think you've made your position quite clear, my dear," Mr. Rose said, speaking for the first time since Louisa had come into the room and introductions had been made. He was sitting in a chair off to the side by the window as though he were merely an afterthought.

Mrs. Rose gave him a pointed glare, and Louisa couldn't help but wonder if she'd made his life miserable. It seemed to be her purpose: to overwhelm and intimidate.

"Very well," Mrs. Rose said. "I shall leave you and the girls to get acquainted. I have other pressing matters that require my attention."

And with that she swept from the room as though a strong gale blew at her back. Louisa found herself sinking against the chair, an equal mixture of relief and dread swirling through her. What had she fought so incredibly hard to get herself into, and how soon before she began having regrets?

"Not to worry. My wife is more bark than bite," Mr. Rose said, as he moved to the chair his wife had vacated. He was well fed, well dressed, and well-mannered.

Louisa felt some sort of response was required, and she had no wish to insult her new employer. While she had little doubt Mr. Rose brought the money into the household, she suspected Mrs. Rose oversaw its departure. "She seems to know her own mind and what she wants."

"We're new money. My lovely wife believes that our daughters' marrying English lords will give us the prestige of *old* money." He repeatedly stroked his thumb and forefinger over his graying mustache. He had kind eyes, not quite brown, not quite green, and a shy sort of smile that seemed out of place on a man who was reputed to be as wealthy, successful, and determined to leave his mark on the world as he was.

Louisa had liked him immediately upon introduction. She wished she could say the same of the formidable Mrs. Rose.

"My wife referred to the vulgar details of your payment. Nothing vulgar in honest work. You aristocrats need to accept that if you're to survive."

"We've done quite well for ourselves for several centuries, thank you very much," Louisa said, grimacing at the haughty tone of her voice, not to mention the audacity of her remark. Was she not practically begging for this position? "My apologies—"

"No need to apologize, my dear. I was once where you are now. Didn't have two pennies to rub together, and I was willing to do what had to be done to survive. So let's talk vulgarities, shall we?"

They discussed her salary, or rather he told her what he planned to pay—five pounds a month plus a bonus on the day each girl married—and as it was an extremely generous arrangement with which only a fool would find fault—and Louisa did not consider herself a fool—she accepted the terms without argument or hesitation. He welcomed her into the household with a firm handshake and a promise to have the papers outlining their agreement ready for her signature when she arrived the following day.

After he walked from the room, all that remained was for her to put the young ladies at ease regarding how her duties would affect their lives. She had a sense, based on Jenny's comments, that the lady enjoyed teasing and having fun. She had no idea what to expect of Kate. Louisa smiled brightly at Jenny since Kate was still absorbed by the contents of her novel. "So as I understand it this will be your first Season in London."

"We were here in the spring, so the summer will be our second season in London," Kate murmured.

Laughing, Jenny did what Louisa had been tempted to do: She snatched the book out of Kate's grasp. With a shriek Kate lunged for it, and Jenny promptly shoved it beneath her bustled skirt, sitting on it and looking quite smug.

"Give me my book," Kate demanded.

"Not until you stop being so rude to our new chaperone. Can't you see she's nervous?"

"I'm not nervous," Louisa protested. She grimaced at Jenny's challenging look. "All right, I am a little."

"You shouldn't be, now that the dragon has left the lair," Kate said, settling back in her chair as though resolved to the fact that her sister wouldn't return her treasured possession.

"Kate is upset that Mother is handling the hunt for our husbands as though it were a business arrangement."

"One should marry for love," Kate said.

"I disagree. One should marry for passion, and love will follow."

"You must have love *before* you can have passion," Kate said.

Jenny looked at Louisa. "What do you think? Which comes first, love or passion?"

Shifting in her chair, Louisa felt acutely uncomfortable with the boldness of her question. "Having experienced neither, I fear I'm hardly in a position to advise."

"Then what makes you think you are qualified to serve as our chaperone?" Kate asked.

"If you'd been listening, silly, you'd know. She gave all her qualifications to Mother."

"I was listening, and I don't care about any of the things she mentioned. I don't want my marriage arranged—"

"Marriages are no longer arranged—"

"The hell they're not. They've fancied up the

process, but it's the same thing. As long as Mother approves of him, it doesn't matter whether or not we love him."

"Which is the very reason Lady Louisa is so important. She will guide us toward only men whom we can love. Isn't that so?" Jenny asked.

Louisa took a deep, calming breath. "That is my hope."

"Have you any candidates?"

"Well, I suppose to begin with, I should find out what you're looking for in a man."

"Splendid!" Jenny pulled the book from beneath her and tossed it into her sister's lap. "There, you see, Lady Louisa is on our side, so victory is assured."

"You make it sound as though you're engaged in war," Louisa said.

"Did you not just meet our mother?" Kate asked. "I could have sworn she was the reason your tummy rumbled."

"Don't be bothered by Kate's sour disposition," Jenny said quickly, before Louisa could respond to Kate's rudeness. "Like Mother, she has her own ideas regarding how one should go about finding the love of her life."

"You don't have to find him. He should find you," Kate said.

Jenny rolled her eyes. "Enough on this subject." She sat up straighter, more attentively. Although neither sister was plump, Kate was considerably rounder, while Jenny was a bit taller, nearer to Louisa's own height.

"Tell us about the prospects," Jenny demanded.

Louisa laughed, a laugh fraught with insecurities as she sought to find a balance in this awkward arrangement: matchmaker-chaperone. It was an emerging position for ladies of quality. As far as she knew no books had been written to explain one's exact duties or responsibilities.

"As I mentioned earlier, I think you should tell me what you are searching for in a husband. Then I can compare your desires against what I know of the available lords, and I hope we'll find a suitable match."

"You want my reality rather than my fantasy?" Jenny asked. "Because as you'll recall, I don't consider them to be the same at all."

Louisa felt the heat of embarrassment warm her cheeks. Americans always spoke so brashly. "Perhaps a little of both would be in order," she said.

"Well, he must be handsome," Jenny said. "Don't you agree, Kate?"

"I care little about his appearance. I care only about how he makes me feel."

"Well, if he's hideous, he will make you feel quite ill."

"He won't be hideous."

"He might be if you don't give Lady Louisa some guidance."

"Ladies," Louisa said before their bickering could escalate further. She hadn't expected her charges to be so vastly different in opinion or temperament. Finding them each a husband

would prove a challenge, a man approved by their
mother almost impossible. "I think it would be
best if you simply each told me what you require."

"Passion," Jenny said.

"Love," Kate countered.

They then proceeded to return to their debate
regarding which came first. Oh, the upcoming
Season was going to be jolly good fun.

Chapter 2

⁓ ⚬⚬ ⁓

"I didn't think matters could get any worse."
Randolph Selwyn, the fifth Duke of
Hawkhurst, moved the glass of brandy from his
lips and arched a brow at Alexander Wentworth,
the sixth Earl of Ravensley, where he stood staring
morosely into the fire, an arm resting on the marble mantel. "You always did lack imagination."

In the plush chair beside him, Michael Tremayne,
the fourth Marquess of Falconridge shook his dark
head and chuckled.

Ravensley jerked around to face his two longtime friends, apparently appreciating neither the
wryly delivered comment nor the subsequent
chuckles. "I see no humor in our present situation."

"Only because you see humor in nothing,"

Falconridge said. "So you lack humor and imagination." He paused for emphasis, his green eyes sharp as he no doubt hit upon the crux of the problem. "And money."

"The humor and imagination I can do without, but I'm finding it increasingly difficult to manage without the money. I'm having a time of it getting anyone to extend me credit. How are you managing?"

Falconridge held up his glass, swirled the liquid around and around, as though mesmerized by the flowing amber. "I'm not. My mistress walked out on me this week. Packed up her baubles and went. Apparently she found a gentleman who could purchase her the useless trinkets I was having difficulty providing."

"I'm sorry to hear that."

"Not nearly as sorry as I am. She was incredible in bed. The best I'd ever had actually."

Hawk knew they wouldn't ask after the situation concerning his mistress, as they knew him well enough to know he'd never taken one. He grew too easily bored with women, had never met one who could hold his attention once the thrill of the chase was past. It was one of the reasons he'd never given serious contemplation to marriage. How did a man force himself to visit his wife's bed, night after night, year after year, until she'd blessed him with an heir and a spare? The duty of procreation effectively removed any sense of enjoyment, any hope for spontaneity, as did the familiar. He enjoyed new experiences. Marriage guaranteed boredom.

"We've all been in this difficult spot for some time now," Hawk said. "Why, of a sudden, are you so bothered by it?"

Ravensley dropped into a chair as though he no longer had the strength to remain standing, as though the burden he carried had suddenly become too heavy. "Louisa."

Hawk's stomach tightened at the mere mention of the woman's name—as irritating a female as he'd ever met. Eight years his junior, she'd been troublesome from the moment he, at the age of fourteen, had met her when he'd visited Ravensley's estate for the first time. She'd caught him and her brother in the stables testing out the old man's pipe. At fifteen, it had been the old man's liquor.

At sixteen, it had been the daughter of the old man's valet—a young woman six years Hawk's senior who took extreme delight in initiating young lads to the joys of manhood when she wasn't seeing after Lady Louisa. In a corner stall in the stables, with the woman and a mound of hay beneath him, Hawk had been lost in bliss until Lady Louisa had suddenly come upon them and shrieked that he was killing her nanny. She'd tried to pull him off, grabbing his shoulder and shaking him. He'd always been grateful that he'd been savoring the initiation and had been in no great hurry to unbutton his trousers, and was merely lying atop the woman, but her harsh breathing at his earnest attentions no doubt did sound as though she was fighting for air. His subsequent yelling for Ravensley and Falconridge—both having experienced the woman's talents earlier—had resulted in their ushering Lady Louisa away, her being none the wiser regarding his true circumstance that afternoon. Ever since that unfortunate encounter, he'd taken great care to avoid her.

"Your sister? What of her?" he asked.

"This morning she took a position as a social chaperone." Ravensley drained the remainder of brandy from his glass. "She's gone to work, for God's sake."

Falconridge shrugged. "It's a reputable position for a lady of quality."

"Wait a moment," Hawk said. "I didn't realize your sister was that old."

"She's not. She is but six-and-twenty, but she has determined no man will ever have her, and, therefore, her age is a moot issue."

"Surely, someone—"

"No," Ravensley interrupted. "No one. She has no dowry. And she is quite right. Without some financial gain to offer a man, her cause is hopeless. And I'm to blame. As head of the family, I should have taken action long ago to ensure that matters didn't deteriorate this far."

"What sort of action could you have taken?" Falconridge asked.

"Married one of these American heiresses who are so set on getting themselves a title."

Hawk got to his feet and replaced Ravensley before the fire, his mood suddenly taking a plunge into the pit of despair at the thought of any proud English lady, especially one of his acquaintances, now serving at the pleasure of others—of wealthy Americans at that. "For whom is she working?"

"The Rose family."

Hawk spun around. "Of New York?"

Ravensley grinned. "My reaction exactly. Wealthy with two very attractive daughters, from what I understand. I've decided the best thing I can do for Louisa is to see that these girls are quickly wed, and that one of them is quickly wed to me. Without charges to oversee, she will no longer be a chaperone, and I will then have the means to provide properly for her. Two birds with one stone, as it were.

"And with Louisa in the Rose household, I have an advantage. She can serve as my spy, offering me advice on how to effectively woo the lady of my choice while keeping me informed of other lords' sad progress. I wondered if either of you wanted to have a go at the other sister."

His gaze darted between Hawk and Falconridge, who was slowly shaking his head.

"You never were good with numbers," Falconridge said. "Two of them and three of us. It doesn't work, old man."

"I'll admit it's not perfect, but it does offer a challenge, and I've found challenges sadly lacking of late. Are you gentlemen interested?"

"I'll confess I'm intrigued by the possibilities,"

Hawk said. "No harm, I suppose, in at least hearing what Lady Louisa has to say about the ladies in question."

Hell and damnation. A man without means was as trapped in an undesirable position as a woman without a dowry.

Hawk detested the shortsighted ancestors who'd come before him and refused to branch into anything beyond agriculture. His own father had failed to notice that tenants were leaving the land in order to work in city factories, and little was going into the family coffers while a good deal was going out. Hawk had nothing to offer a woman except his title, and so he was forced to make his selection based upon what a woman could offer him financially. It was a damned good thing he didn't believe in love.

He'd been toying with the notion of seeking out an American heiress, and so Ravensley's suggestion had some merit to it. And his friend was correct in his assessment: They would have an advantage with Lady Louisa sharing her insights and observations . . .

If only Hawk could focus on her words rather than the lengthy slope of her throat, which gave a man ample room for nibbling. When had her neck lengthened and become so enticing? He'd attended her coming-out ball, but had stayed true to his habit of avoiding her. A woman he could never possess was a tempting morsel he could scarce resist. God only knew what his trusted friend would do to him if he knew the wayward path his thoughts were suddenly traversing.

Along with Falconridge and Ravensley, Hawk was sitting in Ravensley's library where Lady Louisa had been selecting a favorite book to take with her when she moved into the Rose residence the following morning. Now she sat in a chair running her finger around the edge of the leather-bound book in her lap, and he couldn't help but wonder what it would feel like to have her stroke that finger along his shoulder, down his chest, across his belly, down—

"—Your Grace?"

He snapped his gaze up to hers. Had she always had such incredibly blue eyes? So large, so round, so innocent? And her hair was as golden as the wheat that had once covered his land. If he could only spin every silken strand into gold, he wouldn't have to endure the necessity of finding a woman with money to take to wife. And if money weren't a requirement, the possibilities would become infinite.

He cleared his throat. "My apologies. I became distracted."

"It wasn't my intent to bore you."

He'd been far from bored, but he certainly couldn't reveal that bit of information without fear that she might inquire as to what was holding his attention if not her words. And then what would he say? That he'd been dreaming of sending his lips on a journey along her throat?

Not only would that declaration sit poorly with

her, but it might very well end his friendship with Ravensley.

"Again, I apologize. I'm a bit weary this afternoon."

"The result of a late night?"

"Hawk's sleeping habits are none of your concern, Louisa," Ravensley said sternly. He turned to Hawk. "She was asking what you knew of the Rose family."

"Ah. Not much actually. That they are well-off and have two daughters in want of titled husbands." He held Lady Louisa's gaze. Her eyes were the same blue hue as her brother's, and yet they were far more intriguing, far more enticing. "I thought our reason for coming here was so you might tell us what *you* knew of the family."

"So you might court the daughters?"

Was that disappointment he heard in her voice, saw reflected in her eyes?

"So I might contemplate the possibilities, determine the probabilities that one of the ladies might make an agreeable match, and perhaps have you put in a good word for me—for us. For your brother, Falconridge, and me."

Falconridge was sitting on the other side of Ravensley, but he seemed to be paying no more attention than Hawk was. Did any of them wish to marry?

"Rather calculating on your part," she said, not bothering to mask the censure in her voice.

"On all our parts, I would say. It behooves a gentleman not to take the matter of matrimony lightly. So what do you know of the Rose sisters?" Hawk asked.

She opened the book, closed it. "Their mother has charged me with finding them suitable husbands."

"There! See!" Ravensley slapped his hand on an arm of the chair. "You will help us, Louisa, and in so doing, you'll help yourself. We are quite the catch, don't you know. So tell us everything you've learned about the daughters and leave nothing out. We shall sift through the information for pertinent details."

Her gaze darted between the three men, and Hawk wondered at her hesitation, as though she feared disappointing someone.

"Jenny is the older. She is two-and-twenty, while Kate is twenty," she finally said with as much enthusiasm as one reciting memorized passages from a work of literature.

"Are they beauties?" Falconridge asked.

"I can't answer that for you. As I'm sure you are well aware, beauty is in the eye of the beholder."

That statement didn't bode well. Unlike Ravensley, Hawk did not lack imagination. As a matter of fact, at times, it was far too vivid. Her words conjured up visions of women with absurdly large noses, pointed teeth, and coarse hair growing out of warts on their chins. "Would *you* classify them as beautiful?" he asked.

She glanced down at the book. "Yes."

"Charming?"

She lifted her gaze. "They are two very different ladies. It does them a disservice to apply the same description to each of them."

He fought to rein in his impatience. "Then describe each of them separately, which I believe is what your brother asked of you to begin with."

She picked up the book, set it in her lap, and he wondered if she'd been tempted to bonk him on the head with it. Why was she not more forthcoming with the information? What was it about the ladies she had no desire for them to know? If he did learn something unsavory, would it alter his plans? He wasn't certain it would.

Again, she lifted the book, set it down, looked at each of them, and said, "They defy description. They must be met to be understood, to be known, to be adequately appreciated."

"For pity's sake, Louisa, you spent the morning with the ladies, did you not?" Ravensley snapped. "Surely you can provide us with less cryptic information."

"Alex, I have been charged with finding them suitable husbands," she repeated.

"Three candidates have willingly strolled into your library, lambs before the slaughter. I fail to understand why you are not more forthcoming," Hawk said.

"It appears you have a very low opinion of marriage," she said.

"Name me one gentleman who has a high opinion of it. Men marry when their backs are to the wall, and they have no other recourse."

"Are you implying your back is to the wall?"

Damnation! How had this conversation turned to a discourse on him and his views of marriage?

"I believe we have strayed from our purpose," he said. "You are charged with finding them suitable husbands, and here we are."

She took a deep breath, angled her chin slightly, and folded her hands around the book as though she needed it to gain strength. "Yes, well, unfortunately, I do not find the three of you suitable."

Falconridge scoffed; Ravensley shook his head. Hawk could do little more than stare at her in stunned disbelief. He was a duke, had been a duke since the age of twelve. Of course he was suitable.

"I'm sorry, Alex," she said quietly, "but it is not my place to convince you that the ladies are worthy of you, rather you must convince me that you are worthy of an introduction."

"I am your brother!"

"I'm well aware of that fact, and it pains me greatly that I can't recommend you without hesitation." She sighed. "But I can't."

"This is damned ridiculous," Falconridge stated, coming to his feet. "I will not grovel—"

"Sit down," Ravensley said. "She is merely being temperamental."

"I refuse to stoop so low as to have to prove myself worthy to anyone, least of all a foreigner." Falconridge sneered. "Or a chaperone."

Hawk saw Lady Louisa flinch, and his heart went out to her. Obviously none of this was easy for any of them. "See here, Falconridge," he said, "there's no cause to take your frustrations out on Lady Louisa."

Falconridge bowed slightly. "My apologies, my lady. I've been accused on more than one occasion of having too much pride, but, along with my title, it is all that is left to me, so I shall hang on to it for a bit longer if you don't mind. I bid you all good night and shall see myself out."

He'd spun on his heel and was halfway across the room before Ravensley called out, "Falcon—"

"Let him go," Hawk said. "Less competition for us."

Ravensley turned and glared at his sister. "That didn't go well at all, now did it? You somehow managed to insult one of my friends—"

"While you managed to insult me. I am not temperamental."

Ah, but she did have a temper. It was there in her eyes, flaring brightly, turning the blue slightly darker until it resembled the hottest flame in a fire. God help him, Hawk felt his body tightening with desire at the very sight of so much emotion. Had he ever seen a woman exhibit true anger? The women he usually entertained were only too pleased to have his attention. They would certainly never challenge, rebuff, or question him. He fully expected Lady Louisa to fling the book at her brother at any moment. She was grasping it so hard that her knuckles were turning white.

"All women are temperamental," Ravensley stated flatly. "You are a woman, and, therefore, it stands to reason you are temperamental."

"That is a ludicrous assumption, equal to saying all men are dolts."

"Now see here—"

"No, you see."

She rose swiftly. She was breathing harshly, quickly, her breasts straining against the fabric of her gown, and Hawk's body tightened further. He was going to be in a rather embarrassing predicament if he suddenly had to come to his feet. He tried to focus on reading the title of the book she was holding, anything, anything, to avert his attention from her directly.

She was the daughter of an earl, the sister to his most trusted friend, not some common doxy. His reaction was entirely inappropriate, not to mention highly disconcerting.

"It's because of my mistress, isn't it?" Ravensley was saying, and Hawk wondered what else of the conversation he might have missed, what had led to that assumption. "You don't approve, you never have, and yet you must realize all gentlemen of good breeding have a mistress."

"I don't," Hawk said laconically, which brought two sets of blue eyes to bear down on him. He wasn't certain why he'd felt a need to defend himself, to offer up something that might cause him to gain a bit of favor with Lady Louisa. He was attempting to pursue his matrimonial goals, and she served as the shortest, least bothersome path to his destination. Or at least those had been his thoughts before this fiasco of a meeting.

"Lady Louisa, you had stated earlier, before

tempers began to flare, that you did not consider us worthy of an introduction. Would you care to elaborate on how you arrived at your assessment? After all, it is quite possible you have misconceptions where we are concerned."

She hugged the book to her chest as though it could serve as a shield. "When my brother returns home at dawn, after spending an evening in your company, he reeks of alcohol and cheap perfume. He must be assisted up the stairs, and his tongue is quite loose. I shall not embarrass either of us by repeating his utterances. Suffice it to say I know no lady is safe in your presence, you value only the conquest, but not the prize, and are usually quick to discard what you have won. How can I recommend you to a lady for whom I have been given the responsibility of ensuring her lifelong happiness?"

Rubbing his index finger below his lower lip, he studied her solemnly. She knew quite a bit more about him than he realized. Little wonder she'd not favor him with an introduction. "I thought her happiness was dependent upon her acquiring a title. What lady wouldn't be thrilled by the prospect of becoming a duchess?"

"And when the novelty of being a duchess wears off?"

"Hopefully by the time that happens, I shall have my heir and my spare, and I will not fault her for seeking her happiness elsewhere."

"And her pleasure?"

He was taken aback by her question. What did

ladies of quality know about pleasure? In particular, what did Lady Louisa know? Was her knowledge acquired through experience or hearsay? What exactly had Ravensley mumbled as he was carted up the stairs to bed, and what questions might she have asked him in his vulnerable state when he was most likely to have a loose tongue? Seemed it was so loose, Hawk was damned surprised it hadn't fallen out.

Hawk cleared his throat. "Of course. I would never deny a woman the opportunity for pleasure."

She regarded him closely as though trying to determine if his words should be taken at face value or had an underlying meaning. If she were any other woman, he would have intended a double entendre. He was balanced on a fine edge here, feeling as though he were only just seeing her for the first time, and he could not deny he was intrigued . . . was in danger of flirting with her, enticing her to see things his way. Seduction was a great convincer.

"How terribly generous of you," she finally stated.

"I thought so."

"I'm sorry, Your Grace, but you've said nothing to convince me that I should recommend you. If anything, you have managed to reinforce my belief you would be entirely unsuitable."

"Your stance seems a bit harsh."

"Be that as it may, it is my stance. However, on the off chance I have misjudged your suitability,

I won't do anything to undermine your—or my brother's—attempts to win the ladies over, but neither will I encourage you to seek their favor, nor shall I encourage them to favor you."

"Louisa—"

"My mind is set, Alex," she said, effectively cutting off whatever plea Ravensley was on the verge of delivering. "Now, if you gentlemen will excuse me, I have a great many matters that need my attention before I leave on the morrow."

Her repeatedly finding fault with Hawk had effectively doused his desire. He came to his feet easily, bowing slightly. "I appreciate your forthrightness, Lady Louisa."

"I did not mean to be cruel."

"I do not believe you could be cruel if you tried. I further appreciate that you take your responsibilities so seriously."

"If I may be so bold, Your Grace, perhaps it is time you did the same."

"I *am* trying, my lady."

"There are Americans for whom I'm not responsible—"

"But none so wealthy. And while you may find fault with me, allow me to reassure you I'm not one to settle for less when I can have more."

"Yes, based on my brother's ramblings, I understand you are a man who prefers excess in all things."

Hawk was damned tempted to snatch the book from her hands and hurl it at her brother. It was not often he was speechless.

"I believe my point has been taken," she said quietly. "I bid you a good night." Without waiting for them to reply, she strolled gracefully from the room.

"I damned well don't believe her refusing to help us," Ravensley said, once the door closed behind her.

"I have to wonder exactly what you might have said while you were bumbling up the stairs," Hawk countered.

"Nothing of any consequence, I assure you. Late nights, drinking, carousing . . . I suppose I can't blame her for thinking poorly of us. But no matter. We are still the best of the lot, and we should have no trouble winning the hands of the Rose sisters. Some brandy to toast the challenge that awaits us?"

"By all means."

Hawk glanced back toward the door. He feared a greater challenge than gaining the attention of a Rose daughter might be hovering on the horizon. For him, the challenge might turn out to be ignoring the Rose chaperone.

Chapter 3

"**I** can hardly signify that you insulted my friends to the degree that you did."

Louisa understood perfectly that Alex was not only furious but hurt. She'd done more than insult his friends; she'd wounded him to the core. She folded her shawl with extreme care, not because the woolen garment was particularly delicate but because she felt fragile at the moment and needed something comforting to steady her. Speaking the truth had been no easier for her than hearing it had been for them.

"I'm sorry, Alex, but as I stated, I've been charged with finding appropriate husbands for these ladies, and you and your friends are hardly appropriate."

"The ladies are looking for titled husbands. You

don't get much more titled than a duke, unless
you latch on to royalty, and I daresay that's not
going to happen. We are all very nicely titled,
thank you very much."

Louisa placed the shawl in the trunk. She'd dismissed her maid the moment Alex had barged
into her bedroom. While the door remained ajar
and the possibility existed that the servants would
overhear the conversation, they were all adept at
keeping their master's business to themselves. Or
at least they had been when they were properly
paid. Several had sought employment elsewhere.
The three who remained were quite loyal.

"It is the ladies' mother who is so set on their
acquiring titled husbands, not the ladies themselves." She faced Alex. "They are seeking love
and passion. How can I, with a clear conscience,
recommend gentlemen who in all likelihood can
never give them love, who want them solely for
financial reasons?"

"Do you honestly believe you will find a peer
anywhere in England who will not look upon
them and first hear the clinking of sovereigns?"

"We can always hope."

"You are not that naïve. Just this morning you
were lamenting your own impoverished state and
how it guaranteed that you would never have a
husband."

"Yet you were arguing that a man would see
my true worth. Can the same not be said for these
American heiresses?"

He turned to the window, gazing out on the

night-shrouded gardens, his hands clasped tightly behind his back. He seldom got cross with her, but when he did his temper could be quite frightful. She knew he was attempting to regain control of his emotions before he said something they might both regret.

Gathering up her courage, she took a tentative step toward him. "Jenny and Kate are extremely kind and so very young and much more naïve than I. They argue over which comes first: passion or love. Jenny wants passion and Kate wants love, and I'm well aware that in all likelihood they will find themselves married to an aloof lord who will grant them neither passion nor love. While I could argue all night they are my main concern, in reality, it is myself for whom I worry."

She saw him stiffen, his back going straighter than before, and she took another step toward him. "I will be their chaperone for only a short while. It is an odd sort of venture. In order to be successful, I must not be in the position overly long. One Season, two at the most. The heiresses will be married, and I will be searching for another lady in need of my services. I must be known as a chaperone who delivers what she promises: a lord of the highest caliber. You and your friends have proven on more than one occasion that you do not qualify."

He spun around. "If I were to marry one of these heiresses, you would not have to seek another lady to chaperone. You would have an allowance. I would see after your needs, and with a generous settlement, I would be in a position to offer a dowry and find you a husband. Do you not see that we are in the ideal position to help each other?"

"You are asking me to compromise my integrity."

"You owe these ladies nothing!"

"Have you never made a promise?"

"Of course, I've made promises."

"Did you keep them?"

She could see in his startled eyes that he'd recognized the trap she'd set. She loved him dearly, but sometimes he clearly underestimated the cleverness of women.

"Did you?" she prodded.

"Yes," he finally admitted reluctantly.

"Why?"

"Because it was the honorable thing to do."

"Do you expect less of me?"

"I suppose not." He was clearly disgruntled with the truth, but at least his temper had waned. "Still, I think you have vastly underrated us as possible matches for your ladies."

She smiled benignly. "You perhaps. But not Falconridge. And certainly not Hawkhurst."

Without a doubt Hawkhurst was the worst of the lot. Her brother had gotten into no mischief whatsoever before that one had come into his life.

"We enjoy having a jolly good time. I don't see that as a fault."

"Drinking, carousing, and getting into mischief until dawn . . . the very fact you don't see these behaviors as a fault is what makes you so very unsuitable."

"Rather convoluted thinking there, Louisa."

"Not from where I stand. I wish I could recommend you, I truly do, but I simply can't."

"But you won't speak unfavorably about us?"

"Did I not say exactly that earlier?"

"Yes, but you are a woman, and women are fickle."

"You have such a poor opinion of women, it is a wonder you are seeking to find a wife."

"It is my obligation to do so."

"Yet one more reason why you would not be suitable."

He laughed boisterously. "Do you honestly believe any man *wants* to get married?"

"I would think so, yes."

"Trust me, dear sister, when I tell you that *no* man desires marriage."

Louisa had always thought moving out of the home in which she'd been born and raised would come about only when she was moving into the home of the man she'd married. It was a strange experience indeed to stand in a bedchamber that was not hers and to try to envision it as hers—temporarily to be sure—but for several weeks, perhaps months. Perhaps years!

She had stayed at the country estate of friends, but never for more than a few days. She had been a visitor, a welcomed guest.

Within this household, she was something else

entirely. Certainly not family. Not quite a servant. Not a friend.

With a sigh she sat on the bed, on the unfamiliar comforter. She was a chaperone, and this was now her home. In time, she would move on to another. Like a gypsy. With no one place to call her own.

She'd known she'd pay this price when she'd made her decision to place her advert. It was silly to be melancholy because her endeavor had resulted in success.

She watched as her personal maid, Colette, assigned to her by Mrs. Rose, transferred her things from her trunks to her wardrobe. She'd brought all her clothing and feared much of it might be too fancy for one in her recently acquired position. She should blend into the woodwork. During her previous Seasons, her own chaperone, a married cousin, had been exceedingly discreet, and Louisa planned to follow her example. To draw no attention to herself but to be very attentive of her charges and any gentlemen who gave them notice.

When she was finished, Colette had a footman carry the trunks away, then she left with the promise to return to help Louisa prepare for dinner. That was a promising sign. At least Mrs. Rose didn't expect her to eat in the kitchen with the servants.

With a sigh, Louisa got up, walked to the window, and looked out on the street. She was not the lady of the house. She didn't have to see to the meals or discuss daily menus with the cook. It was rather unsettling to be free and yet fettered. What in the world was she to do with her time?

She needed to arrange a social calendar, and in order to do that, she needed to review the invitations that the ladies had received. She also needed to make a list of necessary introductions.

The responsibilities suddenly overwhelmed her, because the truth was that beneath each task was the burden of finding the proper husband for these ladies. Yet how did one know who the proper husband was?

A soft rap on the door had her turning away from the window and her thoughts. Before she could bid entry, the door opened, and Jenny slipped her head inside and smiled brightly. "Are you all settled?"

"For now."

"Care for some company?"

"I'd love some company."

"Wonderful." She marched into the room, dragging Kate, who was holding a book, along behind her. "We thought we could discuss our expectations."

"That's a splendid idea," Louisa said.

"*She* thought we could discuss our expectations," Kate said, jerking her head toward her sister. "I can't see that any discussion is going to make any difference at all."

"I brought the invitations," Jenny said, handing a small bundle to Louisa.

"Lovely. I was just thinking that I needed to

see where you stood among"—how to phrase it politely—"those issuing invitations."

"Don't worry," Kate said. "We get only the finest. Bertie was quite taken with Jenny."

"The Prince of Wales has acknowledged you?"

Jenny shrugged. "He smiled at me. We had a single dance. Nothing more than that really."

"Your mother must have been delighted."

"An understatement," Kate said. "Judging by her reaction, you would have thought she expected Jenny to become a princess. Unfortunately for you, that's when she got the notion to hire a social chaperone."

"Actually, I'm quite pleased that she did," Louisa said.

Jenny sat on the bed. "Now, tell us about you."

Kate took a seat in a nearby chair, surprising Louisa by not opening her book and burying her nose in it.

"There's really not much to say," Louisa said, sitting in a chair and beginning to sift through the invitations. She had to admit to being quite impressed. They were being invited to soirees hosted by the upper crust.

"Have you ever been in love?" Kate asked.

"No." Louisa did not look up.

"Have you ever known passion?" Jenny asked.

Louisa looked up then. "I don't mean to be rude, but truly, you girls need to broaden your horizons. Your topics of conversation seem to be terribly narrow. Tell me what you like to do."

"I like to read," Kate said.

"What a revelation!" Jenny exclaimed, with a roll of her eyes. "She never would have guessed that."

"What do you like to read?" Louisa asked, ignoring Jenny's sarcasm.

"Romantic stories."

"What else do you like?" Louisa asked, encouraged, feeling at long last that she might be making progress.

"Chocolate. Which is the reason I'm more round than Jenny. I like to eat chocolate while reading."

"And she does an inordinate amount of reading," Jenny said.

"I'm not certain it's possible to read too much," Louisa said.

"She never goes anywhere without a book in hand."

"Because I'm easily bored by your company," Kate said. "I must have something to keep me entertained."

"Ladies, I believe we've once again strayed from our topic," Louisa said, before more insults could be delivered. "You were to tell me what you enjoy doing."

"I prefer being outdoors," Jenny said. "I love riding horses and bicycles."

"Bicycles?" Louisa asked. "Aren't they rather unsteady?"

"The high wheeler, yes. I tried that once and took a topple. Have a little scar right above my brow," she said, pointing. "The high-wheeled tricycle is safer, and I've tried it, but I don't really enjoy safe. Do you?"

"Of course, I enjoy being safe."

"But safe is boring," Jenny said, shifting around on the bed until she was lying on her stomach, her chin resting on her hands. "I like excitement."

"So you want a husband who is exciting," Louisa said, striving to narrow the girl's wants down.

"Most assuredly. Handsome, as we've already established. And a fine kisser. Which of the lords have you experienced?"

Louisa felt as though she'd just swallowed the sun, and the heat was radiating out of her body. "I beg your pardon?"

"Which of the lords have you kissed?"

Slowly she shook her head in disbelief. "I've not kissed any."

"Not any?" Kate asked, sounding as shocked as Jenny appeared.

"No, it's improper to kiss . . . at least until you are engaged."

"But how will you know if you like his kiss?" Jenny asked. "What if he's . . . slobbery, like a dog?"

"Well, I . . . I hadn't given any thought to that."

Jenny swung her legs around and sat up. "I'd heard you English girls didn't kiss, but I hadn't really given any credence to it."

"We kiss," Louisa said defensively. "I've been

kissed on the hand, and once a gentleman kissed me on the cheek."

Jenny covered her mouth. "Oh, my dear Lord, how scandalous! On the cheek? Left or right?"

Louisa thought back. "Left."

"Thank God. If it had been your right, you might have had to marry him. A kiss on the right is much more scandalous."

"Leave her be, Jenny," Kate said. "In truth you give your kisses away much too freely."

"I like kissing," Jenny said. She gave her attention to Louisa. "We don't have chaperones in America. We are a bit more free to experience passion."

"But you are not in America now, and you must respect our traditions," Louisa said. "You are seeking to entice a lord into marriage. You must be proper at all times lest you lose his esteem for you."

"He won't like me if I allow him to kiss me?"

Louisa sighed. "He would not favor a woman who was easy to entice . . . into misconduct."

"Then I ask again. How will I know if I will favor his kiss if I do not experience his kiss?"

"Is his kiss so important?"

"Most assuredly. Don't you agree, Kate?"

"It's not often that I agree with Jenny, but on this matter, I must admit, she is right."

"Would you not marry a man because you didn't like his kiss?" Louisa asked.

"Now, that I do not know," Kate said. "It would

depend on whether or not he loved me, I suppose."

Suddenly Louisa felt terribly naïve, young, and unsophisticated next to these ladies. She'd mistakenly thought they were the innocent ones. "So if you won't make your decision based on his kiss, why is it so important that you experience his kiss?"

"Because it might be a factor."

"Handsome and a good kisser," Jenny said. "So let's move on to the next requirement, which is large hands."

Louisa glowered at her. "You are making sport of me."

"No, not at all. Although in truth, I've never had a man touch me intimately, but when I think of him doing so, I think of large, strong hands, hands capable of delivering passion."

Louisa cleared her throat. "I think we need to concentrate on something a bit more measurable from a distance."

"Such as?"

"His sense of humor, his wit, his ability to converse on interesting topics—"

"Where is the passion in all of that?" Jenny asked.

"Passion is not simply physical," Louisa said. "It is the way a man looks at his estate and sees the generations that have come before him. It is his appreciation of Shakespeare. It is his standing by his obligations. It is his courteous nature. His respect for his elders. So much can be determined from a distance."

Jenny sighed. "You're not going to let me slip away to kiss a man, are you?"

"No, I'm afraid not. Our gentlemen require very proper behavior in the ladies they are considering to marry, and I must ensure them that you are as suitable for them as they are for you. I'm beginning to think I must give you an appreciation for our heritage."

"I don't want lessons," Jenny said. "I've had far too many lessons." She pointed to the invitations in Louisa's lap. "So which balls should we attend?"

Louisa began sorting through the invitations again, wondering if she had not set an impossible task for herself.

Chapter 4

The very thought of marriage sent a chill skittering down his spine, but Hawk knew he had reached the point in his life where he no longer had a choice. At four-and-thirty—as his mother constantly reminded him—he wasn't getting any younger. He had a duty to provide a legitimate heir, and he was also obligated to arrange some sort of financial security for those to whom he was responsible. An American heiress would provide him adequately with both.

While the Rose sisters weren't the only heiresses in London this Season, Lady Louisa had tossed down a gauntlet, whether intentional or not. He had decided he *would* marry one of them by God, simply because Lady Louisa was so determined that he wouldn't.

He did love to embrace a challenge.

Standing unobserved near the glass-paned door that led to the terrace, Hawk had watched Lady Louisa elegantly circling the room, introducing her charges to a number of gentlemen of her choosing, men she no doubt considered suitable. Boring and unadventuresome. A pity none of those staid, proper, and well-behaved gentlemen had taken her to wife. Then he would not have to deal with her high idealism now.

The first ball was without a doubt quite important. The impression the ladies made would have an impact on the remainder of their Season. From his observations, he'd managed to deduce that both ladies were exceedingly lovely, graceful, and poised.

But then what American heiress wasn't?

They had money at their disposal, and money was power. Of course, so was a title. Mix the two, and he would be unconquerable. He would be able to do anything he damned well pleased where he damned well pleased when he damned well pleased. Life would be what it hadn't been in a good long while: enjoyable. His burdens would be lifted, his responsibilities would be easier to bear.

He'd spent considerable time plotting the strategy that would result in his achieving his goal of marrying one of the Rose sisters. All that remained was for him to put his plan into action.

The music for the quadrille eased into silence. He watched as each Rose sister in turn was escorted back to her chaperone. He waited while

gentlemen approached, Lady Louisa gave her
charges into their protection, and the ladies were
escorted back to the dance floor. It was time for
Hawk to make his move.

He enjoyed nothing more than he enjoyed the
thrill of the hunt.

She was aware of his approach long before he
came into her field of vision. She felt his gaze, his
attention focused on her as though he had sighted
his prey. She didn't know where that thought had
come from. She knew only that it was the way she
felt.

She shifted her gaze slightly and could clearly
see him striding lithely toward her, something
predatory about his movements. He was a civi-
lized man who suddenly appeared quite uncivi-
lized. He was so incredibly dark, not only in his
looks but in his manner. The name his intimates
used when referring to him—Hawk—seemed
quite appropriate. She'd never referred to him as
such, would never take it upon herself to be that
informal with him.

She could fully understand the reason he'd
gained a reputation for being a man with whom
ladies' hearts were far from safe. As he came to
stand before her, he suddenly appeared to be quite
dangerous.

His eyes darkened, his mouth curved up into a
slow, sensual smile. She'd never before noticed a
man's lips. How soft they looked, how inviting.
She was finding it increasingly difficult to breathe,

as though invisible fingers were slowly tightening the laces on her corset.

"Lady Louisa," he said with a sultry purr that closely resembled the low growl she'd once heard a lion emit during one of her visits to the zoological gardens. "May I have the honor of this dance?"

Her cheeks warmed, and she wondered if her flush was visible. "Your Grace, as I'm sure you are well aware, I'm in attendance this eve as a chaperone, not an invited guest." Initially an embarrassing predicament as acquaintances greeted her and began to comprehend her role. She had effectively taken herself off the marriage market and suffered through looks of pity from those with whom she'd once shared the dream of marriage. They had acquired the dream, while she was left with nothing but a nightmare. But the damage was done, the rumors would spread, and she was certain making an appearance at the next ball would be much easier, and by Season's end all would forget she'd once had hopes of marriage and family.

"I daresay you've done a remarkable job in seeing that your charges are otherwise occupied, in no need of your services at this moment. I can see no harm in your taking a turn about the dance floor as well."

How she longed to accept his invitation, to be whirled across the polished floor as though she hadn't a care in the world. But she couldn't help but wonder: *Why now? Why ask me to dance now when you have never before asked?*

"It would not be appropriate," she insisted, striving to convince herself as well as him. What would it hurt for two minutes, three at the most, to simply enjoy the evening and the attentions of a man?

"I can think of nothing more appropriate than to dance with a lovely lady."

She narrowed her eyes. "What are you up to, Your Grace?"

He extended his elbow. "You seem to be of the opinion that I'm not good husband material, and so I thought a simple demonstration was in order: merely to prove I can be most charming when I set my mind to it. I would ask you be equally charming. If you don't place your hand on my arm and allow me to escort you to the dance floor, all will know you have snubbed me. Not exactly an enviable position for a chaperone to be in, now is it?"

"You have backed me into a rather uncomfortable corner."

Tilting his head slightly, he gave her a devastatingly dangerous smile. "Then allow me to lead you out of it."

Truly, what choice did she have other than to accept his invitation? She tried not to look too pleased that she was going to have an opportunity to move with the rhythm of the music. Without a word, she placed her hand on his arm and allowed him to escort her to the dance floor and into a waltz.

She'd not danced since the Christmas holidays. It felt wonderful again to have her slippers following where a gentleman led. She'd not considered this aspect when she'd made her decision to seek a position as a social chaperone: that she would be relegated to observing the merriment rather than being ensconced in the midst of it. While she'd never had any serious suitors, neither had she ever been relegated to wallflower. She'd had dance partners and a dance card often more full than not.

"How are you enjoying your recently acquired role of chaperone?" Hawkhurst asked.

She nearly tripped over her feet. Had he somehow managed to read her mind? Was her face more expressive than she realized?

"I am enjoying it quite well, thank you."

"It comes with a great deal of responsibility."

"Indeed it does."

"It did not escape my notice that you introduced one of the ladies to Lord Ainsley."

"Yes. Jenny."

"Mmm." He pressed his lips together as though to stop himself from speaking.

"What exactly does that mean?"

"Forgive my boldness, but your brother mentioned that *you* mentioned that Miss Jenny Rose was searching for passion."

Damn her brother! Was nothing spoken between them sacred? She'd worried about the servants gossiping, and apparently it was Alex with whom she should be concerned.

"She does feel that passion is important," she admitted reluctantly.

"Then I daresay it will be a miracle if she finds it with Ainsley."

"I beg your pardon?"

"It is well-known"—he'd lowered his voice slightly, which had her stretching up on her toes to hear him—"that Ainsley has yet to . . . experience passion himself."

"Are you implying he has no mistress?"

"I am implying far more than that. I'm implying he has never known the intimate touch of a woman."

She fought not to blush at words so brashly spoken and forced herself to imitate a smile laced with satisfaction. "Then in my book, he is quite the catch: a man who does not seek frivolous dalliances."

"Is there no passion in your book?" he asked, with a seductive voice that sent warm shivers cascading down to the heels of her slippers.

Why was he having such an effect on her? She had no doubt he was intentionally seeking to rattle her with his inappropriate conversation and sweltering looks that belonged in the bedchamber, not on the dance floor.

"Of course there is passion." She sounded breathless. Surely, they must be dancing too swiftly, and yet she hardly felt her feet touching the floor. "But I don't see that a man needs to be promiscuous in order to be passionate."

"Then how, pray tell, is he to learn how to pleasure a woman?"

She couldn't help herself. She laughed at his audacity. "So you justify visiting brothels as a learning experience? Some sort of school—"

"Quite. Ladies of the evening serve an important function in our society that is seldom appreciated. They ensure a man does not bumble about on his wedding night. They instruct him on how to touch a woman." He lowered his head slightly, the warmth of his breath wafting over her cheek. "*Where* to touch a woman so the act of making love is as satisfying for her as it is for him."

She was suddenly acutely aware of just how large his gloved hands were, how long his fingers. She wondered at the passion they might elicit and exactly how he might use them. What had he been taught? She had little doubt he'd been an adept student. Even now, with only his eyes, his voice, his nearness, his gloved hands, he was managing to create unsettling carnal images in her mind.

"Based on what my brother has revealed about your endeavors, you are no doubt quite the expert."

"I do consider myself such, yes. Would you want a man who did not know the way to lead you on a journey into passion?"

Jerking her head back, she came to a stunned

standstill. "That is quite enough, Your Grace. It is entirely inappropriate for you to speak of such things to me."

"My apologies, but you seemed unable to decipher why Lord Ainsley would be incapable of giving Miss Jenny Rose what she desires, and unable to fathom why it is not such a horrendous thing that men such as your brother, Falconridge, and I do seek pleasure before marriage."

"For the sole benefit of your future wives?" she asked incredulously.

He gave her a decidedly wicked grin and a wink that caused her heart to flutter madly as though it were a trapped bird seeking freedom. "Not solely, of course, but I do think one can argue that at some point, the benefits will accrue to the wife. Now come, the music continues, as should we before we become the fodder for gossip."

He tightened his hold on her and swept her along, giving her no choice except to follow.

"You may justify your behavior as much as you like," she finally managed to say after a while. "I shall not consider you a suitable match for these ladies."

"Then it seems the way to one of the ladies' hearts is through you."

She wasn't exactly certain what he meant by those words, but they definitely carried a hint of a challenge and perhaps a bit of warning. She couldn't have been more grateful when the final strains of the music drifted into silence. He placed her gloved hand on his arm and began to lead her toward the chairs where she'd been when he first approached.

"I must confess that I do not blame you for considering me such a bad influence. In my youth, I was quite the rabble-rouser, and on more than one occasion you caught me engaged in activities that were questionable. Still, I assure you that with the years has come maturity. I would like very much to gain an introduction to Miss Jenny Rose."

"Your Grace—"

"Before you deny me such a simple request, may I remind you that you vowed you would not encourage the lady to favor me, but neither would you undermine my efforts. Not introducing me undermines my efforts, and, therefore, causes you to break your promise. Hardly commendable behavior for a woman who is charged with guarding others. I daresay the Rose family might look upon you with less favor if they thought you weren't a woman of your word."

"Oh, you are ever so clever," she said.

"So I'm told." He winked at her. "Not only clever with my words, but with my hands. Think on that, Lady Louisa. Would you truly deny your charges what I can offer?"

"Arrogance? I believe I would."

"Do not confuse arrogance with confidence."

Before she could comment, she was met by Jenny, whose gaze slowly swept over Hawkhurst as though he were a delicacy she was considering tasting. These Americans were so incredibly brash. It was little wonder they required a chaperone.

They also required an introduction, and while Louisa was hesitant to provide one, she knew it would indeed be an insult to Hawkhurst now that he was here not to introduce him. Of course, as soon as introductions were made, he invited Jenny to dance, and unfortunately, she was available.

Louisa was hesitant to admit that they looked quite remarkable together. Jenny was tall and willowy, the top of her head even with his shoulder. He wouldn't have to lower his head to speak quietly to her. He'd barely have to lower his head in order to kiss her.

Where had that irritating thought come from? She'd definitely not allow any kissing.

"He's certainly a tall drink of water."

Jerking her head around, she discovered Kate was standing beside her. What sort of irresponsible chaperone was she not to have been aware of Kate's approach?

"I beg your pardon?"

Kate nodded toward the dance floor. "The intriguing gentleman with whom Jenny is dancing. Who is he?"

"The Duke of Hawkhurst."

"You don't approve of him."

"I didn't say that."

"Not in so many words no, but the way you were watching him: like you expected him to misbehave. Quite honestly, Lady Louisa, you don't need to worry about Jenny. She can take care of herself."

Perhaps that was the reason Louisa worried so: She feared she would discover she wasn't needed at all.

Not by the English lords, not by the American heiresses. And she desperately wanted to be needed.

Chapter 5

"I see Hawk has made his diabolically clever move," Falconridge said laconically.

"Appears so," Alex replied.

"Who would have thought to do a bit of flirting with the chaperone in order to get into her good graces and thus receive an introduction to the lady in whom one truly has an interest?"

Alex had been surprised that Louisa had accepted Hawk's invitation to dance. But then what choice did she have? She was not in a position to snub a duke publicly. Alex wasn't certain what irritated him more. The fact that Hawk had danced with his sister or the fact that he was now dancing with the lovely Jenny Rose. Dear God, but her name suited her, for she was a blossom among thorns.

63

Clever phrasing, that. Shall have to remember it, he thought. *Might come in useful.*

"She's your sister. She should at least give you an introduction," Falconridge murmured.

"She's a bit cross with me at the moment. I suspect she shan't give me the time of day should I bother to ask."

"Why ever would she be cross with you?"

"Because I took exception to her opinion of us as unsuitable."

"We are unsuitable."

Alex slid his gaze over to Falconridge. Was this the same man who had stormed out of his home, because of his sister's unflattering opinion of him? "You were quite vocal about your objections regarding her opinion."

"I was vocal about my refusal to prove myself worthy."

"Because you don't think you are?"

"Let it go."

"Surely, you jest. So, we have a bit of fun—"

"It's more than that, Ravensley. I have skeletons in the closet that I'd not wish to inflict on any woman."

"Yet you must wed."

Falconridge sighed. "Yet, I must wed, and these heiresses suit me well. They are pragmatic. They do not want love or emotions. They want a title. I want their money. Perhaps a good romp in bed from time to time when it suits. But nothing that arouses any sort of sentiment."

"Then I should warn you that Louisa was kind

enough to reveal that Kate Rose is in want of love; Jenny, passion."

"Then I suppose it is Jenny I should focus on. Passion I can deliver. Love I cannot."

"I daresay I shall be content to have either. All I care about is the weight of the coin purse."

"A rather cold sentiment."

"An honest one."

"A sad one . . . that this is what our lives have boiled down to. Money. It is the root of all discontent."

"Thought it was the root of all evil."

"That as well." Falconridge sighed. "I suppose 'tis time I took a step toward that unattractive part of my life and begin purposely to court a woman with the intention of marriage. Hopefully, Hawk improved your sister's disposition so she'll be willing to give us an introduction." He took a step forward, glanced back. "Coming?"

It irked him to rely on another man to forge the path for an introduction, but then Alex supposed it was no different than asking his sister for the favor. "Do I really have a choice?"

Did any of them?

"I cannot believe you told Hawkhurst that Jenny sought passion."

Louisa had reluctantly made introductions when Falconridge and her brother had approached while she'd been speaking with Kate. Immediately Falconridge had invited Kate to dance, leaving

Louisa free to pull her brother behind a nearby potted frond and give him a good piece of her mind.

"I didn't realize it was a secret," Alex said.

"Not a secret, perhaps, but a confidence. What else have you told him?"

"Nothing of any importance."

She shook her head. Obviously her brother had no idea what was important and what wasn't.

"Do you think Jenny will take a fancy to him?" Alex asked.

"I don't know. She seems to enjoy everyone's company. She is the more easily pleased of the two."

"Upon closer observations, she is also the more attractive. Will you introduce me when she returns?"

"Alex—"

"Louisa, I'm not nearly as bad as you believe. I assure you others are far worse."

She narrowed her eyes. "Lord Ainsley, I suppose."

"Ainsley? Good God, no, the man is a saint."

"I thought as much," she said smugly.

"Would you want to be married to a saint?"

"Better than being married to the devil."

"That might be worth arguing, but I'm weary of being in disaccord with you." Her brother leaned against the wall and crossed his arms over his chest. "Tell me something else about the sisters."

"Alex—"

"Please, I beg of you, give me a leg up. Something. Anything. Just a hint."

He sounded so incredibly pitiful, so desperate. And he was her brother. If Hawkhurst, Falconridge, and Alex were going to fixate on the sisters, Alex was the lesser of three evils. "Kate prefers the waltz. Jenny has no preference."

He seemed relieved that she had shared the smallest bit of information. "Why weren't their dance cards filled?"

"How do you know Jenny's wasn't?"

"Hawk is now dancing with her, and I know you didn't scribble his name on her card."

"Jenny likes spontaneity, and so she leaves every other dance empty so that she has a surprise partner on occasion."

"Spontaneity. I relish that in a woman. Speaks of an adventuresome spirit, don't you think?"

Yes, Jenny was spontaneous, fun-loving. Always laughing and smiling. No cares in the world, apparently. Louisa couldn't help but wonder if perhaps it was more than the lack of a dowry that had resulted in her having no marriage proposals.

"Am I too predictable?" she heard herself ask aloud before she'd even realized she'd formed the question.

"Hardly. Who could have predicted you'd set yourself up to serve as a chaperone?"

She rolled her eyes. "Before that. Do you think gentlemen found me boring?"

He shook his head. "No. I believe it is as you surmised. Many of us need a way to rebuild the family coffers. It has put our own ladies at a decided disadvantage. Primogeniture assures we have few wealthy heiresses of our own. We will be in a bit of a pickle if these Americans are no longer enamored by rank. I don't know why you find fault with us going after their money while they are after our titles."

"In truth, the whole arrangement saddens me. Like Kate, I believe love should have a say in the entire affair."

"Speaking of Kate, you didn't explain why her dance card isn't full."

Her brother seemed determine to learn all he could. "She says she tires easily." Louisa shrugged. "In truth, I think she simply says no to men who don't strike her fancy right off."

"She's fortunate that she can be choosy."

"Indeed she is."

The orchestra stopped playing, and Alex shoved himself away from the wall. "Now, dear sister, please, I beg of you, put me at an advantage where these two young ladies are concerned."

"I thought the evening went remarkably well," Jenny said, her voice a wistful sigh.

Sitting in the carriage, across from Jenny and Kate, Louisa could understand perfectly well the reason Jenny felt as she did. The young lady had danced every single dance, while Kate had danced nearly every dance. Louisa had noticed a decided difference between the young ladies: Jenny welcomed the gentlemen's attentions while Kate merely tolerated them. Those attitudes each carried its own burden when it came to striving to find an appropriate husband for each lady. One who liked all men; one who liked none. How was Louisa to narrow the choices down?

"I thought your brother looked rather like an angel," Jenny said.

Louisa hoped the darkness of the interior of the carriage hid her open mouth and widened eyes. "Alex? An angel?" She laughed lightly. "Hardly."

"Is he a bit wicked then?"

"He has his moments, I'm certain. We don't discuss particulars."

"I thought Hawkhurst looked like the very devil," Kate said.

"But he dances well," Jenny said. "I rather enjoyed having his attention."

Louisa was aware of her hands gripping her fingers. She told herself it was because she didn't want the young lady to finish her Season betrothed to a rogue. It was that concern and not any sort of disappointment because the lady would remove Hawk from the marriage market. She didn't want to acknowledge she had enjoyed his attentions as well, even if their conversation had been inappropriate. Inappropriate, yet interesting. She couldn't envision him ever discussing a topic as mundane as the weather. He would seek to shock, and in the shocking he would excite.

She'd halfway hoped he might ask her for another dance, but, of course, she'd served her purpose, provided him with the introduction he desired. Then he had cast her aside. Conquer and move on seemed to be his preferred style when it came to ladies.

"I noticed you dancing with him, Lady Louisa," Jenny said. "What is your opinion of him?"

"I thought he danced rather nicely," she said.

Jenny laughed, a lyrical sound that Louisa assumed any gentleman would find attractive.

"Come now. I wasn't referring to his dancing, but rather him as a man. Or more importantly, as a husband. He is a duke, after all. That would please my mother immensely."

"And we do want to please Mother, don't we?" Kate asked sullenly.

"I want to please myself," Jenny said. "If I please Mother as well, so much the better. Now, Lady Louisa, tell me what you know of the duke."

What did she know of the duke?

"His family is quite well placed. His father died when Hawkhurst was very young. Twelve as I recall someone mentioning."

"How did his father die?"

"I'm not quite sure. Disease, I believe." A disease one did not speak of, based on whisperings she'd heard.

"How dreadful," Jenny said. "To have such an immense burden placed on young shoulders. I daresay they are broad enough to carry any burden now, though. I thought him a fine physical specimen."

"Capable of providing passion?" Kate asked.

"Quite," Jenny replied. "What of you, dear sister? Did you discover anyone who could provide you with love?"

"Not at tonight's ball."

Louisa thought that an odd comment. "Have you met someone previously?"

Kate sighed. "Tell me true, Lady Louisa. Do you think any gentleman looks at us and sees anything beyond our father's wealth?"

Louisa could see the silhouettes of the two girls shifting as the dim light from the streetlamps weaved in and out of the carriage while it traversed along the London streets. Did she dare lie? Men looked at her and saw no money. They looked at these ladies and saw an abundance of wealth. Was either situation any more desirable?

"Money may be what first catches their attention, but it is your beauty and character that will hold them captive."

Kate released a bitter laugh. "You don't understand. There are times when I wish we lived in poverty. How will I ever know for certain it is I a man loves and not the money that accompanies me to the altar?"

"Which is the reason that I seek passion rather than love," Jenny said. "It matters not why he marries me. It matters only that he can deliver what I need."

"I need love," Kate said solemnly.

Louisa didn't know what possessed her to lean across the space separating her from the two ladies and wrap one of her hands around each of theirs. "I swear to you that I shall do all in my power to ensure the man you marry will want you more than he wants the money."

"Pray tell, how do you think you'll accomplish that?" Jenny asked.

Louisa leaned back. "I shall seek to acquaint you with men who are not desperate."

"Is your brother desperate?" Jenny asked.

"Very."

"And Hawkhurst?"

"Yes."

"And Falconridge?" Kate asked.

"I'm afraid so."

"I saw the three of them congregating from time to time. Are they friends?" Jenny asked.

"Yes, indeed. They have been friends for a good many years."

"Then you must know them quite well. I'm surprised they do not come highly recommended by you."

Louisa felt her stomach tighten. "Quite honestly, several years separate us, and they have hardly ever given me the time of day."

"You can't imagine how horrible it is not to be wanted for yourself," Kate said, turning the subject back to the ladies rather than the gentlemen.

"We are not that different. I'm poor"—how Louisa despised admitting that aloud—"and yet, I have no gentleman caller. I have wished for a bit of money so that I would garner someone's attention."

"Wouldn't it be fun to trade places?" Jenny asked. "Even if for only one evening. For you to live in our world, and for us to have a glimpse into yours."

"I suspect we'd each find life not to our liking," Louisa said.

"Perhaps. But surely, gentlemen danced with you at balls past."

"Of course, but they never wanted more than a dance."

"Not even Hawkhurst?" Jenny asked.

Louisa felt her brow wrinkle. "Quite honestly, we'd never danced before."

"Truly? The way he looked at you . . ." Her voice trailed off.

"What do you mean?"

"Well, he just seemed . . . fascinated."

"Fascinated in learning about you."

"Perhaps," Jenny murmured, with no conviction in her voice. She gazed out the window, as though no longer interested in discussing what Louisa knew of the duke.

Which was just as well. Louisa did not want to get into his rather unfortunate habits, which could very well result in his dying as his father had—of a disease that no one spoke of. She tried to recall what she knew of Hawkhurst's mother and could remember very little about the woman. She was a bit of a recluse, no doubt living in shame because she had only managed to provide one heir—no spare—to the dukedom.

*   *   *

He could still smell her perfume. A faint fragrance that reminded him of lilies at dawn. One of his mother's favorite flowers.

He could still feel her within his arms. Slender. Delicate. Her head barely even with his shoulder.

He could still see the way she looked at him. As though he were capable only of misdeeds, not to be trusted. And certainly not to be recommended to her charges.

Standing with his arm pressed to the mantel, staring into the fire, he downed the remainder of his brandy, hoping it would wash away the memories. Lady Louisa was not the one who should still be haunting his thoughts. It was Jenny Rose who should be traveling through his mind, and yet the reality was that he could barely remember what she looked like.

He heard the door click open, fought back a grimace—because he sought solitude, not company—and peered over his shoulder. Following the ball, he'd returned to his estate, a two-hour ride from the city, rather than his London residence because he'd needed the reminder of his obligations. They were as easy to forget as Jenny Rose's features when he was away from them.

As weary as he was, he still managed a smile. "Hello, Moppet. It's a bit late for you to be up and about, isn't it?"

Dressed in her nightclothes, holding her wrapper close at her throat, his sister smiled shyly as she walked toward him. Her hair, as black as midnight, was braided and draped over her shoulder. She'd always seemed so frail, so fragile. From the moment she'd been born, he'd felt a fierce need to protect her.

"I could say the same of you," she said softly. "I heard you arrive. I didn't know you were going to return home so soon. Won't Mother be surprised?"

"I expect she will be."

She snuggled into the corner of the couch, brought her bare feet up to the cushion, and wound her arms around her drawn-up legs. "Did you attend the first ball of the Season, then?"

"Indeed, I did."

"Was it fun and exciting?"

He gave her an exaggerated scowl that caused her to laugh lightly. She had the most innocent of laughs. He despised that a time would come when the world and its intolerance would strip her of it.

"It is only fun and exciting for the ladies," he explained drolly. "For the gentlemen, it is a great deal of work."

"Oh, bosh, I don't believe that for one second. I'd wager you had a jolly good time. Did you dance every dance?"

"Nearly every dance," he said, to appease her, resenting the ease with which the lie rolled off his tongue.

He walked to the table, where an assortment of crystal decanters awaited him. He refilled his glass before taking a chair, angled in such a way that he could view the fire and Caroline with little more than the slight turning of his head. She had been his mother's secret for seventeen years now, a secret bustled off to various estates whenever company came to call, a secret that would soon be revealed to London. She was of age, and Hawk had every intention of placing himself in a position to protect her and ensure that she married well.

His own marriage to Jenny Rose—he had decided a woman who required passion was a much better suit than one who required love—and the funds the arrangement should provide and make available to him would give him an advantage that if not for Caroline he would care little about obtaining. Not entirely true. After her, he would have his heir to consider. He wanted his son's worries to be fewer, his responsibilities less burdensome. If Hawk had other children, he wanted to provide adequately for them. Yes, the time had come to marry and marry money—the more the better.

"Who was the most beautiful lady there?" Caroline asked.

An image of Lady Louisa darted before him. Beautiful, no. Lovely perhaps. She did not stand out in a crowd, but she did manage to stand up to him, and he found that more intriguing than any physical characteristics she might possess.

"I suppose it would have to be Jenny Rose," he said, before sipping his brandy and gazing into the fire, praying both would burn away his lingering memories of Louisa.

"Describe her to me," Caroline said.

He stared at the writhing flames, conjuring up images of bared bodies tangled beneath red satin sheets, flesh glistening with dew—

He downed the brandy. Cleared his throat. "Honestly, Caroline, I don't remember her features clearly enough to give a description justice."

"Then how could she be beautiful, if you cannot remember her?"

He shifted his attention to his sister. So naïve, so unaware of the trials that awaited her.

"I suppose it is merely that the details escape me, and without details there is little to distinguish her from every other lady in the room."

"Oh."

She seemed genuinely disappointed, studying the sash of her wrapper, which she'd wound around her index finger. "Do you think any gentleman will ever take notice of me?"

"Without a doubt."

His marriage to Jenny Rose would ensure it.

She lifted her gaze to his. "I know I come with a great deal of baggage, Hawk."

"We all do, Moppet. We all do."

Chapter 6

"Men set little store by what is carelessly guarded," the dragon announced at breakfast.

Louisa felt the weight of the woman's gaze on her long before she looked up from her porridge. Mrs. Rose had one brow so highly arched it might have been farcical if not for the heat in the green eye beneath the brow.

"I do hope it is not your plan to make a habit of leaving my girls untended while you see to your own amusements," Mrs. Rose said tersely.

"Mama, it was only one dance," Jenny said. "Quite honestly, I believe the duke was taking advantage of Lady Louisa. He timed their arrival from the dance floor such that she had no choice except to make introductions. Rather clever on his part, I thought, since the lady determines which introductions are appropriate and approaches the man."

Louisa felt her stomach knot at Jenny's words. Last night, for one brief moment, she had dared believe that perhaps it was her he had wanted to dance with. No, not believed. Pretended. Pretended she was the belle of the ball, the one around whom the gentlemen fluttered, like bees to pollen. She did not know who truly deserved more pity: the one overlooked or the one who gained attention because of the coins jingling in her father's pockets.

Mrs. Rose's lips were pressed so tightly together as to be invisible. Louisa did not need anyone taking up for her, but then she wasn't accustomed to being chastised. She had been her father's angel, her mother's darling, her brother's precious sister.

"I assure you, Mrs. Rose, that Jenny has the right of it. The dance was merely a ruse on the duke's part to garner information regarding your daughters and the likelihood that they might favor him," Louisa said.

"There, you see, Mama? No harm done," Jenny said.

"No harm done? If he was a duke, why did he have to engage in a ruse to be introduced? You should have been led to his side as soon as he entered the room." Mrs. Rose gave Louisa a pointed glare. "Why were my daughters not introduced immediately? Is that not what I'm paying you for?"

"Not a ruse to gain an introduction, rather a ruse to gather information, discreetly. We are a very discreet people," she said, surprised by how quickly she was learning to dance around uncomfortable questions.

"Are you saying that your plan all along was to introduce my daughters to him?"

"Yes, madam." How disappointing that the lie came with such ease.

Mrs. Rose harrumphed. "I suppose you spoke favorably on my daughters' behalf while you were dancing?"

"Of course."

"Is this particular duke a relation to the queen?"

"No, ma'am," Louisa said.

Mrs. Rose pinched her mouth. "A pity. Still, he is at the top of the hierarchy. I shall simply have to satisfy myself with that." She held up a finger. "I'm well aware of the order of the ranks, so do not try to deceive me in that regard."

"Mama, I fear you are being too presumptuous," Jenny said. "We only danced. I cannot say for certain whether or not I favor him."

"Whether or not *you* favor him is not the issue. The issue is whether or not he favors you. What was your impression, Lady Louisa? Did he favor my girls?"

"I fear he danced only with Miss Jenny."

"Why not Kate?"

"Because I was occupying the attention of a marquess," Kate said.

"A marquess? That title is second only to a duke, is it not?"

"Yes, madam," Louisa said, wondering why she was asking when she'd earlier declared that she was familiar with the ranking of peers.

"Not bad, but still, I'd rather both my daughters be duchesses."

Jenny rolled her eyes and huffed out a puff of air.

"I saw that look, young lady. There shall come a day when you will thank me for all I've done to get you where you need to be." Mrs. Rose turned her hard look on Louisa. "What did the duke say about Jenny after their dance?"

"I did not speak with him afterward," Louisa said.

"Why ever not? How can you determine how the girls should adjust their behavior in order to impress him favorably if you don't know what his impression was?"

Louisa felt her stomach tighten. She wasn't accustomed to having her every action questioned. "I don't believe your daughters should alter their behavior simply to catch a duke."

"We seem to be at odds regarding our opinions. While I believe my daughters will be the toast of London, I'm not so pompous as not to realize there is always room for improvement. I expect you to advise them regarding how they may make themselves more attractive to these English lords."

"I assure you, madam, they cannot be any more attractive than they already are."

Mrs. Rose jerked her head back slightly. "Are you contradicting me?"

"I believe she's saying that they are perfect as they are," Mr. Rose said laconically from his end of the table. He lowered the newspaper he was reading. "They take after their mother in that regard, my dear."

Mrs. Rose blinked, then smiled at her husband. "I suppose you're right." She looked at Louisa, her smile fading to reveal once again the woman with a definite goal. "I suppose, gentlemen will be calling this afternoon?"

"Undoubtedly," Louisa said.

"I should like to meet the duke or any of his equals. Any rank below would simply be a waste of a pleasant afternoon. Kate, do not encourage a marquess when you can have a duke."

Now it was Kate who rolled her eyes and tightened her mouth.

Mrs. Rose shoved back her chair and stood. "I shall be in my chambers. Send someone to fetch me if a gentleman worthy of my time should come to call. And Lady Louisa, should the duke call, you are to ask him his opinion of my daughters. And if he does not call, you are to call on him and make inquiries as to his opinion."

"Oh, no, madam, I cannot do that."

"Do you wish to remain in my employ?"

Louisa swallowed. "Yes, ma'am."

"Then you will do as I wish or risk my displeasure. And if I am not pleased—"

"No one is pleased," Jenny, Kate, and Mr. Rose said in unison.

Then they all laughed and the tension in the room seemed to ease as even Mrs. Rose's mouth relaxed into what could almost be described as a smile.

"I will not be ridiculed, Mr. Rose," Mrs. Rose said.

"My dear, teasing is but one way to show affection."

She turned her attention back to her daughters. "I will see you both wed before this Season is over. Do you understand me?"

"I will see to your wishes, my dear," Mr. Rose said. "There is no reason to worry yourself over it."

"I'm going to rest for a bit. I shall be ever so grateful when you girls are finally settled into marriage, and your father and I can begin to enjoy the years left to us."

With that parting sentiment, she swept from the room. Louisa breathed a sigh of relief. At least now, she was faced with the possibility that her digestion wouldn't be completely ruined.

"I'm so sorry," Jenny said, when her mother was no longer visible. "I had no idea she would take the news that the duke had danced with you so poorly."

"I can't believe you told her," Kate said. "Where

Mama is concerned, you know as well as I the best plan of action is to say nothing at all."

"Your mother was quite right," Louisa said, not certain why she felt a need to defend the unpleasant woman. "It was poor judgment on my part to accept his invitation for a dance."

"Nonsense. If Kate and I are both otherwise occupied, I see no harm in you having a bit of fun. Don't you agree, Kate?"

"Of course. As a matter of fact, why don't the two of you dance, and I'll simply watch?"

"But what of your marquess?" Jenny asked. "I found him exceedingly attractive."

"Attractive is as attractive does," Kate said.

"What in the world does that mean?"

"I need more than handsome features." Kate looked toward the end of the table, where her father was again partially hidden behind his newspaper. "Papa, may I be excused?"

"Of course," he mumbled, never shifting his gaze from the article he was reading.

Louisa waited until Kate had quit the room, before turning her attention to Jenny and saying, "She does not seem at all interested in finding a husband."

Jenny slid her gaze to her father, before leaning forward and whispering, "She has not yet recovered from having her heart broken."

The newspaper crackled, and Mr. Rose was suddenly glaring over the crumpled paper. "Jenny Rose, you know better than to discuss family secrets."

"I didn't reveal the secret. Only the end result. Honestly, Papa, I don't think you should be forcing her to go out."

"The matter has been discussed and decided." He came to his feet. "You will not discuss it further." He gave Louisa an unexpected hard stare. "With anyone."

And she realized the admonishment applied to her as well.

"I'm not one to gossip, Mr. Rose," she felt obliged to state.

"I love my daughters, Lady Louisa. I will protect them with my fortune, if need be with my life."

"That is quite admirable, sir."

The sternness in his face eased. "I'm certain your father would have done the same for you had he possessed the means."

He walked from the room before Louisa could decide whether or not he had just insulted her father.

"Do secrets abide in your family?" Jenny asked.

Louisa decided there was no hope for it. Her stomach would not tolerate her porridge. She set her bowl aside. "All families have secrets."

"I suppose. You told Mother you knew everything about all the lords. Does that include their secrets?"

"If there are secrets to be known."

"The duke. Hawkhurst. What do you know of his secrets?"

"He is prone to late nights that lead into the morning."

"What gentleman isn't?"

Louisa stared at her. "A respectable gentleman."

"Respectable sounds so boring. Can a respectable man know of passion?"

Louisa could not help but wonder if Hawkhurst had carried on the same conversation with Jenny that he had with her. "Did he speak to you of passion?"

"No, actually, we spoke not at all, which I found most curious. He seemed somewhat distracted. I found both your brother and Falconridge to be much more interesting when it came to conversation." Jenny sipped her tea, and it seemed to Louisa that *she* was now distracted, and she wondered if she was thinking of her dances with both men. If she'd found one more interesting than the other.

And if she had, what then? None of the three was suitable. She had to steer her toward the proper gentlemen.

"If you'll excuse me, I need to look through the invitations in order to determine which ball you should attend next." Louisa pushed back her chair and stood.

"By the by, Kate and I will be having our art lesson in the conservatory later in the morning. You will join us, won't you?" Jenny asked.

"I don't want to impose."

"Nonsense. It will be fun, and it'll give you an opportunity to know us better. And that's essential if you're going to find us the perfect husband."

"I said nothing about finding you the *perfect* husband," Louisa said.

"That's good. Perfection is no doubt overrated. I think I'd like a man with a bit of naughtiness in him. Would that describe your brother?"

"I'm fairly certain your mother would not approve of you spending time with an earl," Louisa said, deftly avoiding answering the question about Alex.

Jenny smiled slyly. "Which makes him all the more enticing."

"I thought you wanted to please your mother."

"Only as long as it pleases me."

Louisa sighed. She now understood why Mr. Rose had offered her such a generous salary. He no doubt understood that the women in this household were impossible to comprehend.

As she walked from the room she remembered Mrs. Rose's earlier demand that she go to Hawkhurst's residence if he did not call on the Roses. Lord help her, she thought she'd never find herself praying for a visit from Hawkhurst.

Hawk found his mother in the garden, a straw basket burgeoning with cut flowers dangling from her arm, while the gardener dutifully cut more for her. For as long as he could remember, it had been their morning ritual. Hawk had been grateful the man's dedication to his gardens had prevented him from leaving when finances began to tighten. His mother so loved her gardens; she spent a good deal of her time simply enjoying them. Hawk knew this latest batch of blossoms would go into a vase in her bedchamber, some in Caroline's. His mother was very particular about the fragrances that surrounded them.

And she had conveniently avoided joining him for breakfast that morning. No doubt because they'd been at odds of late, their opinions differing on what was best for Caroline.

"Good morning, Mother."

With a wave of her hand, she dismissed their longtime gardener before facing her son. She was tall with a willowy grace, her dark hair only just beginning to turn silver. She'd married young, at sixteen, a man many years her senior. Hawk did not deceive himself into believing it had been a love match. No, the love of her life had given her a daughter. His identity remained a secret. So damned many secrets in this family of his.

She smiled warmly, her dark eyes reflecting all the love she held for him. Strange how affection could add to a man's burden.

"I heard you'd arrived home," his mother said. "Bored with the Season already?"

"Hardly. I simply needed . . ." He let his voice trail away. It was one thing for him to be burdened. Another entirely to burden her.

"The reminder?" she asked. "Caroline is not your obligation."

"She is my sister. The daughter of my mother, if not my father. It is enough."

He watched as tears welled in her eyes, and she blinked them back.

"It was never my intent to burden you."

"You did not. Father did. On his deathbed. 'Do not let your mother be unhappy.' I daresay if happiness does not visit your daughter, it will not visit you."

Reaching out, she touched his cheek. "If you are not happy, it will not visit me either."

"What man is happy in marriage?"

"A man who chooses wisely. Have you a prospect?"

"Possibly. I met her only last night. She seemed quite pleasant."

"Pleasant?" Her brow furrowed in slight disapproval. "Pleasant is the manner in which I would describe an afternoon absent of rain."

"I do not know her well enough to classify her any other way."

"Do her interests mirror yours?"

"She will be free to pursue her own interests, so they need not mirror mine."

"Did you ask after her interests?"

"No. They hardly signify. She is in pursuit of a title, and I'm in pursuit of money."

"Ah, she is an American then."

"Yes, Jenny Rose. She has a sister. Kate. But she did not seem as pleasant."

"You spoke with her then?"

"No. I cannot explain why, but I had the impression she did not wish to have my attentions foisted upon her in the least." He saw no reason to explain that it was Jenny's desire for passion rather than Kate's desire for love that had caused him to narrow his choice to Jenny. He doubted his mother would approve.

"I can hardly credit any woman not wanting your attentions," she said.

"I daresay I think it's safe to say Lady Louisa felt the same way."

"Lady Louisa Wentworth?"

"Yes."

"Has she not married?"

"No."

"Been a bit long on the vine, hasn't she?"

"Apparently she has decided to pluck herself from it. She is serving as chaperone to the Rose sisters."

"Interesting. I didn't realize she was *that* old."

"She's not. But neither does she have a dowry. Therefore, her prospects for marriage are decidedly limited."

"So she has decided to make herself a woman of independence. Good for her." She brought the flowers to her face, sniffed the bouquet, and closed her eyes as though lost in memories. She often seemed to drift off to another time, another place, a memory that sustained her during difficult times. In truth he was surprised they'd bantered as long as they had before she lost interest. When she opened her eyes, they had a faraway look in them. "Perhaps Caroline could become a chaperone."

"Lady Louisa has an entrance into society. Caroline has none, not until I give her one. Wealth at my disposal will ensure that the process goes much more smoothly. I do not expect her to marry a man of rank, but certainly she is good enough for some lord's younger son."

His mother flinched.

"I apologize," he said quickly. "My choice of wording was poor. She is worthy of a king, but unfortunately the reality is that a king will not have her."

"Except in the stories you created for her when she was a child."

"It was a world of make-believe, never meant to give her hope, and yet I fear that it did. Sometimes it is as if she truly believes she is a princess." He studied her for a moment, wondering if she might at least admit what he suspected—that her father might indeed be royalty.

"She is our princess," his mother said. "Still, I cannot help but wonder if Caroline wouldn't be happier with a young man from the village."

"Would you have been?" he dared to ask.

His mother rubbed the petal of a lily between her thumb and forefinger. "Happiness eludes cowards. I was a woman unwilling to give up what I valued for what I treasured." She lifted her gaze to his. "What do you treasure?"

"Nothing I do not value. My heritage, my obligations, and my vow to my father. I shall honor them all at any cost."

"And if the cost is *your* happiness?"

"I shall pay it without regret."

"Regret only comes in hindsight, my love."

"Do you have regrets, Mother?" he asked somberly.

Giving him a determined smile, she reached up and cradled his cheek. "None that is impossible to live with."

He swallowed hard. "Was her father married to another?"

She squeezed his chin. "This is a subject we have agreed not to discuss."

"I agreed to nothing. I have a right to know."

"No, my love, you don't. Caroline has a right to know, and should she ask, I will tell her." She patted his cheek. "Don't look so disgruntled. Tell me more about this American girl who has caught your fancy. Will you have much competition for her?"

"It matters not. I will do whatever I deem necessary in order to have her as my wife."

Chapter 7

"So you're the chaperone."

Louisa spun around. A gentleman was leaning casually against the wall, one foot crossed over the other, his arms folded across his chest. His hair was dark, his eyes . . . some dark color, she thought, but couldn't properly identify from this distance.

She'd come to the conservatory, only to discover no one else had yet arrived. "Yes, Jenny said you wouldn't mind if I attended the art lesson."

"I don't mind at all."

He was clearly American and very well dressed for an artist. His trousers and jacket were finely tailored, fitting him as though each stitch had been sewn precisely for him. She supposed that

Mr. Rose was paying him as handsomely as he was paying her.

"Did you travel with the family from America?" she dared to ask.

A corner of his mouth hitched up as though he found both her and her question rather amusing. "Couldn't avoid it, I'm afraid."

"You didn't want to come?"

He shrugged, shoved himself away from the wall. "Lady Louisa, is it?"

She smiled. "You have me at a disadvantage, sir. I'm afraid Jenny didn't tell me the name of her art teacher."

"His name would be Applewhite."

Her heart kicked against her ribs as understanding began to dawn. "You are not the art teacher?"

His grin grew as he bowed his head slightly. "I must confess to not having an artistic bone in my entire body. Allow me the honor of introducing myself. Jeremy Rose."

"Ah." She could see the resemblance now, a younger, slimmer version of the older Mr. Rose, before his dark hair had begun to turn silver, and responsibilities had carved deep lines into his face. She hoped she wasn't blushing too profusely. "I didn't realize there was a son."

"I'm not often spoken of." He leaned toward her slightly. "Black sheep, and all that."

"I'm sure it was simply an oversight—"

"Oh, I'm sure it was intentional."

He removed a silver case from inside his jacket pocket, opened it, removed a cigarette, and went about lighting it. She was fascinated watching him. She'd never seen a gentleman smoke before. It was something they did in rooms where no ladies were present. She'd always thought it would be something wicked to observe. Instead she found herself slightly disappointed by the sight, and not overly fond of the aroma that wafted around him. She wondered if Hawkhurst smoked. Would Jenny find the habit offensive?

"So how is the husband hunting going?" the young Mr. Rose asked, interrupting her thoughts. "Any prospects for my dear sisters?"

"We have quite a few prospects. The challenge is to narrow them down."

He inhaled, blew out the smoke, and seemed to take great interest in watching the end of his cigarette burn.

"Perhaps once you've married off my sisters, you can help me find a wife."

"Are you in the market?"

He laughed. "Not really, but I'd welcome any excuse to be in the company of such a lovely lady as yourself."

She narrowed her eyes. "You are toying with me, sir."

"A bit perhaps. I understand you were properly chastised for dancing last night."

"Where did you hear such gossip?"

"From my mother. She was quite miffed."

"I assure you it will not happen again."

"Oh, it'll happen again." He winked at her. "I plan to attend the next ball."

She hardly knew what to say. Before she could argue further, Jenny waltzed into the room, her eyes alighting at the sight of her brother. "Jeremy! When did you arrive?"

She immediately snatched the cigarette from his fingers, and to Louisa's astonishment, took a long pull on it before tipping her head back and releasing the smoke. Her action seemed somehow quite elegant yet unladylike at the same time.

"In the early hours of the morning," Jeremy said.

"I missed you," Jenny said.

"Missed my smokes more like it," he said.

She laughed before taking another puff. "Lady Louisa, you look scandalized."

"I've never before seen a lady smoke."

"I only do it when Jeremy is home. Mother thinks he's a bad influence."

"I am a bad influence," he said, completely unabashedly, taking the cigarette from his sister while winking again at Louisa.

"Are you flirting with Lady Louisa?" Jenny asked.

"I've asked her to save me a dance at the next ball."

"Mama doesn't approve of Lady Louisa leaving us *untended*," Kate said from the doorway, and Louisa wondered how long she'd been standing there and why it was that she never seemed to notice her.

"Which will make it all the more fun," Jeremy said. He dropped his cigarette to the floor and crushed it beneath a very polished and obviously expensively made shoe.

"How was the Continent?" Kate asked.

"Quite fascinating. Paris, Rome, Berlin, Stockholm, I enjoyed them all."

"Can you imagine being able to travel when you wanted, where you wanted, without any encumbrances or people constantly watching your every move?" Kate asked, and Louisa wondered if she was hinting at a fault with her chaperone.

"Don't be so concerned, Lady Louisa," Jenny said. "She's always envied the freedom men are given."

"It's hardly fair," Kate said.

Jeremy reached out and tweaked her nose. "Life never is, little sister."

"Jeremy, are you going to join us for our art lesson?" Jenny asked.

"Good God, no. I just wanted to make the acquaintance of Lady Louisa—"

"And cause a bit of mischief while you're at it?" Jenny asked.

"Of course. What is life without a bit of mischief?" He bowed slightly. "Lady Louisa, it was my pleasure to make your acquaintance. Don't forget that you've promised me a dance."

"I did no such thing," she blurted. "Your mother is quite right. I should not be dancing."

"We shall see."

He walked from the conservatory before she could say anything else. It seemed American sons

were no easier to deal with than American daughters.

It was really quite thrilling to have the opportunity to apply watercolors to canvas. Louisa had
always enjoyed sketching, but her parents had
never been able to afford for her to have proper
lessons. She thought she could stand within the
conservatory all day testing out this medium,
which was new to her.

"Oh, Lady Louisa, I do believe you're a natural," Jenny said.

Their lesson was to paint a vase of roses. Louisa had painted a single rose.

"The dew drop is a lovely touch, don't you
think, Kate?" Jenny asked.

Kate looked up from her book. "One would
never know that you hadn't taken lessons before."

"I never think to add anything extra to mine,"
Jenny said. "I paint only what I see. Does that
make me boring, do you think?"

"Of course not," Louisa said hastily.

"What do you think, Mr. Applewhite? Am I
your only student who paints exactly what she
sees?"

"At least you paint," he said, giving Kate a stern
look. He was extremely thin and very short for a
man. Louisa actually stood a head taller than he.

Kate stuck out her tongue and turned her attention back to her book, which she'd been reading
the entire time instead of painting.

"You see why I said it would be fine if you

came," Jenny said. "Papa pays for two lessons, and one is wasted."

"I don't like painting," Kate said.

"Or playing the piano," Jenny said. "Or embroidery. Or penning letters. None of the things that a young lady is expected to do." She looked at Louisa. "I don't know how you'll manage to find a husband for her."

"She won't," Kate said.

"I'm sure—" Louisa began.

"Remember, my requirement is love," Kate interrupted, finally looking away from her book. "I absolutely refuse to marry without love."

"And how do you judge love?" Louisa asked.

"If you have to ask, then you have never been loved."

"Kate!" Jenny admonished, but the damage had been done.

Louisa felt the sharp sting to her pride, the brutal flaying of her heart. "No," she said quietly. "If I do not count my father or my brother, then I have never known the love of a gentleman. Am I to assume that you have?"

Kate looked back at her book. "Assume what you wish."

"Kate, you have no reason to be difficult with Lady Louisa," Jenny said. "She doesn't deserve your ill temper."

Kate looked up, regret laced over her face. "I apologize. It is my heart that judges love. It sets no boundaries, sets out no requirements. It is like calling to like, and it recognizes love without consulting me. My heart beats harder and faster when it encounters love, and it quite simply leaves me breathless. I have known love and lost love. And I will not be content with any man incapable of giving me the full measure of his heart."

Louisa hardly knew how to respond to such a heartfelt declaration. What would it be like to have the full measure of a man's heart?

"You think I expect too much," Kate said.

"I think"—Louisa forced herself to smile bravely, a soldier suddenly terrified of the unknown—"you have presented me with a challenge that I shall not take lightly. I shall find a gentleman who is capable of loving as deeply as you require."

Kate smiled, the first true smile Louisa had ever received from her, and it transformed the usual harshness of her features, which tended to resemble her mother's, into the kindness that was more fitting of her father. "I shan't hold you to that promise, Lady Louisa. I know you're in as difficult a spot as Jenny and me when it comes to pleasing our mother."

"Still, I shall try."

"Well, then," Jenny said brightly, "perhaps I should detail what I want when it comes to passion."

"I'll wager you want a well-shaped mouth, skilled hands, and a firm body," Kate said.

Jenny laughed. "You're not far off."

Mr. Applewhite cleared his throat. Louisa had fairly forgotten that he was there.

"Mr. Applewhite, I think our lessons are over for the afternoon," Jenny said.

"Thank you, Miss Jenny. I do have another student waiting on my arrival, and I'm certain she won't mind my arriving early." He gathered up his satchel and walked out of the room.

"He is such a snob," Kate said.

"And Mama's spy," Jenny said. "You do realize he will report every word spoken."

"I don't think we said anything too untoward," Louisa said.

"Miss Jenny?"

They all turned to see the butler standing in the doorway, holding a silver salver.

"Oh, we have a caller," Jenny said, smiling brightly, picking up the card. "And my word, if it isn't the Duke of Hawkhurst anxious to make his mark upon our day. Show him to the conservatory." She glanced over at Louisa. "That's all right, isn't it? This will be a perfect place to showcase our talent."

"Your talent," Kate said, getting to her feet. "I have no interest in the duke. If you'll excuse me . . ."

"Don't tell Mother he's here," Jenny ordered. "I don't want her involved yet."

"Because she'll have you wed before the week is out?"

"Because, in spite of her best intentions, she will frighten the man away."

"The duke has never struck me as a man easily frightened," Louisa said.

"Then let's say she will dim his enthusiasm."

"I shall not breathe a word of his arrival," Kate promised, before waltzing out of the room.

Louisa stepped back from her easel. "We should put this somewhere," she said inanely, referring to her own work, not certain why she was suddenly so very self-conscious that someone might look upon her poor efforts.

"Why?" Jenny asked.

Louisa tried to think of a polite way to say—

"Because mine is so hideous?"

"It's not hideous," Louisa said quickly. "It's . . . it's . . ." She furrowed her brow.

"Hideous," Jenny repeated.

"I'm not certain you were trying."

"Oh, I was trying. I simply have no talent."

"We should tell the duke that this one is yours," Louisa said, pointing to her own work.

"Don't be ridiculous. We Americans may have the reputation of being spoiled, but we don't take credit for what we don't achieve ourselves."

They heard footsteps, and Jenny turned. Louisa could only see her profile, but she could see enough to know the lady was smiling warmly.

"Your Grace," Jenny said, with a well-executed curtsy. "How nice of you to pay a visit this afternoon."

He bowed slightly. "Miss Rose. Lady Louisa."

A time existed when he would have addressed Louisa first, a time before she'd put on the mantle of chaperone.

"Your Grace," Louisa said. "Perhaps we should

adjourn to the garden, where we might have some refreshments."

"Oh, not until he's seen our efforts. Do you paint, Your Grace?" Jenny asked.

"No, I'm afraid I have no talent when it comes to art."

Jenny laughed lightly. "Neither do I. But Lady Louisa is another matter entirely. Come. Tell me what you think of her work."

"Oh, the duke has no time for nor interest in—"

"I'm very interested," he said quietly. "While I may have no talent myself, I'm always in awe of those who do."

Holding his hat in his hand, he walked over until he stood before her canvas. His scent wafted toward her: sandalwood. And something more masculine. He had the scent of a man who had been riding, and she wondered if he'd come by horse rather than carriage.

He seemed to be staring a rather long time.

"It's a rose," she blurted, suddenly very self-conscious of his perusal. She wasn't accustomed to sharing her drawings. They were her guilty pleasure.

A corner of his mouth hitched up. "Yes, I can see that."

"I've never had lessons before," she said, feeling a need to justify the less-than-perfect rendition of a rose that she'd created. All of its flaws were suddenly so glaringly obvious.

"Indeed? One would never know by looking."

"Is that a compliment?"

"No. My compliment is that it is astonishingly good."

"Astonishingly good? So you were taken by surprise? You did not expect it to be good?"

He turned his head, his gaze homing in on hers. "I did not expect to take such pleasure from gazing upon it."

She swallowed hard, not at all certain why she was suddenly so rattled or behaving so irascibly. "I think we should go into the garden."

"Yes, let's," Jenny said. "I'll have a servant fetch us some tea."

She sat so near that if he inhaled deeply he could enjoy the fragrance of her perfume. Strange that with all the scents of flowers in bloom surrounding him, he could still recognize hers. Stranger still, because she was not the lady sitting closest to him.

Lady Louisa sat a short distance away, sketch pad in hand, allowing Hawk the opportunity to woo Miss Rose. Damned if he could think of anything with which to woo her.

"What is she drawing?" Jenny asked.

Hawk jerked his head around to meet Jenny's amused gazed. "I have no earthly idea."

"Really? You were staring so hard I thought perhaps you could see through the paper."

"My apologies. I'm not accustomed to being watched. I find it most disconcerting."

"Surely you have courted others."

"Actually, no."

She angled her head thoughtfully. "Then why me and why now?"

"I'm fast approaching the age when I must see to my duties."

"May I offer you a bit of advice?"

"I would welcome any advice you have to offer."

"A lady does not always welcome honest words."

He chuckled. "I have botched my wooing, haven't I?"

Peering at him over her bone china teacup, before sipping, she said, "Oh, I have every confidence that you can recover quite nicely."

"Do you enjoy the opera?" he asked.

She swallowed delicately, pressed her lips together, and set the cup on the saucer on the table. "Yes, as a matter of fact, I enjoy it immensely."

"I have a box. Perhaps you would be so kind as to accompany me tomorrow evening."

"With my chaperone, of course."

His stomach tightened at the thought of Louisa so very close, but there was no hope for it. "That goes without saying."

"Then I shall be delighted."

"Very good. I shall be by with my carriage at seven." He came to his feet, bowed slightly. "Thank you for a most pleasant visit."

"The pleasure was all mine."

He nodded, turned to the chaperone, who was staring at him oddly. "Lady Louisa. Good day."

"I shall see you out, Your Grace."

She rose to her feet, set her sketch pad aside, and joined him as he headed into the house. "Your visit was rather brief."

"I couldn't think of a damned thing to say, pardon my language."

Her lips twitched, and he could not help but wonder what it might be like to kiss her mouth. Why did thoughts such as those not visit him when he was with Jenny?

"Miss Rose has consented to accompany me to the opera tomorrow evening."

"Then perhaps you should spend what time remains this afternoon studying poetry, so that you might impress her with a bit of well-crafted words."

He grinned. "Surely you are not attempting to help me in my pursuit of a conquest."

She came to a stop in the entry hallway, her smile a bit mischievous. "No, Your Grace, it would be a disservice to the lady were I to do that."

Nodding, he took a step toward the door, stopped, turned. "You were correct in your assessment of me. It is the thrill of the hunt that I take pleasure in. I quickly lose interest in the conquered. Miss Rose does not present me with a challenge, and, therefore, I'm at a loss when it comes to pursuing her. If it is a title she seeks, I have but to ask, and she is mine."

"Do not make the mistake of confusing the daughter with the mother," Lady Louisa said.

Hawk felt a thrill shimmer through him. "You think the daughter would deny me?"

"I think she is a woman with a mind of her own. I cannot speak for what she would or would not do."

"I shall keep that in mind." He turned to go.

"Your Grace?"

He looked back at her. She was gnawing on her lower lip, clenching her hands, and darting a gaze toward the stairs. "I followed you out because Mrs. Rose instructed me to ask you your opinion regarding her daughters."

"Mrs. Rose?"

"Yes, she wants to know if you find her daughters . . . agreeable."

"I find them very agreeable." He tipped his head slightly with further thought. "Too agreeable."

"How can a woman be too agreeable?"

"By not offering a challenge. I'm not certain if these ladies are revealing their true selves."

"Are you revealing yours to them?"

He laughed heartily. "I suppose I am not."

A knock sounded on the door. The footman who had been standing at attention beside it opened it. Ravensley walked in carrying a large bouquet of American Beauty roses. The red rose had been successfully bred only two years before, its name chosen to honor the beauty of the American heiresses now clamoring on England's shores.

"Hawk, fancy meeting you here," Ravensley said.

"Indeed," Hawk replied laconically.

Ravensley tipped his head toward his sister. "Louisa. Will you let Miss Jenny Rose know that I have come to call?"

"She's in the garden. If you'll come with me . . ."

As Ravensley walked by, Hawk grabbed his arm. "You have set your sights on Jenny?"

"Indeed I have. She led me to believe last night that she would welcome my courtship."

Well, Hawk thought. *The hunt just got more interesting.*

Chapter 8

"**P**ray do tell me you're not planning to wear *that* again."

Louisa turned from closing the door to her bedchamber to find Jenny standing in the hallway wearing a lovely dress of lavender, with a modest décolletage, and a skirt with a train that flowed behind her. It wasn't the gown she'd worn to the ball earlier in the week.

The same couldn't be said of the gown that Louisa was presently wearing. It was the one she wore for all her evening entertainments. "No," Louisa said. "I am not *planning* to wear it. Rather I *am* wearing it."

"But you've already worn it once this week."

"Miss Rose—"

"Jenny. We really must do away with this formality."

"Miss Jenny, then. That's as far as I'll go toward informality. However, regarding my gown, I fear it is the only evening wear I possess."

"I don't understand you English girls. How can you catch and hold a man's attention when every time he sees you, you're dressed exactly the same?"

"I'll admit to not understanding you American girls and your extravagances. I daresay I've not seen you wear the same clothing once since I walked through your door."

"And I daresay that you won't." She angled her head. "You're not quite as . . . robust as Kate, but you're almost as tall as she. And while your hair is not nearly as outlandish as hers, I can see hints of red when the light catches yours just right. And your skin tone is more in line with hers. Come along. Let's see what we can find of hers for you to wear. Most of hers are unused while mine are not."

Louisa laughed lightly. "Don't be ridiculous. Hawkhurst will be here any moment—"

"Let him wait."

Louisa stared at her, deciding another tactic was in order. "I'm not going to wear your sister's clothing."

"Why not? Afraid a gentleman might actually take notice of you?"

Louisa felt her mouth drop, her eyes widen. "I beg your pardon?"

"You dress dowdily, like a spinster aunt who has given up on ever finding passion."

Striving not to feel the sting of that sentiment, which struck just a little too close to home, Louisa lifted her chin. "I'll have you know that this gown was quite the rage three years ago."

"Yes, well"—Jenny took Louisa's arm—"let's find something for you that's quite the rage now."

Louisa dug her slippered feet into the carpet. "Jenny, I'm not going to wear one of Kate's gowns."

"Have you ever worn a Worth?"

Louisa licked her lips, shook her head. "No."

"Have you never wanted to?"

"Of course, I've wanted to, but they are notoriously expensive. Besides, if I were to wear it tonight, and then she wore it to a ball, people would know that I had borrowed it—"

Jenny laughed before Louisa could finish explaining the mortification of people knowing that she was borrowing clothes.

"Don't be ridiculous. Kate has a hundred gowns. We'll select one, and you may borrow it for the entire Season."

"Your mother won't like it at all."

"We won't tell her."

"You don't think she'll notice—"

"No. She pays scant attention to our gowns, too busy with her own wardrobe. Come on, it'll be fun."

"Jenny, seriously, the duke—"

"Can *wait*." She leaned forward, and whispered

conspiratorially, "A lady should never give the impression that she is too eager to be in a gentleman's company. Now, come along. While we don't want to appear too eager, neither do we want to appear as though we have no interest at all."

She opened the door to her sister's bedchamber. "Kate, help me find a gown that Lady Louisa can wear this evening."

Kate was sitting on a divan. She looked up from the book she was reading. "What?"

"She wore this gown to the ball. She can't wear it to the opera."

"She's the chaperone. What does it matter?"

"It matters," Jenny said, as she opened a set of doors that led into a small room where gowns were hanging.

So this is what true wealth is like, Louisa couldn't help but think. A room filled with evening gowns. A sitting area. Mirrors placed in such a way that a lady would be able to view her front, sides, and back—all at the same time, by simply looking in one mirror.

Louisa had heard the rumors that American heiresses owned hundreds of gowns, but she'd never believed it . . . until now. Until the evidence surrounded her. And such beautiful, exquisite gowns, with pearls and beads, velvet and lace.

"Her coloring isn't anything like mine," Kate said.

"No one's coloring is like yours. Honestly, sometimes I can't decide if your hair is red or orange," Jenny said distractedly as she began moving gowns aside.

"I can't decide if yours is red or brown," Kate said.

"Depends on the lighting." Jenny turned around, holding up a lovely gown of pink tulle and black velvet. "This should do nicely. Where are the accessories?"

Without hesitation, Kate walked to a dresser.

"Honestly, this is simply too much," Louisa said, clutching her hands to prevent her fingers from reaching out to touch a gown more beautiful than any she'd ever worn. To wear a Charles Worth gown had long been a dream of hers, but if she wore it, how could she return to her simpler gowns? Was it better to have one night of feeling like a princess, then spending the remainder of her life knowing what she would never again have, or was it better never to have and never know?

"If you don't like it, we can find another," Jenny said.

"It's lovely, but the duke—"

"Again, he can wait. Believe me, gentlemen appreciate us much more when we make them work a bit to gain our attention." She smiled brightly. "Surely you wouldn't deny Kate and me the fun of transforming you into an American heiress."

"But your mother—"

"I asked Father to take her out for the evening."

Kate approached, holding pink kid gloves, pink silk stockings, and pink silk slippers with black bows. Louisa had accessories, but they did not match any particular outfit down to the tiniest detail. Rather she purchased items so they had multiple uses, could be interchanged without seeming out of place. These accessories could be worn with only this gown.

"Jenny feared Mama would push the duke into asking for her hand before he left," Kate said.

"Your mother isn't that bad," Louisa said, again not certain why she took up for the woman. Perhaps because she had no mother to see after her, and a part of her envied these girls, thought they should appreciate their mother a bit more.

"She's awful," Kate said. "Now, Lady Louisa, do let Jenny and me have our fun. We often dressed each other when we were younger. I must admit that each of us takes pleasure in making the other look her best. You won't be disappointed."

"It seems like so much trouble—"

"Nonsense. Besides, won't the duke be the envy of everyone when he arrives at the opera house with two lovely ladies on his arm?" Jenny asked.

Louisa knew that she should leave this room immediately, but for three years she'd worn the same gown to every evening function that she'd attended. To have one night—

"Is it truly a Worth?" she heard herself asking.

Smiling warmly, Jenny said, "Are ladies such as we deserving of anything less?"

He was unaccustomed to waiting being forced upon him. During the hunt, he would often bide his time before making his calculated move, but as a rule, ladies did not seek his displeasure by delaying their entry.

Jenny Rose was another matter entirely. She had the upper hand, and well she knew it. Hawk stood in the entry hallway, holding his top hat and walking stick in one gloved hand, attempting to rein in his impatience. He was anxious to be about the seduction. It had even occurred to him to seek out her parents and ask for their daughter's hand in marriage.

If a title was what they desired for her, then why was courtship even necessary? It was a colossal waste of his time and energies and simply delayed the introduction of his own sister into Society.

Hearing light footsteps, he glanced up at the sweeping staircase and felt as though someone had taken his walking stick and given him a hard jab in the chest. She was absolutely stunning. A vision in pink. Her hair was swept up off her alabaster shoulders, a band of gold circling the top of her head, holding pink ostrich feathers so they curled over her hair. She came to stand before him, the hue in her cheeks matching the hue of her gown. Had he ever seen so much of her shoulders, her throat, her chest? The swell of her breasts was merely a hint, yet his body reacted as though all were revealed.

"—lovely, don't you think?"

He jerked his head around, the heat of embarrassment traveling along his neck, threatening to strangle him. What had Jenny Rose been saying?

He forced himself to nod, smile, and hold her gaze when he desperately wanted to take another long, lingering look at Lady Louisa, from the silly ostrich feathers perched atop her head to the tiny pink satin slippers peeking out from beneath her hem. "Miss Rose, my apologies. I must confess that I'd not expected your chaperone to dress so . . ."

"Becomingly?" she offered.

"Inappropriately," he stated succinctly.

"Oh, come, Your Grace. I find your custom of chaperones tedious, and this way I can simply pretend I'm going out with a friend and a gentleman." She winked. "Much easier to escape the watchful eye of a friend, don't you find?"

Her eyes and the moue of her mouth held promises of mischief not spoken. He couldn't understand why he wasn't enthralled with the prospect.

"If we do not get on our way, we shall be tardy and miss the beginning of the opera," he pointed out.

She laughed lightly. "I daresay that my interest in the opera is such that it has never bothered me in the least to miss the beginning."

"If you have no interest in the opera, then why did you consent to accompany me?"

She wound her arm around his. "Why because I have an interest in you, Your Grace."

He felt the heat intensify at his neck and darted a glance at Lady Louisa. She was studying a glove as though she'd never before worn one, and he couldn't help but realize how awkward it was to be a chaperone—a young chaperone—when a couple was engaged in a courting ritual.

"We should be off," he announced, and thought Lady Louisa looked as relieved as he felt.

The footman opened the door, and the ladies preceded Hawk into the night. Lady Louisa's gown dipped almost as low in the back as it did in the front, and with the help of the gas lamps bordering the walk, he could make out the line of her spine. He'd always favored a lady's neck, her shoulders, trailing his mouth along her spine, feeling her shiver beneath him. He was in a frightfully uncomfortable state by the time they reached his coach. He helped Miss Rose inside, then held his hand out to Lady Louisa. He seemed unable to stop himself from squeezing her fingers, halting her progress.

"I don't believe I've ever seen you look quite so lovely," he said quietly.

Her eyes widened, and she ducked her head as though suddenly embarrassed. "My charges are determined that I should reap the benefits of living within their household. My attire was their idea, not mine."

"So you did not wish to take my breath away?"

She seemed momentarily flummoxed. Not that he could blame her. What had he been thinking to reveal that sentiment?

"Quite honestly," she finally said, "my only thought was to do whatever necessary to get

Jenny down the stairs. She is quite headstrong."

"Not unlike you."

"I prefer to think of myself as determined."

"Are you two coming?" Jenny called out. "I thought we were in a hurry."

Indeed he was most anxious to get this night over with. He helped Louisa into the coach, then made his own way inside, taking the seat opposite them so he traveled backward. A footman closed the door, and before Hawkhurst had taken a breath, the coach was on its way.

It irritated him that he could smell Louisa so distinctly, that he was so much more aware of her. He should have invited both sisters; then perhaps they could have left the blasted chaperone at home.

"You don't strike me as a man who would enjoy the opera," Jenny said, suddenly bursting into his thoughts with a voice much too loud for his tastes. It was the way of these Americans to speak as though the entire world wished to hear what they had to say.

"I inherited the box from my father. My mother enjoys the opera."

"Oh, is she in London then?"

"No, she prefers the country, but I keep the box available for when she might come to the city."

"It seems you are a most thoughtful son, much more so than my brother, I daresay."

He shifted his gaze to Louisa. She was staring out the window, her profile limned by the light from the streetlamps. He'd never sought to seduce a woman who brought a chaperone along. It was a rather uncomfortable endeavor.

He turned his attention back to Jenny. It was difficult to tell in the shadowy confines of his coach, but it seemed she was watching him quite intently. He wondered if his appearance pleased her. Then he cursed himself for caring. She wanted only his title. It was all he intended to offer.

"I was unaware you had a brother," he said, only because the silence stretching out between them was beginning to test his patience.

"Yes, Jeremy. He's twenty-eight. Unfortunately, I don't see him nearly often enough. He spends a good deal of his time traveling. He just returned from a lengthy sojourn in Europe."

"How fortunate for him that he is in a position to do as he pleases."

"You are not in a position such as that, are you, Your Grace?" she asked.

"No, Miss Rose, I am not."

"Neither am I. I find that to be most unfortunate. What would you do if you *could* do as you pleased?"

"It is not so much what I would do as what I would not do. I would not marry."

"Truly? My brother is of the same mind. I don't understand. Why do men abhor the thought of marriage do you suppose?"

"Why do women adore it so?" he countered.

"Because we have been brought up to believe it will bring us happiness. Will your wife be a happy woman, Your Grace?"

Louisa swung her head around, and even in the darkness, he could sense the dare in her gaze. To reveal the truth: that any woman married to him would be more likely to be miserable than happy.

"I'm certain she and I could come to an understanding that would result in her happiness," he finally admitted.

"Well, that is all a woman could ask, I suppose."

But he feared that beneath her words, he heard the censure and the acknowledgment that a woman—especially a woman in her position—could ask for a great deal more.

It was an awkward thing to be a chaperone, to be privy to conversations that should have been private. To witness a gentleman's attempts at seduction, a woman's flirtations. To be present and yet invisible. To hold one's tongue when it wanted to wag incessantly. To be merely an observer, not a participant in the evening.

It was especially awkward when the gentleman insisted that she sit beside her charge at the front of the box while he sat at the back. Louisa had wanted to be irritated with Hawkhurst; instead, she'd been touched that he refused to relegate her to the role of inconsequential companion.

She fought to focus on the performance, to appreciate fully this rare moment of actually attending an opera, but instead she found her mind drifting to thoughts of the man sitting behind her. The way his gaze had roamed over her as she'd descended the stairs: almost feral in its intensity, it had set her heart to racing. She was not a newcomer to men's attentions, but they rarely lingered long once the reality of her financial situation became apparent.

Even wrapped inside the shadows of the coach, she'd been aware of his gaze, homing in on her with startling precision. She'd been acutely aware of his scent filling the small confines. When she closed her eyes, she could see the fierce pride in his stance as he'd stood in the entryway, a man at a disadvantage who failed to give quarter. She'd been cognizant of her own position, its unfairness; but she'd never considered how difficult it would be for a man to pretend interest, for a man literally to hold his hat in his hand and hope he would be found worthy.

She nearly leapt out of her skin when Jenny touched her arm, leaned over, and whispered, "I'm going to visit the ladies' toilette."

"Can you not wait for the intermission?"

"Afraid not, but I won't be long."

"I'll go with you."

"No need for you to miss the performance when the gentleman who could get me into mischief will be staying behind."

"But still, to let you go out alone—"

"I'm only going to the room designated for ladies to freshen up. I'm hardly likely to be ravished in the hallway. I'll be fine. Besides, it's the duke you're to keep an eye on and keep in line. Not me."

Louisa had to admit Jenny had made a valid point. What mischief could the lady get into when the main mischief-maker remained? Louisa nodded. "All right then."

Smiling sweetly, Jenny patted Louisa's arm before rising. She took a step back, whispered to Hawkhurst, then disappeared through the curtains at the back of the box.

Louisa was suddenly very much aware that she was alone with Hawkhurst. She forced her attention to the stage. It would not do to fantasize, even for a moment, that she was the reason he was in attendance this evening. She heard a scuffling sound, then he was sitting beside her. She was incredibly grateful that she wore gloves to absorb the sudden dampness of her palms. She focused more intently—

"Are you enjoying the performance?" he asked quietly.

"Yes, thank you."

"I have never understood the appeal of opera."

"And yet you keep the box."

"For my mother, as I said."

"It seems an unwarranted extravagance when one is having a difficult time making ends meet."

"On occasion I . . . sell the seats for the evening for a good deal more than they are worth."

His voice was tight, and when she looked at him, she could see what it had cost him to admit what he did, and she couldn't understand why he had chosen to confess to her. Perhaps because their situations were so alike. "To Americans?" she asked.

"No. To my fellow Englishmen who suddenly find themselves with more money than they know what to do with."

"I assume you're referring to the upper class that has emerged through hard work."

"Indeed. They have means but not the legacy. It is an odd arrangement, and they are encroaching ever more upon our . . . small, intimate society."

"Mr. Rose says that our aristocrats must accept that their future holds work if they are to survive."

"He may have the right of it. Still, it is a dismal prospect."

"Less dismal than starving to death."

He flashed a grin. "Are you a realist, Lady Louisa?"

She straightened. "I like to think so, yes. It's the very reason that I took a position as chaperone. Because I grew weary of waiting for life to offer me something when I was fully capable of acquiring my own happiness."

"Being at another's beck and call brings you happiness?"

"It brings me independence, Your Grace. I cannot say that marriage would have done the same. While I will admit that being waited upon is quite pleasant, I find it exceedingly satisfying to know

I'm in charge of my actions in a way that I have never been before."

She glanced over her shoulder at the still curtains. What was keeping Jenny?

"How did your brother fare with Miss Rose yesterday afternoon?" Hawkhurst asked.

"Not very well, I'm afraid."

He leaned nearer, bringing his wondrous scent with him. She wondered why she'd never found the scent of any other man quite as appealing.

"She did not fancy him?" he asked.

"Her mother did not fancy him. Unfortunately, Mrs. Rose had chosen that moment, shortly after his arrival, to come out to the garden. She was less than impressed with his title. She forbade him to call upon them again. I felt rather sorry for him." His pride had been bruised, his manhood battered, and while Louisa questioned his appropriateness as a husband for her charges, she'd still taken offense at Mrs. Rose's treatment of her brother.

"A pity," Hawkhurst muttered.

"There is insincerity in your tone, Your Grace. Do not for one moment think that I do not recognize that Mrs. Rose's attitude gives you an advantage."

"As I said, I enjoy the thrill of the hunt, and without competition—"

"Make no mistake," she said smugly. "You have competition."

"With whom?" he fairly growled, coming even nearer, until she could almost feel the heat leaving his skin.

"I'm not at liberty to say."

"Damnation, Louisa—"

"Do not use profanity or that tone of voice with me. I have been honest regarding my opinion of you as a prospect. I will not reveal anything that might give you a further advantage than you have already gained."

"I'm not as bad as all that."

"Do you deny that you imbibe to excess?"

"On occasion, perhaps, I drink a bit too much."

"Do you deny that your sexual appetites are insatiable and that you take more than one woman to your bed at a time to appease your needs?"

Closing his eyes, he pressed two fingers against the bridge of his nose as though to push back some sort of pain. "What else has your brother said?" he asked, with the low growl she was coming to recognize that he used when he was incredibly displeased.

"I should think that was quite enough."

"Indeed." He took her hand, turned it, and placed his fingers against her gloved wrist. She could feel the heat of his touch. "Your heart is racing. Is it the thought of such wickedness or my nearness that causes such a reaction?"

"Neither. I simply have a very rapid heart." She tried to tug free, but he held fast.

And worse, he managed to draw her nearer, until she felt his breath skim over her cheek.

"I was all of twenty," he rasped in a seductive voice. "It was one night, and they were twins who proposed the notion to me. I'm not one to turn away opportunity, especially when it comes in the form of a lovely lady . . . or two."

She was finding it increasingly difficult to breathe. "Jenny will be returning at any moment. It would not be wise to be found in this compromising position, and if someone else should look over—"

"They will think we are merely whispering about the opera. They cannot detect your blush, or the speed of your heart, or the scent of desire that is growing—"

"Release me now, or I shall be forced to slap you, Your Grace," she said.

He did release her, as though she'd suddenly become too hot, a fire that could scorch.

"My apologies." He leaned back slightly. "You are the way to Jenny, yet, I seem to insult and offend you at every turn."

"Perhaps because you do not truly wish to marry her," she said quietly.

"What a gentleman wishes and what a gentleman must do seldom coincide."

"The same holds true for a lady."

"An unfortunate state of affairs."

"Indeed."

"I think it would be best if I return to my chair."

He took her hand and this time, although he merely pressed his lips to her gloved knuckles, still she felt the moist heat of his mouth. "Pink becomes you."

She wondered if he'd say the same if he could see that she was pink from the top of her head to the tips of her toes, pink with embarrassment, flushed with pleasure.

"Thank you, Your Grace."

She thought she heard him chuckle quietly as he returned to his seat, giving her the impression that he did know that more than her gown was pink. She glanced back over her shoulder, cursing Jenny for taking so long. It seemed her chaperone was in need of a chaperone.

"I have to go," Jenny whispered.

"Another moment more," he said quietly, nibbling on her ear, causing incredible sensations to travel the length of her body.

"I'll be missed, and what if they come looking for me?"

"They won't find you back here in the shadows."

They were in a hallway, ensconced in a dark corner, near an empty box that was reserved for royalty, who'd had the good graces not to attend that evening.

"I can't believe your chaperone let you come out alone," he said.

Laughing lightly, she leaned her head back,

giving him easier access to her throat. "As most, she believes it is the gentleman who is the cause of mischief, not the lady."

"And you like to cause mischief."

"As I have told you. I require passion, and one cannot test the waters of passion with a chaperone looking on."

"You Americans are so bold."

Smiling wickedly, she pushed him away. "We know what we want, and we're not afraid to go after what we want." Reaching out, she touched his cheek. "Now I *must* go." She kissed her gloved fingertips and pressed them to his lips. "I will send word when I can determine how to arrange another meeting."

"Even if it is for no more than a moment, it will be enough."

She felt her heart being crushed and shook her head. This was not love, it was passion: the manner in which he looked at her, touched her, kissed her. They'd not known each other long enough for it to be love. "It will be soon, I promise."

Before he could say anything to convince her that a few more moments wouldn't put them at peril of being discovered, she lifted her skirts and hurried down the hallway until she reached the doorway that led into the duke's box. She slipped inside and took her seat.

Lady Louisa leaned close. "What kept you?"

"I'm sorry. I had a bit of a headache brewing, and the performance wasn't helping matters, so I sat for a while with my eyes closed."

"Should we leave?" Lady Louisa asked, the concern in her voice causing Jenny to feel guilty about her lie.

"No, I'm fine now." She sat back with a contented sigh. She was more than fine. Every lady needed a good ravishment now and then.

Chapter 9

After listening to opera for most of the evening, Louisa thought the coach seemed unnaturally quiet as it journeyed through the fog-shrouded streets of London, its passengers either too weary or too preoccupied to carry on any sort of meaningful conversation. She'd never traveled with a gentleman other than her brother or father. She didn't know why she'd expected there to be ample discourse. The hushed and shadowed confines seemed to call for something other than the type of discussions she was accustomed to engaging in during dinners.

She told herself that she was merely a deterrent to naughty behavior, that she was not supposed to engage Jenny or Hawkhurst in conversation, and yet . . .

"Thank you for sharing your box with us this evening," she heard herself say before she could think better of it.

She saw his teeth flash as he smiled. "It was my pleasure."

He fairly purred pleasure like a contented cat—a very large cat—that has lapped up the last of the cream. Did he have to constantly make innuendos? Or did she simply interpret everything he said as though it had some scandalous meaning?

"I'm always amazed by how quiet it gets when the fog rolls in," she said, anything to fill the silence.

"I find it a good time to be reflective," he said.

Jenny laughed. "Then you must be reflective quite a bit, because it seems there is always fog."

Louisa heard Hawkhurst chuckle. "Perhaps too reflective. What sort of weather do you enjoy?"

"Sunshine," she answered without hesitation. "Why would anyone like any other sort of weather?"

"I enjoy when it rains," he said. "What of you, Lady Louisa?"

She was suddenly very self-conscious and wished she'd kept quiet. "I like cold days when I can snuggle before a fire, which is a good thing as the manor at our estate is quite drafty."

"I've heard most are," Jenny said. "From what I've been told, it can be quite a shock to an heiress to discover that the manor house has not been kept up as well as the London residence. Is your manor home drafty, Your Grace?"

"There are spots where one can catch a chill, but I have tried to keep it well maintained for the sake of my mother."

"You care for her a great deal," Jenny said.

"My father, upon his deathbed, charged me with seeing that she was always happy. A drafty home that makes one frequently ill doesn't lead to happiness."

"My mother once told me that I should pay attention to the manner in which a man treats his mother, that it is often a foreshadowing of the way that he will treat his wife."

"I'm not familiar with that philosophy," he said.

"Is that a polite way of saying that my mother utters nonsense?"

Again, he flashed a smile. Louisa wished she could look away, wished she could ignore the conversation, wished she wasn't intrigued by the glimpse she'd been given into his relationship with his mother. It was much easier to dislike a man who showed no kindness toward the woman who'd given birth to him.

"I promise you," Hawkhurst said, "that I shall not look upon my wife as I look upon my mother."

"But if you are kind to your mother, it stands to reason that you will be kind to your wife," Jenny said. "So it is simply a point in your favor."

Louisa did look away then. She didn't want to see that speculative gleam in Hawkhurst's eyes as he looked at Jenny, the challenging smile that she was giving him, as though daring him to come up with ways to earn more points.

Louisa wondered if she should sit down with Jenny and tell her all the things she knew about Hawkhurst that would take the points away. She shouldn't be favoring him, she shouldn't be enjoying his company or looking at him with speculation and a hint of promise.

But Louisa was having a difficult time standing behind the conviction of her beliefs. He was not suitable . . . and yet she was no longer entirely certain that she could proclaim him unsuitable. What had he really done to fall out of favor with her?

"That would be lovely," she heard Jenny say. Jenny touched her arm. "Wouldn't it?"

"I'm sorry. I really wasn't paying attention."

"His Grace wants to take us rowing on the Thames tomorrow afternoon. Won't that be great fun?"

"Of course," Louisa managed to say. "Great fun, indeed."

It had seemed like the perfect plan. Remove Miss Rose from her home during the afternoon when gentlemen were most likely to call. Make her unavailable for their attentions and flirtations. What Hawk had not counted on was the closeness of her chaperone within the small rowboat he'd rented.

Holding a parasol at the perfect angle so that it cast shade over both ladies, Louisa sat behind Jenny. She wore a light blue dress with a high

collar, buttons in the front, every one snug and
secure in its place. Nowhere on the material
could he see signs of fraying or fading, and he
wondered if this dress had also once belonged to
one of the Rose sisters. Like Jenny, Louisa wore a
wide-brimmed straw hat decorated with satin
ribbon and dried flowers. It shaded her face and
made the parasol seem superfluous.

Hawk had removed his jacket, rolled up his
sleeves, and set himself to the task of rowing
with a great deal of enthusiasm, making his muscles burn in order to distract himself from the
fact that Louisa sat so damnably near, a portrait
of perfection, gazing off to the side, absorbed in
the scenery. He could only be grateful that her
attention wasn't focused on him, and yet even as
he thought it, he was somewhat irritated that she
could dismiss him so easily when he was having
a hell of a difficult time ignoring her.

"Are we engaged in a race, Your Grace?" Jenny
asked.

Slowing his frantic movements, he shifted his
gaze to her. Was she not the one who should be
garnering all his attention? He gave her what he
hoped was a seductive grin. "My apologies. I suppose I was simply . . ."

Smiling, she angled her head thoughtfully.
"Demonstrating your strength?"

"I will admit to enjoying sports and competition."

"I don't know how much competition truly

exists if the others on the river don't realize a contest is taking place."

Almost a dozen other boats were floating nearby. Hawk had planned to have a calm and relaxing outing. Instead, he'd fairly worn himself out.

"What sort of sports do you enjoy? Other than rowing?" she asked. "Croquet perhaps?"

He scowled; Jenny laughed lightly, and Hawk found himself wishing that he could say something that would bring Louisa's laughter into the mix. Had he ever heard her laugh, truly laugh? Not scoff, or scorn, or berate with a harsh clearing of her throat? He'd heard her light laughter, but he wanted more. He wanted her holding her sides, her smile wide, her eyes bright.

"I do not consider croquet a sport. It is merely a game, one that allows for flirtation more than anything else. I enjoy lawn tennis," he admitted.

"My brother is fond of that sport. I would enjoy it more if I were allowed to wear trousers."

That comment brought Louisa's head around and a bit of satisfaction to Hawk. So she *was* listening to the conversation, not completely distracted by the fauna. He tried to imagine Louisa in trousers, shook his head. It was Jenny who was interested in wearing men's clothing.

"I daresay ladies wearing trousers is something that shall never come to pass," Hawk said.

"I disagree," Jenny said. "At least in America. Years ago, Amelia Bloomer advocated women wearing baggy trousers like those worn by Turkish women. Even your Rational Dress Society approves of Miss Bloomer's notions."

"It is not *my* Rational Dress Society," he grumbled.

That drew a light laugh from Louisa, and he welcomed the excuse to shift his attention to her. "I suppose you are a member of that ludicrous society."

She ducked her head. "I support Viscountess Haberton and Mrs. King's notion that a lady should not have to wear more than seven pounds of clothing."

"If that is their stated philosophy, then I suppose I support them after all, because I prefer women with no clothing at all." As soon as the words were out of his mouth, as soon as Jenny—whom he'd forgotten was sitting right in front of him—gasped, as soon as Louisa stared at him openmouthed, he regretted that he'd felt a need to shock Louisa, to ensure she keep her distance. Which was a ludicrous action on his part when she obviously had no interest in him whatsoever. So instead of building a barrier that would keep him from even being tempted by Louisa, he had effectively ruined his chance of making a favorable impression with his intended lady.

He shifted his attention to Jenny, where it should have remained all along. "My apologies. That was an entirely inappropriate comment for me to make in the presence of a lady as delicate as you."

"I have an older brother with whom I'm very

close, Your Grace. I'm well aware that men prefer women without clothing."

"Still, it has been my experience that a man is better off not voicing his preference."

"It seems we are prone constantly to disagree, Your Grace. How is a woman to know what a man prefers if he is not confident enough to share his preferences—even if it is a mere whispering in her ear?"

Her suggestive voice, her flirtatious smile should have had his body tightening in response. Instead, he found himself put off by her brashness, could not envision leaning near and whispering anything of a seductive nature to her. She was too easily conquered, not a challenge in the least.

Louisa, however, looked properly appalled by the direction of the conversation. He met her gaze only to have her quickly avert it, once again seeming to find solace along the banks of the river. He wondered if she'd ever been kissed. If a gentleman had ever whispered his longings near her ear. And if he had, what exactly had he said? Had he whispered memorized poetry, or had the words come from his heart?

"I believe you've made your chaperone uncomfortable," he said.

"Nonsense," Louisa answered quickly. "I'm paying no heed at all to your conversation."

She grimaced just as Jenny said, "If that were true, you wouldn't have known what he said."

Jenny then proceeded to laugh as though she thought everything were great fun, while Louisa looked over at her charge apologetically, and even with the lacy parasol casting a shadow over her face, Hawk could tell that she was blushing profusely. He wondered if the blush ran the length of her body.

"I'm sorry," Louisa said. "It is a bit difficult not to hear when the boat is so small."

"No need to apologize," Jenny said. "Honestly, I suspect it must be rather uncomfortable for you to watch us skirt around the mating rituals. And I suppose you know all the ways to evade one's chaperone so one can test the depths of a man's passions."

Hawk watched in fascination as Lady Louisa's blush darkened.

"I can't say that I've spent any time evading a chaperone," Louisa said.

"You *can't* say or you *won't* say?" Jenny challenged.

"Allow me to be clearer. I have spent no time evading chaperones."

"I believe quite strongly that every woman should evade a chaperone at least once in her youth. How else is she to experience a kiss?"

Louisa's gaze slammed into his. Her blush deepened even more as her gaze dipped, and he wondered if she was studying his mouth, curious as to what his kiss might be like. Then he cursed himself for giving a care about her thoughts. How was it that she managed so easily to distract him from his purpose?

Suddenly she looked away, and said on a sigh

as soft as a summer breeze, "I'm amazed by the lovely weather we're having this afternoon. We could not be more fortunate."

Jenny laughed. "Are you attempting to change the subject?"

"Quite."

Jenny laughed again. Louisa gave her an impish smile that made Hawk feel as though he'd taken a swift kick to the gut and almost caused him to release his hold on the oars. He imagined Louisa nestled up against his body, curled against his side as they lay beneath silk sheets that would serve to cool the heat of their fevered skin.

Once, if he could have her but once, this fascination with her would desert him. It was because she was unobtainable and untouchable that his attention kept shifting to her.

"Is there anything in these waters that will snap at my fingers?" Jenny asked.

He shifted his gaze to her. They seemed effectively to have moved off the topic of kisses and evading chaperones. Thank goodness. "No, your fingers will be quite safe."

An image of nibbling on Louisa's fingers popped into his head. He thought of her holding the book in the library, how slender her fingers were, how rounded her nails. He thought of them digging into his backside as she squirmed beneath him—

Shifting on the bench, he began rowing in earnest while Jenny slowly, seductively removed a glove. If Louisa wasn't here, he would have taken that bared hand, pressed it to his lips, circled his tongue over her knuckles . . .

He would have trailed his mouth across her wrist, along her forearm. He would have kissed the inside of her elbow, inhaled the perfume she would have placed there. He would have slowly journeyed along the inside of her arm, stopping only when he reached her shoulder. He would have nibbled on the sensitive skin at the base of her neck, heard her sharp intake of breath, shifted his gaze up to meet hers, stared into her cornflower blue eyes . . .

Damnation. Louisa again, worming her way into his fantasies. It was Jenny dangling her bare hand over the side of the boat. It was Jenny's fingers tripping over the current. Jenny's green eyes that he should envision gazing into.

Why could Jenny Rose not have a hideous, old, and unsightly chaperone? Why did she have a chaperone who was playing havoc with his fantasies, his desires, his yearnings? Why did her chaperone continually distract him?

Louisa was aware of each stroke of the oars, each bunching and relaxing of the muscles in Hawkhurst's forearms. The man's form had been sculpted as though by the gods—simply to torment women with his perfection. Even turning her head and focusing on the greenery along the banks did her little good, because her peripheral vision was exceptionally irritating, taking note of Hawkhurst almost as though she were facing

him. She'd actually considered turning complet-
ing around, presenting him with her back—but
she feared the rudeness of that gesture. After all,
he was a duke.

Not to mention a friend of her brother's.

And it appeared he had Jenny's complete interest. Why else would the young woman be hinting
at escaping her chaperone for a moment of privacy in order to have an illicit kiss?

Louisa was grateful for the wide brim of her
straw hat that shaded her eyes as well as the parasol. She hoped both darkened her face enough
that the numerous blushes she'd felt making their
way up her neck and into her cheeks had not
been visible to the duke. What would he make of
a woman so easily embarrassed?

She and Jenny were complete opposites, and
Louisa felt rather boring sitting in the same boat
with her. Again, she couldn't help but wonder if it
was more than her impoverished state that had
kept gentlemen callers away.

Occasionally her gaze shifted to a gentleman in
another boat. None had the duke's virility; none
seemed to have his determination to reach the
end of the river. She smiled at that thought. Of
course he had no intention of rowing until he
reached river's end, but he was putting his all into
the effort, as though he sought to escape something.

Or perhaps he was simply showing off. She
doubted any man could keep up with him. He'd
mentioned sports, which had surprised her. She'd

assumed his life of debauchery would leave little time for sporting pleasures, and yet she couldn't deny that he had a very healthy bronzed tint to his skin. She wanted to ask after his interests, but she was not the one with whom he should be conversing.

As a chaperone, she should be invisible, a role for which she'd apparently been preparing all her life. To be present, but unnoticed. To be available if needed, to be disregarded if not.

Unlike Hawkhurst, who would be noticed even if he dressed in clothing that matched his surroundings. He was not a man to be overlooked. He stood out. Even here on the Thames, with others in similar boats, wearing similar shirts, trousers, and straw hats. While most continued to wear their jackets, Jenny sat on Hawkhurst's . . . a bit of cushioning he'd said with a grin . . . a gentlemanly gesture Louisa would not have expected of him.

But she didn't quite trust it. He was seeking to woo the American heiress—no doubt at any cost, even if it meant creating a false perception of him as a man and potential husband. While Mrs. Rose wouldn't look beyond his title, Louisa was certain that Jenny would.

She couldn't help but respect the girl for that bit of wisdom. She had little doubt that Jenny was worthy of a duke, would make an exceptional duchess.

But she sincerely hoped that she wouldn't settle for this duke. Although for the life of her, she was no longer certain why she thought it would be a horrible thing to be married to Hawkhurst.

And that worried her even more, because how could she properly advise Jenny when Louisa was losing her own perspective on what a suitable man should be?

Chapter 10

The two outings with Hawkhurst had signaled the start of a whirlwind of activities that seemed to know no end: gentleman callers in the afternoon, theater and concerts and dinners in the evenings. Always Jenny and Kate ushered Louisa into their wardrobe room and insisted that she select something different to wear.

That morning Louisa stood in the confectioner's shop, studying all the varied offerings in the display case, trying to decide which she should select. It was the first time in days that she'd worn her own clothing in public, something that had been worn on more than one occasion. She drew comfort from the familiar.

And dearly appreciated that she had a few hours to herself.

Last night Louisa had accompanied Jenny to a concert at the Royal Albert Hall. The Duke of Pemburton had been Jenny's escort. Louisa had always thought highly of the duke, had actually encouraged Jenny to welcome his suit. By evening's end, Louisa had decided that marriage to Pemburton would bore Jenny to tears and leave her permanently bent over as she strived to hear the man's mumbling conversations. Why could he not speak clearly, succinctly, and a bit more loudly?

He was only forty for goodness' sakes.

It seemed no one had succeeded in catching Jenny's fancy to such a degree that he was all she spoke of. Much to Louisa's chagrin, Jenny spoke of Hawkhurst the most—not so much Jenny's interest in the duke, but her perception that the duke was interested in Louisa. Ludicrous ramblings.

Upon arriving home last night, Jenny had declared that she intended to sleep in. Kate had begun reading a new novel and didn't want to be disturbed this morning. Which left Louisa to do entirely as she pleased.

And what made matters even more exciting was that Mr. Rose had given Louisa her first month's salary. She was practically a woman of independent means. It was an incredibly heady sensation: to have money that was hers to spend on anything she wished.

She contemplated paying her brother a visit, giving him half her money, but, damnation, she'd worked hard for it, swallowed her pride, earned the right to clutch the money in her little hands. Or hear it jingling in her purse as it were.

She'd never before experienced such a sense of accomplishment. It was intoxicating. Had her almost giddy. She wanted to skip across a park as she had when she was a child. She wanted to sing, dance, and purchase new slippers.

On the other hand, she thought it would be prudent to retain as many of her coins as possible, but the appeal of spending just a bit was overwhelming. Mr. Rose had told her that the carriage was hers to use, and so she'd had the driver take her to a nearby section of shops. She'd told him that she'd rent a hansom to return her to the Rose residence. She'd spent the morning peering in shop windows until the urge to spend became too great. Then she'd ducked into this sweet shop, determined to make at least one small purchase.

And now she was overwhelmed by the varied selections. She couldn't remember the last time she'd visited a sweet shop. With her father, when she was much younger, she supposed. He'd had a weakness for sour cherry drops, while she'd simply adored toffee. When poverty visited, one was required to sacrifice the pleasures of extravagance. Louisa had gone a good long while without the taste of sweets upon her tongue. She hardly knew how to end her hiatus: to go with her favorite or to sample something she'd never before experienced. She leaned nearer to the glass case, studying the various assorted colors. Four for a penny. Perhaps she would have two toffee and then—

"Attempting to sweeten your temperament?" a low voice asked near her ear.

Jerking upright, she twisted around and glared at the man who stood there, grinning foolishly as though he'd made some grand joke. He wore a frock coat, a gray waistcoat and gloves, and dark gray tie. She couldn't deny that regardless of what he wore, he was a man who drew a lady's eye. "Hawkhurst."

"Lady Louisa." He glanced around. "Where's Miss Jenny?"

"Still abed."

"So they sent you to fetch some sweets?"

She angled her chin slightly. "No, actually, I'm here shopping for myself. I couldn't decide between the toffee or the fruit confections."

"I see the dilemma."

Did he really? she wondered. He'd never struck her as a man with a sweet tooth.

"Your Grace!" the clerk behind the counter said enthusiastically as he bustled over. "Here for your weekly purchase I assume?"

Well, it seemed Louisa had judged Hawkhurst's fondness for sweets unfairly.

"Indeed, but please see to Lady Louisa's needs first."

"Of course, Your Grace." The clerk turned his attention to her. "What will it be, my lady?"

She nibbled on her lower lip and decided on a compromise: something familiar, something new, and something remembered. "Two toffees, a pear drop, and a sour cherry."

"Very good. And what will be your pleasure, Your Grace? The usual?"

"Yes, please, a dozen brandy balls."

Louisa rolled her eyes and muttered. "I should have known."

"Should have known what precisely?" Hawkhurst asked.

"That you would ask for something with a bit of wickedness in it."

"They're rather tasty. I'll let you try one."

"No, thank you."

"They won't make you drunk. Even if you eat a hundred. I tried once."

She stared at him in astonishment. "Surely, you jest. A hundred at one time?"

"One right after the other." He leaned near. "I was all of fourteen and made myself quite ill."

"Was that when you decided to sample my father's liquor?" she asked, a brow arched. Although his skin was swarthy, she thought she detected a blush working its way along his strong jaw line.

"You always did come upon us at the most inopportune moments," he said, his voice low, as though he was imparting secrets.

Her stomach quivered, and she didn't want to think about all the women he may have spoken to, in the dark, using that voice.

The clerk brought over their two small sacks.

"Put the lady's purchase on my account," Hawkhurst said, much to Louisa's astonishment. She was fairly certain that his financial situation mirrored her brother's.

"That's very kind of you, but quite unnecessary," she said. "I'm in possession of my own funds."

"Please, I must insist."

She thought about arguing, but she didn't wish to make a public spectacle of herself. Nor did she wish to cause him embarrassment. She sensed his purchasing her sweets was more of an issue of pride, not because he cared enough for her to want to give her a gift. Besides, others were coming into the shop, and she didn't want rumors to begin circulating. "Thank you, Your Grace, that's most generous of you."

"Think nothing of it."

He followed her out of the shop and glanced around again. "Are you alone?"

"Yes. I'm a chaperone, so I require no company. It's quite liberating."

"I admit to finding it rather odd that a single woman of marriageable age is gallivanting around the town without benefit of protection."

"How you find it does not concern me." It was amazing how he could so easily prick her temper. In an effort to make amends, she held up her small sack. "Thank you again."

"I must confess to having no willpower when it comes to sweets. A park is nearby. Will you join me while I indulge in enjoying at least one brandy ball before I head home?"

"I'm not sure that would be appropriate."

"Yet you believe it appropriate to be walking about London unescorted?"

"I won't get into mischief unescorted."

"Nor will you if I escort you. I shall be the perfect gentlemen."

She refused to acknowledge the disappointment that hit her with that declaration. Finding himself alone with Jenny, he would no doubt strive to take advantage and be less than a perfect gentleman, delivering the kiss of passion that she required.

"Besides," he continued, "we're out in public. You're completely safe. And I wish to ask you some questions about Miss Jenny Rose."

"What sort of questions?"

"The questions of an interested man."

She'd known he was interested, of course. She considered denying him the opportunity to seek her counsel, but spending time with him at the opera and on the river had served to give her doubts regarding her original opinion of him. Besides, she knew Jenny had enjoyed his company much more so than she'd enjoyed the company of Pemburton. And Hawkhurst was a duke, which would please Jenny's mother immeasurably.

"I suppose I could spare a few moments," she said.

"Afterward, I'll be more than happy to provide you with a ride home. My carriage is nearby."

"I can rent a hansom."

He arched a brow. "You have the ability to rent a hansom and to pay for your own sweets?"

She couldn't prevent a self-satisfied smile from spreading across her face. "I've been given my wages for the month. Oh, Hawkhurst, I have the means to provide for myself."

"You don't say?"

"I do say, and it's most addictive," she said. He began walking, and she fell into step beside him. "I can understand why someone would seek employment. The receiving of money for services gives one such a sense of accomplishment. I can hardly wait until next month, when I will receive another five pounds."

"Good God, they're paying you five pounds a month?"

She couldn't resist a triumphant nod. "Indeed. And I shall receive a bonus on the day that each girl marries."

"Perhaps your brother will have no reason to seek a wife in possession of money," he said.

They'd entered the park. The flowers were in riotous bloom. A few couples strolled about, but it wasn't yet the height of fashion to be seen in the parks; had it been two hours later Louisa doubted that the bench he escorted her to would have been available. He took his place beside her. The bench suddenly seemed incredibly narrow. She peered inside her sack rather than look at him.

"Do you think I should give a portion of my earnings to Alex?" she asked quietly.

"Not necessarily. You earned the money. It should be yours to do with as you please."

She studied the amber toffee. "I feel selfish hoarding the money when I know Alex is in such dire need of it."

He touched her chin, turned her face toward him. There was a kindness in his eyes that she'd have never expected of him, and she couldn't help but wonder what other surprises he might be hiding.

"Your brother needs a good deal more than five pounds."

"But it is a start—"

"It is a start for *you*. The responsibilities for his estates fall to him. He will see to them."

Another surprise. She'd not expected him to acknowledge who, indeed, was responsible for the estates.

"Through marriage?" she asked.

"We do what we must." His hand fell away. "Which brings me to Miss Rose. Does she enjoy my company do you think?"

"Truly, Your Grace, she hasn't specifically addressed her feelings in regard to you." Louisa popped the confection into her mouth.

"What does your woman's intuition tell you? And don't think for a moment that enjoying your sweet will end our conversation. I won't think you rude if you talk around it."

So much for that ploy to prevent further conversation with him. She had indeed thought she was delaying the inevitable.

"I believe she finds you interesting. She certainly laughs when she is with you more than she does with others."

"Hardly a resounding endorsement of her

affection. Rather she could be laughing because she considers me a buffoon."

"You're hardly a buffoon."

"A compliment from you? Beware, I may faint dead away."

Her mouth twitched at the teasing glint in his eyes. She remembered Mr. Rose explaining that teasing was but another way to show affection. But there was no affection here. Never had been really.

"I don't know what possessed me—"

He leaned near. "You find me charming."

"I do not."

"Not at all charming?"

She held up her little finger and pressed her thumb near its tip. "Perhaps that much."

He gave her a triumphant grin. "At least it is a start. Before I'm done, I shall claim that entire pinky."

She laughed. "I believe you overestimate your powers of persuasion."

"We shall see," he said quietly, an undercurrent of challenge and something that warned her that flirting with him in the least was a dangerous undertaking.

He was much more experienced, and she suddenly felt very much out of her element.

Sucking on her toffee, she watched as he slid a brandy ball into his mouth. He seemed to do it with deliberate care, as though he sought to draw attention to his lips. She wondered if his kisses would taste like brandy, and how would a lady know if he'd been drinking or sampling sweets?

"If a gentleman were to bring Miss Rose a small token of his affection, what would you suggest, what would please her the most?" he asked, bringing an effective end to their lighthearted banter and reminding her that she wasn't the object of his quest and would never be the object of his affection.

She fought back the unwarranted disappointment. She was simply the means to his end, and she would do well to remember that.

"If it is to be *his* token, *he* should be the one to determine what to give."

"But I want to ensure that the lady takes pleasure in it, and that is part of the gift. Making inquiries until I determine what would be the perfect gift."

She couldn't help herself. She laughed at his reasoning, to hide the fact that she was touched by it. It did indeed increase the value of the gift to know that he'd given the purchase of it such thought.

He arched a brow. "You find my attempts at wooing amusing?"

"No, I find your attempts at manipulating me amusing."

"Am I so easy to read?"

He held her gaze, a challenge in his dark eyes. Slowly, she shook her head. "No, you're not at all easy to read."

"I don't think I'd make such an unwanted husband for a woman who desires a title."

"Their mother wants the title. They want passion and love." The last of her toffee melted in her mouth. She swallowed. "I was always rather envious of these American ladies. It's not something that I admit with any sort of pride. And yet, having spent some time with them, I'm not certain which is worse: to be ignored because you have no dowry or to be sought after because you have so much."

"I should think being ignored is much worse." He shook his sack and held it toward her. "Have a brandy ball."

She gave him an impish smile. "Are you certain it won't make me drunk?"

"I'm positively certain."

She reached into the bag, removed a dark ball, and plopped it into her mouth. It was surprisingly good.

"Would you like a toffee?" she asked.

"No, thank you. I would like to know what sort of sweets Miss Rose might like."

"You are single-minded in your purpose."

"I'm not sure why you find fault in that habit. It is the sign of a man destined to achieve greatness."

"By marrying well," she said.

"It is the only recourse I have."

"As I mentioned during the opera, Mr. Rose believes that the aristocracy must begin working if they are to survive."

He scowled at her. "Don't speak such blasphemous words."

"Before you indicated that you agreed with his assessment."

"I did not wish to get into a debate."

"Would it be so awful? I'm not talking labor, but I'm talking positions that require agile minds."

She suddenly became very uncomfortable under his scrutiny, as though she'd said something terribly improper, rude, possibly even vulgar.

"Are you implying that I have an agile mind?" he finally asked.

"I'm implying that there is more to life than gambling, womanizing, and drinking. There is pride, a sense of accomplishment."

"If I can manage to get my estates back into working order, I shall have accomplished something of value."

"Why do you suppose it is that those within our circle frown so on working?"

"Because our ancestors worked so damned hard to become powerful enough that they didn't have to work." He leaned over slightly. "How are you enjoying the brandy ball?"

She wondered if he was attempting to turn the topic away from what he was being forced to do: marry for money rather than love.

"It's quite good."

"Have you ever taken a sip of brandy?"

She shook her head.

"You should do that sometime, now that you're a woman of independent means."

"I rather like it, you know," she heard herself

say before she'd thought about what she was going to reveal.

"The taste of the brandy ball?"

"Having this independence." She twisted slightly to face him. "I can do anything I want, whenever I want. I'm not observed. I'm not guarded. I fancy this new life."

Very gently he tucked some stray strands of her hair behind her ear, his gloved fingers lingering near her cheek. She tried to squelch the shiver of anticipation that went through her, but it seemed to have a mind of its own, determined to elicit heat and yearning. It was an awful thing to desire what one could never have: the love of a gentleman.

"You were very courageous to do what you did," he said quietly, his gaze holding hers.

"I was very desperate." And suddenly very breathless. What power did he have over women that he could steal their breath with little more than a touch?

"But you took steps to right matters. There are ladies who would have simply . . . withdrawn."

And if she were wise, she would do exactly that right this moment. Withdraw from his touch, his nearness. She swallowed hard.

"We English are a strong lot, and sometimes I think we forget." She rose to her feet. "I really should get home. I have social engagements to arrange."

He stood. "I promised you a ride in my carriage, and while I may not be a man you trust to do right by your wards, I'm a man who keeps his promises."

It wasn't that she didn't trust him to do right by Jenny or Kate. It was quite simply that she didn't trust him. He'd been too pleasant by half.

She wasn't fooled for a moment. He had told her that he understood the way to the heiresses was through her, and he was coming very close to luring her into believing that he was not as awful as she'd originally surmised. And yet she knew his history. She couldn't look past it.

Refused to look past it, because she feared if she did not hold his past against him, she might decide that he was very worthy indeed. Not for the Rose sisters. But for her. And that was most frightening of all. To suddenly find herself wanting *him*.

Louisa returned home to find Jenny sitting in the solarium, still in her nightclothes, her feet curled beneath her, the sun coming in through the windows making her hair appear to have been laced with strips of red.

"Are you ill?" Louisa asked.

Jenny glanced over her shoulder, her hand clasping her wrapper close to her throat. She smiled softly. "No."

Louisa sat in a bright yellow-and-orange chair. Everything in this house was so garishly bright. She found it all rather hideous. She supposed good taste was something that could not be purchased. "Is everything all right then?"

"Just thinking about the parade of men who will come through the parlor this afternoon. Father took us on a tour of a factory once, and when I'm sitting in the parlor with gentlemen arriving, I feel rather like a cog on the assembly line watching as the unfinished product passes by."

And here Louisa would have given almost anything to have gentlemen passing through her parlor.

"If you're weary of gentlemen callers, I could let it be known that this isn't your day at home."

Jenny twisted around in the chair until her back was pressed against one arm and her legs were draped over the other. "I'm not weary of the gentlemen. I'm weary of the parlor. Father is taking mother to Brighton for a few days of sun and sea air. I was thinking while they're away, we should have an afternoon tea party."

"We can arrange that easily enough," Louisa said warily, suspecting there was a bit more to this tea than Jenny had revealed because she had a mischievous glint in her eyes. "I'm certain if we sent out the invitations this afternoon, posthaste, that ladies would be available."

Jenny sat up. "It's not the ladies I'm interested in. It's the gentlemen."

"Afternoon tea is usually reserved for the ladies."

"We shall have a 'gentlemen's tea with sport.' A bit of lawn tennis, croquet, flirtation while the sun shines. A string quartet to provide music. Perhaps a little dancing across the grass. It should be fun.

We shall keep it small, intimate. Invite a duke or two, a marquess, and a couple of earls."

"Your mother doesn't favor earls."

Jenny winked at her. "Mother shan't be here."

Two days later, Louisa couldn't deny that the afternoon tea party appeared to be a resounding success. Even Kate was lively and animated, apparently enjoying herself as much as Jenny. Louisa had been quite surprised when Kate had embraced the idea with enthusiasm. Now Kate and Jenny were taking a turn on the tennis lawn, facing Falconridge and the Duke of Stonehaven.

Louisa sat on an iron bench beneath a tree, sketch pad in hand so she wasn't too obtrusive, periodically counting heads to ensure no one was getting into idle mischief, although truthfully the only two she truly needed to worry over were Jenny and Kate. Five young ladies and fifteen gentlemen, including her brother, were in attendance, and Louisa was feeling quite ancient. Most of the ladies had only recently had their coming out—hence the reason they were still unmarried and available for flirtation. Some had the silliest of laughs, and the conversations she'd overheard held no substance.

Had she been that . . . young . . . when she was younger?

A shadow crossed over her face, and she looked over to see that Hawkhurst had approached, quietly, across the lawn. He tilted his head slightly toward the bench. "Do you mind?"

"No, of course not." She flattened her skirt against her hip to give him a bit more room.

"Why aren't you playing?" he asked.

"Because I'm the chaperone," she answered tartly. "I fail to understand why you seem unable to comprehend that fact and continually question my actions."

"I simply wonder at the difficulty of watching others play while you must, for all intents and purposes, work."

"I'm quite content, thank you."

"I admire your determination not to be bothered by the unfairness of your situation."

"My situation was brought on by my choice. There is nothing unfair when your path is dictated by your choices, and as I explained during our time in the park, it is quite liberating to be able to do as I please."

"Except now, if you pleased, you could not play tennis."

"Then it is rather fortunate I do not wish to play tennis."

He chuckled, low, a sound that seemed to dance along her skin.

"I'm not certain I've ever known a woman who accepts the limits of her life as easily. I wonder if Jenny will be as accepting should Stonehaven ask for her hand."

She refused to give him the satisfaction of looking at him. She did not want to see those dark, enigmatic eyes. It was difficult enough simply having his masculine scent competing with that of the flowers. "I suppose he, too, is a man who knows naught of passion."

"On the contrary, he may be a bit too familiar with it."

She swung her head around. "I'm not going to play a game of trying to decipher your cryptic statements. Either be clear or be gone."

Smiling warmly, he twisted slightly, placing his elbow on the back of the bench so that his fingers were dangerously close to touching her bared neck. He leaned near, and whispered, "He suffers from the French disease."

Staring at him, she shook her head. "I'm not familiar with that illness."

He touched his finger to the back of her neck, where no cloth covered her skin. She wanted to move away, should move away, but she was certain he'd touched her only in an effort to unsettle her. She refused to be unsettled.

"If a gentleman is not particular about the beds he visits, he can find himself suffering from some nasty symptoms that are rather unattractive," he said.

"Are you perhaps referring to syphilis?"

"Sadly, I am indeed."

"Dare I presume you are familiar with the symptoms because you have suffered through them?"

"No, I'm quite particular about the beds I visit."

The undercurrent of experience and desire vibrated through his voice. She did not want to contemplate the beds he might have visited.

"You have leveled quite an unflattering accusation against him."

While she had pinned most of her hair up, she'd left tendrils curling along her neck. He tugged on several, absently wrapping the strands around his finger.

"I'm simply pointing out that it would be unfortunate should she marry him."

"Out of the goodness of your heart, I suppose you wish me to warn her?"

"It is your duty as her chaperone is it not?"

"And I suppose you will tell me that the Earl of Langley is also diseased."

He shook his head. "No, but his mother . . . quite in her dotage. He needs someone who can watch her, feed her, bathe her, make her final months upon this earth less miserable."

"Hah! I saw his mother not more than two weeks ago, and she was fit as a fiddle."

"It is a deceptive illness."

"I know she is not ill, and I suspect Stonehaven isn't either."

"But he could be."

"But you don't know that he is."

"I would not presume to ask. And the earl's mother . . . you must admit, she is up in years. At any moment she could require constant care."

The ease with which lies rolled off his tongue was irritating to say the least. Impatiently, she reached back and slapped his wrist. "Release your hold on me, sir."

Surprise flitted across his face, and she wasn't

certain if it was because she'd slapped him or because he hadn't realized that he was toying with her hair.

"Lady Louisa! Hawkhurst!" Jenny neared, breathless, her cheeks pink. "I believe you two are the only ones yet to play. Come, you must have a turn at lawn tennis."

Louisa shook her head. "I'm not one of your guests; I'm your chaperone."

"Nonsense. This is an informal, private party. The rules are as we choose them to be. Are you up to the challenge, Your Grace?"

Hawkhurst came to his feet, a dare in his eyes as he looked at Louisa. "I believe I am."

Jenny reached down and tugged on Louisa's hand. "Come on, then. For the sake of women everywhere, you must give him a sound beating. The gentlemen have yet to win a single game."

"I'm really not certain—"

Jenny bent down until they were eye level. "Why not? You're too young not to have any fun at all. And Mother isn't here to spoil things. Please?"

She wasn't certain why Jenny was so insistent, but where was the harm in it? From the court she could keep an eye on everyone.

"Oh, very well," she finally said, with little enthusiasm.

"Splendid!"

It felt good to have the wooden racket biting into his fingers, good to have it erasing the memory of the silken texture of her hair touching his skin. He'd not even realized what he was doing. He'd been concentrating on weaving fanciful lies, and instead she'd somehow managed to weave a web of interest around him.

She took her position as chaperone so incredibly seriously: her brow furrowed, her attention intense, and when she'd caught him in a lie . . . her triumphant smile . . .

Dear God, but he'd never been so mesmerized. He should borrow the paste that Caroline used for her scrap album and use it to adhere himself to Jenny Rose. She was the one whose hair he should be twisting around his finger, the one from whom he should be eliciting smiles and laughter. The one who should have his attention and his stories.

Louisa came with nothing, absolutely nothing, not a penny to her name. Not entirely true. She had all of five pounds, while he required thousands. Continuing to flirt with her, to give her any attention at all could spell disaster for them all.

Now she hit the ball, and he watched as it soared over the net. He smashed it, returning it to her. She screeched and ducked.

"Have a care!" Stonehaven called out. "You're playing against a lady."

A lady who irritated him, pricked his anger, and of late had begun to stir his desire.

"My apologies," Hawk said. "I don't seem to know my own strength."

"Are you certain that's it?" Louisa called back.

"Quite." Why was it when she was near, he was

continually distracted? "Let's begin again, shall we, calling that last volley a practice?"

She looked at him warily before moving back to serve. He either needed to pour his efforts into winning or settle for defeat—whichever would bring the game to a hasty end so he could turn his attention to Jenny.

She was the one who should be intriguing him—not the damned chaperone!

He had the most sensual mouth. Full lips, questing tongue. And when he released one of his deep-throated groans, Jenny quite simply wanted to gobble him up.

His hands remained respectful, cradling her waist, inching up her ribs, stopping just below her breasts. But his mouth, his mouth was decidedly wicked, trailing along her throat, his teeth nipping at her buttons until he skillfully loosened one, then two, then three, giving his tongue the freedom to taste hidden flesh.

She'd despaired of ever having a moment alone with him.

"We should get back," she muttered, but her words lacked conviction.

"A moment more."

"You say that every time."

"Would you rather I willingly give you up?"

"A time will come when you'll have to. My mother is insisting that I marry a duke."

He tensed, stilled. She felt his fingers digging into her ribs.

"You're hurting me."

Immediately he loosened his hold and pressed his forehead to hers. "You take delight in tormenting me, in offering me glimpses of what I cannot keep."

She cradled his handsome face. "I torment us both."

Before he could respond, she slipped free of him and darted around the corner, quickly buttoning her bodice. She knew she was playing a dangerous game. If they were ever caught . . . it would be the ruin of them both.

Chapter 11

A week later, with the chandeliers glittering above him and the ballroom filled to over-flowing, Hawk stood beside Falconridge, their backs pressed to the wall, watching, waiting, and in Hawk's case, temper simmering.

He did not like the way the man held her as they danced—as though they shared secrets, se-crets to which he was not privy. Intimate secrets, as though the man had held her bare ankle in his hand, run his palm along her calf, pressed his mouth behind her knee.

"Who the devil is Louisa dancing with?" he ground out.

Out of the corner of his eye, he saw Falcon-ridge jerk his head around. He could feel the in-tensity of his friend's gaze, but he couldn't see it because he was unable to tear his attention away from the merry couple on the dance floor. Louisa wore a different gown from the one she'd worn to the opera or the one she'd worn to the first ball. Trust a woman to have a few coins and start expanding her wardrobe. Although he might find fault with the frivolous purchase, he could find no fault with the lavender gown. She looked positively ravishing.

"The gentleman would be Jeremy Rose," Falconridge said.

"The heir to the Rose fortune," Hawk said speculatively. Perhaps Louisa was much more cunning than he realized. Ensconce herself in the Rose household, use her coins to make herself appear exquisite, snare the heir who would no doubt inherit millions.

"One of the heirs," Falconridge said. "The Americans don't hold to our tradition of primogeniture. From what I understand, the Rose fortune will be divided equally into thirds."

"The daughters may inherit the money, but not the businesses."

Falconridge shrugged. "I don't know the particulars of how the estate will be settled, and I daresay we're a bit premature in our speculation. James Rose seems in fine health. Have you settled on a sister?"

"Jenny has reserved the next dance for me. I noticed Kate is not here this evening. I saw you spending some time with her during the afternoon party."

"Indeed. A most unfortunate encounter. Even if she were here this evening, she is the last one I would want to marry. She speaks of nothing except love. She wants poetry, flowers, and chocolates. She requires much too much work and effort."

"You believe you will find an heiress who doesn't require excessive attention?"

"I have devised a plan that I believe will result in my marrying an heiress without much effort on my part."

"Care to share this amazing plan of yours?"

"Not really, no."

"Well, my plan is to woo Jenny for a bit more, then go to her father and ask for her hand."

"Then why the interest in the man with whom Lady Louisa is dancing?"

"Merely keeping a watch over Ravensley's sister since he isn't in attendance this evening."

"Where is he, by the by?"

"No doubt licking his wounds again. Apparently Mrs. Rose is not impressed with his title."

"Yes, I've heard. She is insisting that Jenny marry a duke, but I believe a clever man could convince her otherwise."

"And you believe you're a clever man?"

"I'm not going to give up as easily as Ravensley."

"You're interested in Jenny?"

"I'm interested in any woman who can fill my coffers."

Hawk wondered if Falconridge was a serious

threat to his plan to acquire Jenny. The music drifted into silence. Hawk shoved himself away from the wall. "It is time for me to pour on the charm," he said lightly.

A strategist did not let the enemy know he had uncovered his weakness. Damnation, now he was thinking of his friends as enemies.

"The beauty of my plan is that no charm is needed," Falconridge said.

Hawk turned. "Then why are you here?"

"Merely to observe and take pleasure in the fact that I will soon be beyond all this."

"And does your plan include moving Jenny beyond all this?"

"I cannot say for certain, but it is possible."

"You are becoming a very irritating friend."

"I have become a desperate one."

Hawk shook his head. "I wish you luck with your endeavor, whatever it is."

Falconridge's mouth turned up only slightly, his eyes seemed to dim, not to match the merriment of the ball. "Won't need luck."

Whatever his plan was, Hawk truly hoped it turned out well for him, although he also hoped that it wouldn't place his quest of Jenny in jeopardy. Why was Falconridge always so tight-lipped? Perhaps because he didn't want to hear Hawk voice his suspicions of the success of any plan that required little effort.

He thought of Louisa, who had stopped waiting for a gentleman to call and give her the life she deserved and instead had taken matters into her own hands. She had coins to spend, a smile that was more dazzling than the crystal chandeliers in the room, a laugh that wafted over to him, and the attention of a man reputed to be worth millions. She had set a fine example, an example Hawk intended to follow.

He wanted to catch her eye, to receive some sort of acknowledgment of his approach, but she was busy talking with the younger Mr. Rose and a young woman whom Hawk did not recognize, introducing them perhaps. All three laughed as though they hadn't a care in the world. Envy did not suit Hawk, but he certainly felt it sitting upon his shoulder.

"Looking for me, Your Grace?"

He snapped his head around at Jenny's words, hoped the heat of embarrassment that suddenly warmed his face wasn't visible. "Indeed, I have been looking forward to our dance."

He offered his arm and forced all his attention on the woman who placed her hand on it. "Your brother seems to be enjoying himself," he heard himself say before he could prevent the words from tumbling out.

"Indeed. I think he's trying to get Lady Louisa into a bit of trouble. He taught her to play chess last night, and she soundly beat him. He said he's never known a woman who is as much a strategist as she is."

"He enjoys her company then," he murmured, as they reached the dance area, and he took her into his arms.

"Oh, they get along famously well."

"How does your mother feel about their ... friendship?"

"I don't think she's too keen on it, but Jeremy is her only son and can do no wrong in her eyes, so I suspect she will hold her tongue."

"I have been given the impression that your mother is very particular about whom her children marry."

She laughed gaily. "She has her opinion, and we have ours."

"And who will have the final say?" he asked.

"When it comes to my marriage, I will."

"And if I were to speak with your father—"

"Are you proposing?"

Was he? Good God. An unexpected shiver of dread coursed through him. "I'm merely attempting to assess my chances of success."

"My father will not force me to marry anyone I don't wish to marry. I believe that I have mentioned that passion is my criterion. I'm very fond of you, Your Grace, but as of yet, I have been unable to experience your passionate nature. I must also confess, I'm in no hurry to wed or even to be spoken for. I intend to spend this Season sampling the selections. Perhaps next Season I'll make my decision."

"Sampling the selections?"

She smiled. "Oh, yes. My chaperone is so very attentive that I must proceed cautiously and slowly so as not to arouse suspicions." She winked at him. "Perhaps you could arrange another outing to the opera. Remember, Your Grace, it is passion I seek above all else, and I will not be content with less."

"I would like to escort Miss Jenny Rose to the opera again," Hawkhurst said. "But she insisted I must verify her schedule with you."

Louisa fought not to be disappointed that Hawkhurst was continuing his pursuit of Jenny or that the young lady was encouraging it. She was finding it increasingly difficult not to be aware of every nuance associated with him when he was near. She looked at her dance card, where she had been making notes. The duke was rudely looking over her shoulder.

"Thursday, she has a dinner engagement with Lord Bertram."

"Mmm," he rumbled near her ear, and she heard the censure in his muttering.

With impatience, she glanced back at him. "And what, pray tell, is wrong with Lord Bertram?"

He glanced around, before leaning nearer, bringing his unsettling scent of musk and maleness that much closer to her. "Boils upon the buttocks," he whispered.

She narrowed her eyes at him. "If that were the case, the man would be unable to sit, and I have seen him sit on numerous occasions."

"He has them frequently lanced."

She couldn't help herself. She grimaced as an image filled her mind . . . "I don't believe you."

"Ask him."

As if she would ask a man about the very personal nature of his buttocks.

"Who else seeks her favor?" he asked.

"That is none of your concern."

He narrowed his dark eyes. "Do I see the Marquess of Umberton on your list?"

She sighed. "And I suppose you find fault with him."

"He is known to drink heavily before noon."

"Ha! You forget how well I know you, Your Grace. The same could be said of you."

He gave her a devilish grin. "I cease at dawn." He held up a finger. "And I do not resume until twilight."

"And you find that admirable."

"I find it more admirable than a man who is constantly at the bottle. I also believe I spotted Lord Ketchum's name on your list."

"I know he does not drink."

"Webbed feet."

She stared at him. "I beg your pardon?"

He held his hand up, his fingers spread wide, and drew imaginary lines connecting them. "He joined me at the seaside once. We went swimming. He's a remarkable swimmer. Has webs between his toes. Like a duck."

"That's ridiculous."

"I thought so as well, but there you are. Who says God doesn't have a sense of humor? Who else?"

She dropped her hand to her side. "None of your affair."

"It does not seem right that a lady as lovely as you should be using her dance card to keep records of another lady's social engagements."

She didn't think her snort was too unladylike. "I'm not here to dance."

"Yet you were dancing."

Was that a frisson of anger she heard opening in his voice?

"I do not see that my actions are your concern," she said.

She watched his jaw clench. He was angry. Why? Why would he care?

He cleared his throat. "Dance with me then."

"Mrs. Rose would be none too pleased if she caught wind that I'd danced with you again."

"You are the daughter of an earl. Who gives a damn whether or not she is pleased?"

She spun around and faced him. "You are as irritating as my brother. You don't understand the importance of my position."

Heat flared in his eyes, his nostrils flared. "Do not for one moment mistake me for your brother."

She furrowed her brow. "He is your friend."

He shook his head as though straining to rein in his temper. His behavior was most odd. She did wish her experience with men was such that she could decipher subtle nuances in behavior.

"Take a walk about the garden with me," he said.

"I must see after Jenny."

"She has another dance after this one and one after that. I daresay her dance card is filled and then some. Please, Louisa. Step outside with me."

Louisa. Not Lady Louisa, as though there was an intimacy shared between them.

"On one condition. That I may ask a question of you, and you will honor me with the truth."

His gaze grew intense. "Ask."

"Does Lord Bertram truly have boils?"

He straightened, pressed his lips together, and shook his head. "No."

"And Lord—"

"You said *a* question. I have fulfilled my obligation, and now you must carry through with yours."

"You are attempting to discredit other lords so that your own shortcomings might be overlooked," she stated, hating that she'd allowed him to manipulate her, that she'd actually believed his lies.

He extended his arm. "I believe we could both use some fresh air, and as you are a *chaperone*—as you repeatedly remind me—and not a debutante, no one should think anything of our leaving together."

"It would, however, be best if we weren't touching, if we weren't giving any sort of indication of intimacy."

"Very well. If you will lead the way."

She thought she might be leading the way straight into hell. Still, she made her way to the glass-paned doors that had been left open to provide some additional air in the room. Dancing tended to make one extremely warm, as did having a gentleman so near. She was grateful to see that they weren't the only ones walking along the lighted garden path, and she couldn't help but wonder if a time would come when chaperones would be a thing of the past. Already, her role was not so much guardian as advisor.

"It's a lovely evening," she said quietly. Anything to break the silence that seemed to have come upon them as soon as they'd stepped outside.

"Do you not miss it?" he asked.

She glanced over at him. "Miss what?"

"The attention."

She laughed lightly. "I was never one to receive much attention. No dowry, you know."

"Yes, that does make it difficult for a lady."

"It makes it impossible."

"Your brother believes that, if he were to marry well, he could see you nicely situated in marriage."

"Ah, but now I have experienced independence, and I'm not entirely certain that I want to return to the way things were. Why do you know that this afternoon I actually went shopping again without an escort? At my leisure. I was amazed. It was quite . . . liberating."

"And dangerous," he fairly growled.

"I was perfectly safe. There were constables about."

"A woman needs protection."

"Protection, a chaperone, a dowry, a husband . . . I cannot say that any of those things is precisely what a woman *needs*."

"And what do you perceive as a woman needing?"

"I daresay, I think the Rose sisters have the right of it: passion and love. Unlike them, though, I do not think the order is important as long as a woman acquires both."

"A husband can provide those things."

"Not always, Your Grace. I would have thought your mother would have taught you that."

"And what do you know of my mother?" he asked, a frisson of anger working its way through his voice.

"Only what I have heard. Your father died when I was but a babe, but I know he was considerably older than your mother. Was it a love match?"

"No, I suspect not."

His voice contained a profound sadness.

She stopped walking and touched his arm. "My sincerest apologies. That was not only rude but insensitive."

"Did your father love your mother?" he asked.

"Yes, I believe he did. Too much perhaps. He indulged her every whim. It is part of the reason that we are in poverty now."

"Can a man love too much?" he asked.

"I suppose not. But he can love rather foolishly."

"With that sentiment, I will not argue."

A couple passed by them, and Louisa decided it was best to stay on the move. She began walking again, and he fell into step beside her. "You wished to speak with me about something?" she prodded.

"Yes. It is no secret I'm in dire financial straits."

"No, Your Grace, it is no secret."

"I need your assistance—"

"I cannot give it, as I have already explained."

"Answer me this: How will Miss Rose deduce that any man is one of passion if you never grant her a moment alone with him?"

"You are not suggesting that I grant you a moment alone with her?"

"I'm merely curious." He took her arm, led her off the path, into the shadows of the trees. "If her criterion is passion, how can you judge that a man may provide what she desires?"

"I'm certain there are ways."

"Don't be naïve, Louisa. Passion must be experienced in order to be proven, and if you will not allow her a moment alone with me, then you must serve as messenger."

With one bare hand—when in God's name had he removed his glove?—he cradled her cheek and tilted her head back slightly, just before he bent down and lowered his mouth to hers. The first brush of his lips was as gentle and warm as summer rain, a tantalizing touch, a mere whisper . . .

She should have pulled back then, stepped back, retreated. Instead she held her ground as though she were on the cusp of battle. She was aware of his other hand circling her waist, aware of him pulling her nearer until her breasts were flattened against his chest, her heels rising of their own accord to bring her nearer, a blossom turning toward the sunlight, and then his growl rumbling along his chest, vibrating against hers, as he returned his mouth to hers, hungrily, greedily. His eagerness took her by surprise, and when she parted her lips, his tongue swept inside, to claim, to conquer, to seduce.

To elicit passion.

Passion. Which had always been only a word. Spoken. Understood. But never experienced.

Until this moment.

Heat poured into her, sluiced through her. She felt as though every nerve ending had been ignited. She was vaguely aware of her arms wrapping around his shoulders, hands rubbing his neck, her fingers toying with the ends of his hair.

Passion. Dangerous, dangerous passion.

If he were to lift her into his arms and carry her to a hidden corner of the garden, she would not object.

She'd been chaperoned all her life, and until this moment, she'd never truly understood the reasoning for it.

Now she understood all too clearly.

His kiss alone caused her body to thrum with yearning, his intoxicating scent heated her with desire, weakened her knees. All her senses were heightened, even as they all seemed to blur into one.

He drew back, breathing heavily, and even in the shadows of the garden, she could see the fervor burning brightly in his dark eyes. "Do inform Miss Rose," he rasped, his voice hoarse, "that I am fully capable of delivering the passion she so fervently desires."

With that, he spun on his heel and stormed away, leaving her bereft and weak. She backed up until her knees rammed into a stone bench. She dropped onto the cold slab, fighting to draw in each labored breath, her body trembling with needs unfulfilled, with desires unleashed.

She pressed her gloved fingers to her swollen, wet lips. She could still taste him—brandy, from drink or sweet, she did not care—an addictive flavor that longed to be tasted again.

Passion? Oh, my word yes, the duke certainly was capable of delivering passion . . . and a good deal more.

Chapter 12

What in God's name had possessed him to take Louisa into his arms? To press his mouth to hers, to devour greedily what she so innocently offered? She was not the one he should desire, not the one who should haunt his every waking moment, his every lurid dream.

After leaving her in the garden, he'd immediately left the ball, located his carriage, instructed the driver to go home without him, that he would walk to his residence, and now he was prowling the streets like some ravenous beast, his hunger unchecked. He could still taste her upon his tongue, thought he might forever taste her, even when he kissed another.

He had not originally taken her into the garden for the purpose of seduction. He had intended to plead his case, to be honest and forthright, to strip himself bare if need be in order to gain her as an ally . . .

Instead, he had been mesmerized watching the light from the gas lamps play over her features. And when she had cut him off, refusing even to consider a request from him . . . he had reacted with poor judgment. Diabolically poor judgment.

If he'd ever held any hope that she would help him, he'd certainly dashed it all to hell with his actions. He had behaved exactly like the blackguard she'd accused him of being. He wondered if she took great satisfaction in being proven correct.

On the other hand, it had been impossible to gauge what thoughts might have been running rampant through her mind. She had looked at him like a woman fully aroused, and that had made his walking away doubly difficult.

He told himself it was because she was forbidden—as she was the sister of a friend, his overwhelming desire for her was entirely unacceptable—that he felt this overpowering need to possess her. If he could have her but once . . . conquer and move on—like Victoria's armies—as was his usual habit he could more readily concentrate on the task at hand: gaining a wife who could provide him with the funds he needed to protect his sister, protect his family.

He staggered to a stop, the neighborhood familiar. Not where he'd planned to end up, but it would do for the moment. He opened the gate, walked through, and closed it behind him. Then he strode up the cobbled walkway. He was in need of a friend and, more, an accomplice.

He arrived at the door of a home in which he was as welcome as his own. Or at least he'd always felt that way. He wondered if Ravensley's parents had looked on him as unfavorably as his sister did.

He did not hesitate to open the door and stride through the foyer as though he owned the residence. This time of night he had a good idea where he'd find Ravensley. The lights were dimmed in the hallway leading to the library. In truth, he was surprised Ravensley hadn't returned to burning candles rather than gas. He was well aware that it was difficult to revert to less-than-modern conveniences.

When he reached the library and opened the door, he was taken aback by the darkness. The only light came from a low fire burning on the hearth. He had to fairly squint to see Ravensley sitting in a chair by the fireplace.

"Ah, the duke, my well-titled friend has come to call," Ravensley called out, his words slightly slurred.

"Into your cups, are you?" Hawk asked as he walked to a nearby table and helped himself to a generous portion of bourbon before sitting in the chair opposite his friend. "You weren't at the party this evening."

"No need. I'm not welcome in the Rose household, don't you know? My title is not worthy of a

Rose daughter, and should I marry one, I will find her cut off with no settlement arrangements. Unfortunately, I do not have the luxury of marrying a woman who cannot provide me with sovereigns."

"But you attended their tea party."

He shrugged, sighed as though it sapped his strength to move at all. "This evening I had no desire to be tormented by gazing at what I could never possess. What brings you about this time of night? Must be long past midnight."

"It is." Hawk sipped the bourbon, welcomed its tart taste. "Jenny is forbidden to you, but not to me, yet I'm having difficulty obtaining her affections. Your sister refuses to assist me in my pursuit."

Ravensley laughed bitterly. "You knew that already. So what has changed?"

"I'm not accustomed to not gaining what I have set my sights on."

"And you want Jenny?"

"At all costs. The sooner, the better. I cannot be distracted from my purpose."

"What distracts you?"

Not what but who. Your damned sister, he almost yelled. He effectively had to make himself unavailable in order not to be lured by her innocent charms. He would never see her again once he took Jenny to wife, as she would no longer need a chaperone. Their marriage would solve all his problems, problems he'd not even realized he had.

"It is of no consequence. But I have given a good deal of thought to my strategy, and I believe, with your assistance, that I could be wed before the Season is done. I realize I'm asking a good deal of you, because you favor her; but again, you have no hope of obtaining her, so I'm asking you to put our friendship above your wants—which again will never be realized."

"And how exactly do you plan to accomplish this?"

Hawk gazed into the fire, watched the flames, dancing and writhing. For Caroline, he vowed, and tossed back the bourbon.

"As you eluded to some weeks back: by killing two birds with one stone. Miss Rose wishes to experience the passion of my kiss. I intend to be caught delivering it."

"Are you certain you're all right?" Jeremy asked.

Sitting in the carriage, listening as the wheels clattered over the street, Louisa forced herself to smile. He'd seen her come in from the garden and had been solicitous ever since: fetching her champagne, insisting she dance with him again, making her laugh by sharing funny stories from all his adventures traveling. He'd been jolly good fun and almost managed to make her forget about her encounter with Hawkhurst in the garden.

"Yes, I'm fine thank you."

"I've never seen a woman return from a walk

about the garden quite so pale. Usually the outdoors puts color back into her cheeks."

"It was simply a bit too warm out there."

"I thought I saw the duke accompany you through the doors," Jenny said.

"He was with me only for a moment," Louisa said hastily. "He had to leave."

"Your brother wasn't there this evening," Jenny said.

"No, I suppose he had other things to do as well."

"A pity. I rather liked dancing with him." She gazed out the window.

Louisa could not help but wonder what she would say if she knew that her mother had promised Alex that he would not see a penny if he pursued her daughters. Dear Lord, Louisa wasn't certain if she'd ever met a woman as nasty as Mrs. Rose. Was it all money, titles, and prestige?

"A penny for your thoughts," Jeremy said.

Louisa laughed lightly, wondering if pennies were all this family thought about. "None, really. I'm simply tired."

"You're a lousy liar," he said, "but I won't press matters."

They rode in silence until they arrived at the Rose residence. Once inside, Jenny said, "Jeremy's right. You are rather pale." She took Louisa's arm. "Come on. Father's brandy will put the color right back into your cheeks."

"I'm not pale," Louisa protested. "I'm naturally very light of complexion."

Jenny smiled brightly and leaned near. "It's an excuse, Lady Louisa. I want to hear the details of the walk in the garden, and a bit of brandy always makes the telling so much easier."

"It was merely a walk—"

"Shh. Say no more until we are settled in the library," Jenny said.

"Am I invited?" Jeremy asked.

"Of course. You shall do the honors of pouring the spirits," Jenny said.

"This is highly improper," Louisa said.

"Nonsense," Jenny said. "It is late. No need to be my chaperone. Be my friend. I could use a friend."

Something in her voice made Louisa realize she was serious. "Are you lonely here?"

"Of course I am. I know so few people, and Kate has withdrawn—" She shook her head. "I love the balls, but it is amazing how lonely one can be in a room filled with people." She wound her arm around Louisa's. "Now come, let's relax with a bit of brandy—"

"I've never had brandy," Louisa said, allowing Jenny to lead the way. Although she had tasted it in the form of sweets that Hawkhurst had shared with her. She wished she could stop thinking about him, and she feared brandy would only serve to remind her of him. She considered asking for something else to drink, but she didn't want to appear rude.

"It's wonderful for helping one to relax," Jenny said.

They went into the library. She and Jenny took seats by the fireplace on the far side of the room, while Jeremy walked to a table of decanters. He handed them each a glass before returning to the table to pour himself one. Then he sat on the couch that was set between the two chairs, lounging with his legs stretched out before him, his jacket and waistcoat scandalously unbuttoned, seemingly quite comfortable and at ease, a position Louisa had never seen a man take. Not even Alex. He lifted his glass. "To uncovering the truth behind the trip into the garden."

"I'm not going to drink to that," Louisa said, smiling at him. She thought he was quite charming. She was halfway tempted to try to find him a wife.

"So something wicked must have happened there," Jenny said.

"No, not at all," Louisa said quickly. She took a sip of the brandy, quite pleased with the taste, and looked at the empty hearth.

"Come, Lady Louisa, you are among friends," Jeremy said. "Did the blackguard take advantage?"

She jerked her head around. "Of course not. And why do you call him a blackguard?"

"Is he not?"

She took another sip of the brandy. It was one thing for her to have a low opinion of Hawkhurst; she didn't much like that these Americans might, even if the low opinion was well earned. "He was simply curious as to how a gentleman might persuade Jenny that he was of a passionate nature if he never had a moment alone with her."

"Excellent point," Jeremy said. "Too much chaperoning goes on over here as far as I'm concerned. In America, I've found it's quite sufficient for mothers to keep an eye out, fathers to threaten . . . no need to hire."

"Lady Louisa is serving as my *social* chaperone. While she keeps a more watchful eye than I would like, her main purpose is to guide me away from fortune-hunters and wastrels and guide me toward men of quality. That said, I must state that there are many ways for a man to prove his passion," Jenny said, returning the discussion to the preferred topic. "A man who is truly passionate would know that. Passion must occur outside the bedroom before it can occur inside the bedroom."

Louisa's cheeks grew warm as she stared at Jenny, then shifted her gaze to Jeremy, who appeared amused. She thought of the passion she'd experienced in the garden. That had certainly taken place outside of a bedroom, but, she realized, only because a bedroom wasn't near.

"Tell me, dear sister, what do you know of passion outside a bedroom?" Jeremy asked laconically.

"I believe the purpose of this late-night gathering was to find out what happened in the garden with the duke." Jenny finished off her brandy and held out her glass to her brother. "More, please."

He quirked a brow, grinned, and shook his head. "Who are you of a sudden? Oliver Twist?"

"Don't be difficult. I could make this a ladies' only meeting."

Seemingly without taking offense, he got to his feet and went to the corner to do her bidding.

Jenny leaned toward Louisa. "Passion is evident in the way that a man holds my gaze as we waltz, the way he holds me in his arms. If you look closely, you can see in his eyes . . . a burning that causes your flesh to heat long before he touches you. I will go to my wedding bed a virgin, but I fully expect the man I marry to entice me with the promise of passion long before."

She moved back as her brother returned with her glass.

"Whispering secrets?" he asked.

"Merely explaining what I want from a man. Something I'm certain the Duke of Hawkhurst would have no trouble delivering."

Louisa felt decidedly uncomfortable as memories assailed her: his touch, his scent, his groans, his taste, the look of him ensconced in shadows . . .

"Interesting. It seems the color has returned to your cheeks with a vengeance, Lady Louisa," Jeremy said.

She cleared her throat, shook her head. "It's the brandy."

She took a sip as though to emphasize her point. Hawkhurst wanted Jenny. If he could deliver passion such as he had with his kiss in the garden to a woman he didn't desire, she feared

Jenny might ignite into flames if he got hold of her. "Do you favor him, then?" Louisa asked.

Jenny raised a brow in an arch that very much imitated the one for which her mother was famous. "Hawkhurst?"

Louisa nodded.

Jenny shrugged. "He is extremely handsome. A fine physique. A marvelous dancer. And he has a bit of the devil in him. I enjoy his company. But I need a bit more wooing before I can claim to favor him."

"Wooing," her brother grumbled. "You do not make it easy for a gentleman."

"Nor should we." Jenny held up her glass. "More."

He groaned as he got to his feet. "What of you, Lady Louisa?"

Louisa downed the brandy in a very unladylike manner and held out her glass. "Yes, please."

Perhaps more brandy would wash away the images of Hawkhurst, would ease the pain that had settled into her heart because the kiss he'd delivered had not been for her but had been for Jenny. Louisa was merely the messenger, and she supposed she should take that role to heart.

Louisa forced herself to lean forward, and say, "Hawkhurst kisses with a great deal of passion."

Jenny's eyes widened. "And how do you know this?"

"In the garden. He was upset because he could not get you alone, and as a chaperone, I have no one watching me, and so he asked me to deliver the message."

Jenny grinned impishly. "So he *told* you that his kisses are passionate? Any man can make such a claim."

Louisa shook her head, more than a little uncomfortable with what she was about to reveal and resenting Hawkhurst for putting her in this uncomfortable position. "He demonstrated quite skillfully."

"Who demonstrated what?" Jeremy asked.

Louisa squeaked, flung herself back, her hand knocking the glass and causing some of the brandy to spill.

"Damnation," Jeremy said, stepping back, somehow avoiding having any brandy splash on him. "I didn't mean to frighten you."

"It seems Lady Louisa has firsthand experience with the duke's kisses," Jenny said.

"I'm not sure I like hearing that," he said. "Did he take advantage in the garden?"

Louisa reached up and took the glass from Jeremy. "Please let's not discuss it any further. He merely wanted me to plead his case. Which I will not do."

"Because you disapprove of him?" Jenny asked.

"He tends to take pleasure in late nights, heavy drinking, and dallying with an assortment of women. From what I understand, he is unable to commit to even one for any length of time. I think you would be miserable."

"But shouldn't Jenny make that determination?" Jeremy asked.

Should she? And if she chose Hawkhurst, what then?

Why did it bother her so to think of him belonging to another? He would never belong to her. Surely, was there not some small part of her that had begun to enjoy his company, had begun to think of him as hers?

Chapter 13

He stood in the corner, watching, waiting, a predator that had sighted its prey.

He did not try to convince himself that he was not the lowly scoundrel that Louisa had accused him of being. He did not pretend not to know that his soul would rot in hell for eternity because of the actions he was about to take.

He was not proud of his plan, but then pride was a luxury that a desperate man could ill afford. Jenny Rose was in no hurry to wed, others were in danger of capturing her interest, and Hawk needed to marry in order to provide adequately for those he loved and ensure that he keep his distance from Louisa.

Fortunately, as a result of some information Ravensley had shared, he knew that Jenny considered it a lark to escape her chaperone for an opportunity to experience a lover's kiss. While he'd been dancing with her, he'd whispered near her ear that during the sixth waltz of the evening, he sought an opportunity to prove his prowess with a passionate kiss and would be waiting for her in the library to deliver said kiss.

Ravensley was also aware of the rendezvous. He would lure Jenny's brother to the library partway through the sixth waltz with an invitation to join him in a glass of Pemburton's finest brandy. Instead, he would find his sister in Hawk's arms, his mouth latched upon hers, with the shoulder of her gown pushed down just enough to leave no doubt that his actions, if permitted to continue, would be far from honorable.

Young Mr. Rose would be incensed on his sister's behalf. Ravensley would feign being appalled. Miss Rose would be duly embarrassed by being caught in the arms of a cad . . . and Hawk would be honor-bound to preserve the lady's reputation.

Jenny was presently dancing with Falconridge. The next dance was the sixth waltz. It was time for him to prepare to meet his prey. To take the final step toward fulfilling his obligations, to ensuring that he was in a position to protect Caroline.

"Louisa!"

The harsh whisper came from behind her. She turned to see her brother barely visible behind the broad leaves of the potted frond. She'd been relieved to see him at Pemburton's ball. He'd even danced with Jenny. She didn't like the idea of his moping around simply because Mrs. Rose didn't think him worthy, and while Louisa might not have considered him acceptable a few weeks before, she was beginning to reassess her evaluation of him as a potential husband.

He pressed his lips together, rolled his eyes, and jerked his head back, obviously having a desire to speak with her in secret. What was this then?

She glanced around; everyone was otherwise occupied. She slipped around behind the plant. "What is it?"

"I needed to speak with you privately."

She pressed her lips together. "Obviously. I need to be watching my charges, so what is it?"

"Actually, it has to do with them." He closed his eyes. "One of them at least. Jenny."

She touched his arm, and he opened his eyes. "I know you must still be feeling the sting of Mrs. Rose's unkind words—"

"No, no," he said hastily cutting her off. "I'm beyond that. My concern now is you."

She furrowed her brow. "I beg your pardon?"

He took her gloved hand in his, his expression earnest. "I know this position means a good deal to you, and that you need nothing untoward to happen, nothing that will challenge your reputation as a trusted chaperone. What you said about my being unsuitable, it was true. I can see that now. I can also see that if you recommend a gentleman who is not of the highest caliber, you risk your ability to continue to serve in this capacity."

"I accept your apology."

"I'm not apologizing, Louisa. I'm striving to convince myself that what I'm about to do must be done. For Jenny's sake, but more for yours, because it simply would not do for this travesty to happen under your watch."

She furrowed her brow, alarm beginning to skitter through her. "What are you rambling about?"

"I have never betrayed a confidence, but I fear my friend has put me in a rather unconscionable position. If his plan succeeds, it will ruin your reputation as a chaperone. My loyalty is being tested, but I know that I have no choice except to remain loyal to you, dear sister."

"Alex—"

"Hawk intends to compromise Miss Jenny Rose during the sixth waltz. He has arranged an assignation in Pemburton's library—"

"He what?" she interrupted, scarcely able to believe what she was hearing.

"He has asked her to meet him in the library for a kiss. But I fear it will be more as he has asked me to wait a few minutes. And then I am to bring her brother with the ruse of sampling Pemburton's fine brandy—"

"No," she said, glancing at her dance card. The sixth waltz was next. The strains of the music that accompanied the previous dance were fading. "You have to stop him, Alex. This is not the way to do it, to ensure that she marry him."

"He will not listen to me, and if something

should happen and she was caught with both of us—you can well imagine that her reputation would be left in tatters and yours along with it. No one will hire you again to serve as chaperone—"

She waved off those concerns and began to look frantically around the room. She couldn't see Jenny. She turned back to her brother. "The library, you say?"

"Yes."

"Do not take her brother there. I will do what I can to extricate Jenny from this situation with no harm to her reputation." She squeezed his arm. "Thank you."

He gave her a funny look that she couldn't quite decipher: one of guilt or shame. Maybe a little of both, but she had no time to contemplate it further. She had to get to the library as quickly as possible and pray that she wasn't too late.

She slipped into the library. Closing the door immersed her in total blackness, the draperies drawn across the windows, no fire flickering on the hearth. Of course. Illicit assignations required darkness. Well, she was here to put an end to that notion. This was a modern house, with electricity recently installed. She needed only find the—

An arm snaked around her waist and she found herself pressed up against a hard, firm body. Hawkhurst. His scent filled her nostrils, his mouth blanketed hers, and his tongue breached her half-hearted attempt to deny him access.

Lord help her. She'd not forgotten the magic of

his kiss, the heat it generated, the sensations of desire, yearning, and passion that it invoked. She should push him away. Instead, with a soft moan, she drew him nearer, raking her fingers up into his hair.

She should break free, make him aware that she was not the woman he sought, not the woman he'd planned to ruin, not the woman he intended to marry.

One more sweep of his tongue, and she would do just that. She would alert him to his mistake.

One more moment . . . of feeling wanted, of feeling beautiful, of feeling desired.

His kiss stirred at her insides, curled her toes, reached deeply, and sent incredible sensations skimming along her nerve endings. His large hand cradled the back of her head, angled it, as his tongue delved deeper, more frantically as though he couldn't have enough of her.

Pain speared her heart because she knew it was Jenny whom he thought he could not have enough of. Jenny whom he thought he was holding in his arms. Jenny whom he wanted so desperately that he was willing to compromise her in order to ensure that he possessed her for all eternity.

Breaking off the kiss, he released a feral growl, a low groan as his hot, wet mouth trailed along her throat. She dropped her head back, rasped his name, her voice barely a whisper. One second more, then she would speak aloud, one second more and she would alert him to his blunder—

He began pushing her back—unerringly

avoiding tables and chairs—and she realized that
he must have memorized the room, become familiar enough with it that he knew the path to his
destination. Or perhaps he'd simply been in the
room long enough for his eyes to adjust to the
deep, lingering shadows.

His hands, his mouth did not stray from their
course, even as his legs guided her. The back of
her knees struck something, and she found herself falling onto plush cushions. A couch, she realized. Long and wide, crafted for a gentleman's
pleasure and now serving at hers.

Hawkhurst followed her down, his breathing
as harsh as hers, robbing them both of words,
allowing only the release of muted groans and
soft moans. His nimble fingers made short work
of lowering her bodice and his mouth closed
over her breast. Lost in the sensations, bucking
against him, she pressed her head back against
the pillows.

This was madness.

She felt as though she were on fire, felt as
though she must have him nearer, or she would
die. She was barely aware of unbuttoning his
waistcoat, his shirt, but suddenly her hands were
traveling over the heated flesh of his chest, her
fingers enticed by the soft hair.

He shifted, bunching her skirts at her waist. She
felt the first probe of hot flesh to hot flesh . . . was
shocked by it, even as she found herself arching
toward him, needing, wanting, desiring—

The pain came swift and sharp, the fullness of him filling her as his mouth captured her cry . . .

Then the stillness, the hush of harsh breathing.

"Next time," he rasped, "there will be no discomfort."

She should have told him there would be no next time, but a part of her embraced the promise, held it close as though he'd made it to her and not another, as though he would fulfill it, as though she would again have the opportunity to hold him close and be held near by him, to feel the weight of his body pressing down on her, to thrill at so intimate a joining.

He began moving against her, and the discomfort he'd alluded to began to ease and in its place came sensations unlike anything she'd ever experienced: a tightening that spread out to encompass every inch of her body. She released a tiny squeal, and his mouth returned to hers, hushing her even as it worked to increase her pleasure—

Because that was what this was. Pleasurable. Intensely pleasurable. Almost painful and yet not. It was indescribable. But she wanted it, wanted it with a desperation that almost frightened her—

Felt herself climbing toward a pinnacle—

Then a million brightly colored stars burst through her body in a maze of sensations that had her arching as he threw his head back, his satisfied groan echoing around them.

* * *

Dear God in heaven, what had he done?

She was lying beneath him, her breaths coming fast and harsh in the darkness, a woman pleasured, seeking to regain her equilibrium.

While he doubted that he would ever regain his.

He heard the door click open—

"Damnation!"

He rolled off her, barely had time to fasten his trousers before light filled the room. He heard her horrified squeak, sought to move himself into a position to protect her modesty as best he could.

As he turned to face the expected intruders, he was vaguely aware of her scrambling off the couch.

"Alex, I can explain—" she began.

"You have nothing to explain," Hawk heard himself growl, as he stared at Ravensley and the young Mr. Rose.

To his surprise, Ravensley appeared to be in stunned shock. Rose didn't even try to hide his fury. It marched over his features like Victoria's armies set on conquest.

"You bastard," he ground out as he crossed the room.

Hawk saw the balled fist—damn but the man had large hands—but he stood completely still, not bothering to turn away or duck from what he knew he deserved. Rose's fist landed squarely against his cheek, beside his nose, beneath his eye. Pain ricocheted across his face, pounded through his skull as he stumbled to the floor. He was vaguely aware of Louisa's tiny screech, the ringing in his ears muffling the sound.

Hit me again, he thought. *I deserve a harder blow than that, damn you. Hit me again.*

He watched as Rose removed his jacket and draped it carefully around Louisa's shoulders, drawing it close, and buttoning a center button, even though she'd somehow managed to straighten her clothing. Still, her hair was askew, and she looked like a woman thoroughly ravished. Perhaps because she had been.

He couldn't meet her eyes, couldn't bear to see the accusation he was certain he'd find there.

"I'll inform my father that you'll be at the house at eight o'clock in the morning to set this matter right," Rose said. "If you're so much as a minute late, you'll get a face-to-face introduction to the firing end of my gun."

Rose ushered Louisa out through a door that led onto the gardens. Hawk assumed he'd discreetly get her to the carriage and then find his sisters and get them all safely home. He looked over at Ravensley, who was staring at him as though he didn't know him.

"You said your plan was to be caught kissing her," Ravensley said slowly, as though needing to search for each word before he spoke it.

Hawk looked away as he pushed himself to his feet. His clothes were disheveled, and he, too, would use the back door to leave the party.

"A kiss!" Ravensley roared.

Hawk wasn't aware of the fist coming at him until he felt its impact slam his jaw upward, knocking his head back until it slammed against the marble mantel. He dropped to the floor. A blurring Ravensley crouched in front of him.

"She is my sister! May you rot in hell for what you did here tonight!"

He heard Ravensley's loud, angry footsteps as he stormed from the room, a man who could still exit through the front door. Hawk lay back on the floor, not certain he would ever again be worthy of exiting through anything other than a rear door. *Rot* in hell? He had a feeling he was going to *burn* in it for eternity.

Louisa was cold, so terribly cold, even though she sat in a tub of hot water, the mist rising, falling, circling around her. Jeremy had been so solicitous, so kind, assuring her over and over that she was innocent in all of this, not to blame, and that everything would be all right.

Only how could it be all right when they all thought that Hawkhurst was going to marry her? A man in need of money marrying a woman without money? They were all mad not to see the truth of the situation.

She was equally at fault. She shouldn't have gone to the library alone to confront him. When his mouth left hers after the first kiss, she should have spoken aloud, should have announced that it was her—rather than whispering his name in ecstasy. When he had laid her down on the couch, she should have gotten back up. When he had lifted her skirts, she should have shoved them back down.

While he'd certainly been eager, he'd not forced her. She could have said no at any moment, and she was certain he would have heeded her request. But she'd wanted one more moment, one more touch . . . a little something to last her a lifetime.

Tears filled her eyes.

"It's all right," Jenny said, wiping a warm cloth over Louisa's face.

With Louisa's hair draped over the edge of the tub, Kate sat behind her, brushing out the tangles.

"No need to cry. Papa will make everything all right," Kate continued.

Papa. Their father. Not hers. Because hers was dead. And not her brother, because he'd simply stood inside the doorway like a buffoon and done nothing.

No, not nothing. He'd brought Jeremy Rose to the library, knowing, knowing that Louisa would be there, most certainly alone, with Hawkhurst. Why had he done that when she'd specifically asked him not to? Why had he betrayed not only his friend, but her? The pain sliced through her. A more miserable night she'd never known.

"Nothing needs to be done," Louisa said quietly. "We are the only ones who know, and if we keep quiet, it need go no further."

Jenny released a laugh laced with incredulity. "Louisa, the man comprised you in the worst possible way."

Worst possible way? She could think of worse ways, and she'd certainly not objected at the time. Rather she'd relished his attentions.

Jenny held her gaze. "If you hadn't gone to meet him, it would have been me that your brother and mine would have walked in on."

Louisa felt the tears burn her eyes. "Don't you see? That's the very reason that I can't marry him. It was dark. He didn't know it was me. He doesn't want me."

"He doesn't want me either," Jenny said. "He just wants my money, and obviously he's willing to do anything to get it."

"Well, you did say that you wanted a man who could deliver passion," Kate said. "And based on the way Louisa looked when we first stepped into the carriage, I'd say the man delivered that without question."

They'd stopped calling her Lady Louisa, as though tonight's unfortunate incident—Louisa thought she would always think of it as "the unfortunate incident"—had transformed them into longtime friends, had created a bond that until now had been lacking.

"Kate!" Jenny chastised. "That's a horrible thing to say."

"It's the truth."

Louisa felt the continual tugging on her hair cease. Kate came around and knelt beside her. "The encounter was passionate was it not?"

Louisa was no longer chilled as images swamped her. Even though it had been dark she could see him so clearly in her mind, still feel the touch of his mouth and hands, the weight of his body . . .

"Kate, that's an entirely inappropriate thing to ask," Jenny said, but her voice held no conviction.

"You're as curious as I am," Kate said. "So don't be a hypocrite about it."

"I may be curious, but I would never ask, although I think Louisa's blush has given you the answer to our continual debate. There can be passion without love."

And with that truth voiced aloud, Louisa burst into tears. Because all his touches and kisses and sweet murmurings had been intended for another woman. And on the morrow, she would have to face him again. How could she after the intimacy they'd shared?

Chapter 14

"**Y**ou were supposed to secure a duke for my daughters, not acquire one of your own!"

Mrs. Rose had been ranting, huffing, and puffing ever since she'd joined the somber assembly in Mr. Rose's study and learned that the Duke of Hawkhurst would be arriving any moment to make his intentions clear regarding Louisa.

It did not help matters that Louisa was harboring such guilt. She did not want to explain that in a darkened room, he'd thought she was another. She did not want to have to confess that she'd willingly allowed him to harbor those thoughts. She'd accused him of being without scruples, and yet it was she who was responsible for bringing them to this devastatingly ruinous moment.

"Now, dear, let's not be that way," Mr. Rose said gently from where he sat behind his desk. "The girl is under our protection, after all."

"She is a paid servant," Mrs. Rose said.

"A chaperone is not a servant," Louisa retorted, stiffening her back and sitting up straighter.

Mrs. Rose stopped her pacing. "How badly were you compromised?"

"With all due respect, Mother," Jeremy said from his place behind his father, where he stood with his shoulder pressed against the wall and his arms crossed over his chest, his raw, skinned knuckles visible. "There are not levels of being compromised. One is either compromised or she isn't. I can attest to the fact that Lady Louisa was compromised."

"Rather fortuitous that your brother invited Jeremy to join him for some brandy," Mrs. Rose said snidely. "I cannot help but believe this was all arranged in order to ensure you achieved exactly what you sought."

"Mama," Jenny said, exasperation in her voice, "we all know it was arranged—but Louisa was not at its heart, not part of its planning. It was a trap set for me, and poor Lady Louisa sprang it. And unfortunately got caught in it."

"Unfortunately indeed. It should have been you. He is your duke and Lady Louisa took advantage of the situation to ensure that she ended up with him rather than you! She knew full well what she was getting herself into, and she calculatingly barged ahead—"

"Enough!" a voice barked from the doorway.

Louisa jumped to her feet and spun around, unable to refrain from grimacing. The Duke of Hawkhurst stood just inside the study door— obviously deciding that since he was expected, he needed no servant to introduce him. One side of his face was badly battered and bruised, the area beneath his eye terribly swollen. It had to be incredibly painful.

"You are speaking about the daughter of an earl and my future duchess. I would take care with the words you choose to use, madam," Hawkhurst said, a warning shimmering beneath his voice that had Mrs. Rose taking a step back, Mr. Rose coming to his feet, and Jeremy taking a step forward.

Jenny and Kate exchanged glances as though Hawkhurst's words pleased them. No doubt because they gave the impression that he intended to marry Louisa. Well, she needed to set everyone straight on that account.

She cleared her throat. "Your Grace, it seems you and I have several matters to discuss."

"Indeed we do, and none of them concern these people. I would appreciate their taking their leave."

Jeremy took another step forward. "You can't possibly believe after what happened last night that I'm going to leave you alone with her."

"The damage has been done, and the time for protecting her is long past," Hawkhurst said. "The rectifying of this situation does not require an audience."

"The hell it doesn't," Jeremy said. "I'm not leaving this room, so you may have the opportunity to intimidate and bully her—"

"I've just stated that she's to be my future duchess. The terms of that arrangement are none of your concern."

"I have no plans to marry you," Louisa said.

Hawkhurst swung his gaze around, clearly dumbfounded by her remark. She had to resist the temptation to cross over to him and press her cool palm against his poor cheek.

"I beg your pardon?" Hawkhurst said.

Louisa shook her head. "I won't marry you."

"Why ever not?"

Taking a deep breath she walked up to him. Closer to him, she could see that his chin sported an ugly bruise as well. Jeremy had done significant damage. She didn't resist this time. She reached up and touched the bruise. He flinched. She lowered her hand, blinked back tears.

"I am not what you need," she whispered. "I have all of eight pounds to my name. I am not who you want, I am not the one you were expecting to arrive in the library last night. Only a few people know what occurred, and they will hold their tongues. My reputation is intact. No reason remains to take drastic measures."

"And if you are with child?" he ground out.

She stared at him. "But . . ." She couldn't find the words. "But it only happened once."

He leaned nearer. "That, sweetheart, is all it takes."

Her knees were suddenly weak, and her legs had no more consistency than her morning porridge. She must have looked on the verge of swooning, because his hand was suddenly supporting her, and he was leading her to a couch. As soon as she was near enough, she sank onto the stuffed cushions.

He knelt before her. "Surely you are not that innocent."

Pressing her hand to her mouth, she shook her head. "My mother never spoke of such things to me before she died. I had a notion of what occurred, but I was unclear on the particulars. And who was there for me to ask? Alex?"

With gentleness she'd not have expected of him, he reached out and, with his fingers, feathered stray strands of her hair back from her face. "So now you see the need for us to wed."

Again, she shook her head. "Not unless I'm with child. When will I know?"

"Not for a few months. The fact that there is a possibility that you are with child means we must wed now. I will have no scandal surrounding my heir."

"Your heir?"

He grimaced, then winced. "Or my wife."

This was wrong. All of the reasons for him marrying her were wrong, and yet if she was with child, no reason was more compelling than protecting the child. She looked past him to the one person she'd never thought to turn to for advice.

"Mrs. Rose, when and how will I know if I'm with child?"

Mrs. Rose squared her shoulders as though about to face unpleasantness. "It is much easier for a woman to know for certain that she is *not* rather than that she is. There are signs I will not mention in front of gentlemen, but a doctor can't confirm a lady's delicate condition for a few months."

With the confirmation of Hawkhurst's understanding of the situation, Louisa couldn't help but wonder if he'd placed another lady in this predicament—and been unwilling to marry her. How else would he have known?

Gathering her strength and conviction about her like a well-worn cloak, Louisa came to her feet, waited until Hawkhurst had also come to his. She met his gaze. "In a few months at the latest, Your Grace, I shall give you my answer."

With that, she walked out of the room that had become as quiet as a tomb.

His mother would never forgive him. He'd never forgive himself. He didn't want people to know his child's birth date and count backward, raise eyebrows, and give a pompous, knowing look.

He threw the brandy to the back of his throat, felt it burn its way down.

He'd wanted to rush after Louisa, drop to his knees in front of her, beg her to reconsider, but he had some pride when it came to his manhood. With both Rose men watching, he'd prepared to take his leave.

Mrs. Rose had stepped forward to stop him. "It appears you are still on the market, Your Grace. Would you care to join us for breakfast?"

He had politely declined.

He had returned home to pace the quiet halls that were devoid of all servants except his valet. The man stayed with him, because he had a penchant for rat fight betting and with a run of luck he'd managed to put aside some money for a rainy afternoon. Hawk was beginning to wonder if the sun would ever again shine.

He'd not handled the situation at all well. His face ached. His anger seethed just below the surface, anger at Louisa for coming to the library to begin with. If she had stayed away, his trousers would have remained buttoned, her skirts would have remained lowered.

But she had waltzed into the room, a temptation beyond measure. The fire in his blood had instantly boiled. Have her once and be done with it. Conquer and move on.

And yet he sat there tonight wanting her more than he'd ever wanted her.

He poured more brandy into his glass and downed it.

There could be only one explanation for his continued interest in her. He had yet to conquer her. She had refused his proposal. She had walked out on him.

He heard the harsh laughter echoing around him, realizing belatedly that it was his own.

The woman was driving him to madness.

He had possessed her, and when he walked into the Rose study he should have been barely aware of her existence. Instead, he had been conscious of every subtle nuance: her fragrance, her hair simply pulled back and held in place with a ribbon. The slight redness in her eyes that told him she'd been weeping. The touch of her fingers against his chin had shot desire straight down to the heels of his shoes. Jeremy Rose had been right not to leave, because Hawk had wanted nothing more than to take Louisa into his arms and have her again.

Slowly, he wanted to take his fill of her. Remove every stitch of clothing.

Their coming together had been unsatisfying in its swiftness. If he could have her but once more at his leisure, then he would never need her again. Once more. That was all that he required.

Acquiring *that*, with her present attitude, seemed impossible.

He was splashing more brandy into his glass when he became aware of the footsteps. Since he was without a proper butler, his friends were in the habit of simply coming into his home as though it were theirs.

He glanced over at Falconridge. "Fetch a glass."

His slurred words surprised him. How much had he drunk already?

"Good God, what happened to your face?"

"It ran into a fist. Two actually."

"The rumors are true then?"

He twisted his head around, forced himself to focus his attention on Falconridge. He did wish the man would quit swaying. It made it appear as though there were two of him, darting in and out of hiding. "What rumors?"

"That you compromised Lady Louisa and will soon be taking her to wife."

"Ravensley tell you that?"

"No. I heard it at the club. Wagers are being made on the precise date when the nuptials will take place."

Hawk sat upright too fast. His head spun, and he thought he might be ill. "They're discussing Lady Louisa at the club?"

"Did I not just say that?"

Hawk dug his elbows into his thighs, buried his face in his hands. "How did they hear?"

"Haven't a clue."

"Ravensley."

"Why would he implicate his good friend and his sister in a scandal?"

Hawk lifted his head slightly and peered at Falconridge over his fingertips. "Only the Roses, Louisa, Ravensley, and I knew what had transpired. I alerted him this morning that I'd asked for her hand, and she denied me. He is the only one with anything to gain."

"No offense intended, but I don't see how acquiring you as a brother-in-law can be considered a gain."

"It eliminates me permanently as competition for Jenny Rose."

Falconridge appeared adequately horrified. "You can't be serious."

"There can be no other explanation. It is appalling what we will do for money."

Falconridge turned and stared at the cold and empty hearth. "I daresay that I don't know if I've ever heard truer words spoken."

"He's returned."

Louisa looked up from the invitations she'd been perusing. Jenny stood in the doorway to her bedchamber. "Who's returned?"

"The Duke of Hawkhurst. I think he's come to ask for your hand in marriage again."

"Why would you think that?"

"Because he wants to see *you*, and he has brought you a small gift."

"Tell him I'm not at home." She lowered her gaze to the invitations. Much to her astonishment, Mrs. Rose had not immediately dismissed her because of the unfortunate incident, and Louisa needed to arrange a schedule of activities for the girls for next week.

"I think you should hear what he has to say."

Louisa lifted her gaze. "Why? I've made my position perfectly clear."

"What is the worst that could happen if you marry him?"

"The worst is that I could be married to a rake

and a scoundrel. He has admitted that the only thing that appeals to him is the chase. Well, I was well and truly caught, without even having experienced the pursuit. I see no point in entertaining him further."

"I don't think he's as bad as all that. I've seen the way he looks at you."

She laughed. "The way he looks at me? As though I'm the irritating younger sister of his good friend. Or his past good friend. I'm not even certain that Alex was incensed by what happened. If not for the kindness of your brother, I would have been totally without support. And that hurts as well if I'm truthful about it."

"As well it should. I expected better of your brother." She stepped farther into the room. "I fear I'm partly to blame for what happened, and I'm not sure why. Your brother informed me of Hawkhurst's plans. He knew I had no intention of going to the library, so I don't know why he sent you to rescue me when he knew I was in no need of rescue."

Disappointment roiled through Louisa. Her brother had betrayed her much more thoroughly than she'd thought. It made no sense. Why would he do that?

"I did not see you in the ballroom."

"I must admit to having a weakness where sampling passion is concerned. The duke is a very virile man and I was incredibly tempted to taste what he was offering, but I wanted no more than a taste. I did not wish to eat the entire meal, so I asked Falconridge to take me on a turn about the garden—to remove temptation."

Louisa sighed. "I wish you'd confided in me."

"I should have, and I'm sorry I didn't, but I thought my not going to the library would put an end to the duke's pursuit."

"You did not want him pursuing you, but you think I should marry him?"

"As I said, he looks at you far differently than he looks at me. I truly believe you shouldn't discount his feelings. He brought you a gift, Louisa. It's so incredibly romantic."

"Nothing he can say will change my mind."

"Then where is the harm in seeing him?"

The harm was that he could possibly melt her resolve. No, she could be strong. She would be strong. She set the invitations aside. "Very well."

She followed Jenny down the hallway and stairs to the foyer. Jeremy, ever her protector, was scowling at the duke.

As she neared, Louisa felt her heart tighten at the sight of Hawkhurst. The bruises on his face had deepened to a ghastly purple, and she thought his eye might be more swollen than before. He was holding a small paper sack. Recognizing the emblem drawn on it, she couldn't help but smile.

"What have you there, Your Grace?"

"A small token of . . . my esteem. A dozen toffees."

"And here I'd taken a fancy to brandy balls."

His mouth curved upward, and he grimaced. "I beg of you, do not make me smile."

"Your bruises look quite painful."

He shifted his gaze to Jeremy. "They have served their purpose exceedingly well. I was wondering if we might take a turn about the garden."

"Jeremy and I will be more than happy to serve as chaperones," Jenny said.

"I don't require a chaperone," Louisa said.

"From the likes of him, I think you do," Jeremy said.

Louisa rolled her eyes and shook her head. "Very well. If you'll come with me, Your Grace."

She gave the sack to the butler with instructions to have it delivered to her bedchamber. Then she led the way into the garden with Jenny and Jeremy trailing behind them. The duke did not offer his arm, but rather walked with his hands clasped behind his back. Night had fallen, and the gaslights created a muted glow that served to create an intimacy that reminded her of their first kiss in a garden.

"It seems our indiscretion is the talk of London," he said quietly after a time.

She stopped walking and stared at him. "You told—"

"I've told no one. Falconridge heard the rumors. He came by to confirm them."

She sighed. "Damnation."

"My sentiment exactly."

She thought she heard humor laced in his voice, when there was certainly nothing humorous about this situation.

"Be that as it may, the rumors change nothing," she said.

"They change everything. Your reputation is in tatters—"

"Which would only make a difference if I cared, and I don't."

"Well, I do care!"

She heard a footstep, turned, and held up a hand to stop Jeremy's advance. "It's all right."

"You speak to her with respect."

"I'm trying. She's a bit on the stubborn side and doesn't seem to be hearing what I'm saying." Hawkhurst turned back to her. "Less than a month ago, you were concerned that if you recommended me to your charges, your reputation would be suspect. How can you say now that your reputation does not matter? Do you think you will not be let go? Do you think you will be able to find another position? And even if our actions have not effectively ruined your chances of continuing on as a chaperone, how can we not take action when our sins could very well cause our child to suffer? If we marry posthaste, we can limit the damage."

Our child. Our child. Our child.

Louisa wrapped her arms tightly around herself, suddenly dizzy. "If I'm not with child, we are both condemned to a life of misery."

With his thumb and forefinger, he took hold of her chin and tilted her head back until she was forced to look into his eyes. "We are condemned anyway. My behavior has sullied my reputation as a gentleman. I will no longer be welcomed in the finer homes, and I shall be labeled exactly as you view me—unsuitable to be the husband of an heiress. While you, sweetheart, will no longer be a woman of independent means. Mrs. Rose is certain to dismiss you once she learns of the rumors going around. Tell her," he ground out.

"I'm afraid he's right," Jeremy said quietly. "It pains me to say it, but with last night's encounter being whispered about . . . you are well and truly ruined."

"You will not be able to find another position in another household," Hawkhurst added. "No one will hire a chaperone who was caught in a compromising position, just as no one would hire a servant who has been caught pilfering the silver."

She'd never known such despair. Her career as a social chaperone was coming to an end with ugly accusations and innuendo. What was left to her? Nothing.

She was not certain she could force herself to live under the same roof as Alex. He'd known she was in the library, and he'd brought Jeremy to it. Why?

Without a position she had no funds. She would be on the street. And if she were with child . . .

"But you don't love me," she said to Hawkhurst, hoping, praying, wishing that he would deny the charge, even a bit.

"Love is not something I required for a marriage."

"Well, I did. I'm not like Jenny, requiring only passion."

"It is not a half-poor substitute." He glanced over his shoulder, his voice filled with anger. "Could you at least step beyond hearing?"

Jenny and Jeremy backed up several paces, and Hawkhurst turned back to Louisa. "I won't say it won't be difficult, because it will be. I will not say it is what I *want*, because it is not. But I think you could say the same. Marriage to me is obviously not what you *want*."

She heard him swallow.

"But in the past few weeks, I have come to gain an appreciation for your determination and your ability to take charge of your life. You have a strength of character and strength of purpose that I believe would serve our marriage well. I'm fully aware that I gain the most with this arrangement, but I promise you that I would not hinder you in any ventures you wished to pursue. My weaknesses have brought us to this, and I shall spend the remainder of my life making it up to you." He dropped down to one knee, took her hand in both of his, and looked up at her. "Will you please do me the honor of becoming my wife?"

She felt the tears burn her eyes, could hardly see him through their thickness. Dear Lord, such a proud man down on bended knee, in front of Jeremy Rose, in front of a man who would never have to bow down to anyone.

She could not refuse so heartfelt a request. Swallowing hard, she nodded. "Yes," she rasped.

Pressing his lips to the back of her hand, he said in a low voice, "Thank you."

With her free hand, she touched his bent head, threading her fingers through his thick hair. Everything would be all right. She would do everything in her power to see it was so.

Chapter 15

"I'm marrying Hawkhurst."

Alex met Louisa's announcement with little more than a nod. Looking slovenly with his clothes wrinkled and askew, he lounged in a chair, one leg bent, one outstretched. He'd barely acknowledged her when she'd walked into the room.

"You smell like a brewery," she said.

"Pray tell, dear sister. How do you know what a brewery smells like?"

"I know the odor of alcohol, and I assume a brewery is merely the odor intensified. You are also sorely in need of a bath."

"If I had a valet, perhaps I could have a bath. The servants have all abandoned me."

"Poor, poor Alex. You keep waiting for life to

happen to you. Don't you see? You must take charge, you must make—"

"I did!" he yelled coming to his feet, wavering, and dropping back into the chair. "I did take charge."

"What did you do?"

Shaking his head, he looked away.

Dread piercing her heart with confirmation of what she had feared most of all, she took a step nearer. "You did more than betray me by bringing Jeremy to the library. You started the rumors."

"Hawk told me that you refused to marry him."

"Why was it so important to you that I marry Hawkhurst?"

He shook his head again. "Not that you marry Hawk. That he not marry Jenny."

Anger pierced her soul, sorrow her heart. She loved him, and yet he had betrayed her as she never would have betrayed him. He was the one constant in her life she'd always thought she could depend on, but he'd selfishly put his own wants above all else. She felt an uncharacteristic need to lash out, and while it made her feel small and petty, she couldn't seem to stop herself from wanting to hurt him as he'd hurt her.

"Mrs. Rose wants a prestigious title for her daughters. I daresay she would consent to letting them marry the Prince of Darkness if he knocked on her door." She took another step toward him. "But she will not let them marry an earl."

"She will have no choice if I'm all that remains,"

he rasped, his voice hoarse, and she wondered if all his drinking had burned his throat raw.

"Are you so greedy that you will do anything? Ruin my reputation? Break my heart? Conspire to have me marry a man for whom you knew I had naught but loathing?"

He laughed harshly. "You have a rather strange way of showing your loathing. My God, Louisa, you were lying beneath him—"

The crack of her palm connecting with his cheek resounded throughout the room. "How dare you? How dare you find fault with me when you live the debauched life that you do?"

"Who do you think taught me the debauchery?"

Why, oh why, was he working so terribly hard to hurt her? What had become of the brother who had once been her champion? Rather than rise to the challenge of overcoming their unfortunate circumstance, he'd resorted to trickery and betrayal, while Hawkhurst had turned out to be far more honorable than she'd ever given him credit for, honorable enough to protect her reputation. How could she have so vastly misjudged both men?

"I pity you, Alex."

"I pity us both."

As the coach traveled over the rough country road, Hawk watched his wife worrying her gloved finger, the finger on which, little more than an hour before, he'd placed a thin band of gold. He wasn't certain he'd ever attended a more somber affair. The private ceremony had taken place in a small chapel, the only guests in attendance Jenny, Kate, and Jeremy Rose, and Falconridge.

By all rights, as her husband, he could sit beside her, but he feared if he got too close, she would arrive at his ancestral home looking like a woman who had been thoroughly ravished, because she would be.

Louisa wore a silvery gray travel dress that modestly covered her from her chin to her toes. The last thing Hawk should have been was aroused, because nothing about her attire was the least bit arousing—except that she was in it.

He found himself envying cloth simply because it rested next to her skin. She was now his wife. It made no sense that he wanted her with a fierceness that was almost frightening.

In order to distract himself, he thought of the lavish wedding he'd hoped marriage to Jenny would have allowed him to give Caroline and felt a pang of guilt because his own wife had been given such a simple wedding. She'd not been even properly given away.

"I fear you are in danger of rubbing a hole in your glove," he said.

She lifted her gaze to his. "Everything happened so quickly. I can scarcely wrap my mind around it all."

"I'm sorry your brother wasn't in attendance," he said.

She gave her head a quick shake. "I'm rather glad he was absent, actually. I'm quite cross with him. He set out intentionally to ruin me, to ruin us both. His most-trusted friend and his sister. What sort of man does something as unkind as that?"

"A desperate one."

"You say that as though you approve of what he did."

"No, I do not approve of his actions; but then neither do I approve of mine. Still, I understand the desperation that caused us both to act stupidly."

"He wanted Jenny for himself."

"I believe Falconridge did as well. And Stonehaven and Pemburton. I knew Jenny had no wish to marry this Season, and so I attempted to press the matter. Rather bad planning to take your brother into my confidence."

"He was quite into his cups the last time I saw him. I'm angry at him, and yet I do worry about him."

"I'm certain he'll make out just fine, and marriage to me will give you plenty of other things to worry over."

"You have been Alex's friend for as long as I can remember, and yet I can't recall ever being a guest at any of your residences or meeting your mother," she said, as though needing to change the subject.

"My mother is a bit of recluse. She prefers her privacy."

"I shall strive not to be an intrusion—"

"It is your home now. You may do as you wish."

"How do you think she will take our marriage?"

"She has long wanted me to marry. She will be thrilled beyond measure."

She glanced down at her gray-gloved hands. "I meant specifically how will she take your marrying *me*?"

"She will be delighted."

She quickly lifted her head, and he could see all the doubts in her blue eyes. "Delighted that I bring naught but myself and scandal to this marriage?"

He furrowed his brow. "What of the eight pounds? Do you not still have it?"

She appeared horrified, and he quickly regretted his words. "I'm sorry. I was attempting to lighten the mood by teasing you. You've not smiled since I set eyes upon you this afternoon."

"I see little to smile about. You needed a wife with money and you have married a woman with all of a hundred and eight pounds."

"A hundred—"

"The Roses gave us a wedding present. I suppose I should have told you earlier."

"I'm quite surprised they would give us anything."

She shrugged. "I think it was from Jenny and Kate more than from their parents."

"And Jeremy Rose as well? He seemed quite fond of you."

She did smile then, as though some memory

delighted her. He was taken aback by the spark of jealousy that struck him.

"I think it is just his nature to be kind," she said.

"And what is your opinion of my nature?" he heard himself ask before he could stop the words.

"Dangerous," she said quietly, before glancing out the window at the passing scenery. "I think it is your nature to be dangerous. I've always thought you appeared to be rather predatory."

He wasn't certain whether to take insult or pride in her view of him. Insult he supposed. After all, to her, just as he'd feared, he had been a danger. He released a harsh chuckle.

"Do share the joke," she urged. "I could use a bit of laughter."

"I was merely thinking of that night in your library when you proclaimed me unsuitable, and I argued against your reasoning. It seems you know me better than I know myself."

"I'm not certain I knew you as well as I thought. My reason for going to Pemburton's library was to assure you that you needn't take such drastic measures, that I was going to begin advising Jenny to seriously consider your suit."

He stared at her in stunned disbelief. "What changed your mind?"

He could see the blush warming her cheeks. "Well, all thoughts of saying anything at all deserted me when you kissed me—"

"No," he interrupted, needing no reminders of

his shameful actions. "What changed your opinion of me?"

"I'm not sure. I think . . . I think I began to feel like a bit of a prude. Jeremy Rose stays out until all hours. He drinks, he smokes, and on occasion, I have heard him use profanity, but my opinion of him is not any less. I began to think that perhaps I had set too high a standard for you." She peered over at him. "And you make me laugh."

"Laugh?" he asked, chuckling. He'd always prided himself on his ability to stir passion, but she'd changed her opinion of him not because of his seductive kisses but because she found him humorous?

She nodded. "With your outlandish tales about all the lords. Were any of them true?"

"No."

"I thought not." She looked back out the window as though very satisfied with her deduction.

He contemplated telling her that he'd told his outlandish tales, because he enjoyed listening to *her* laughter, but in the end, like her, he merely stared out the window.

His home was as large as any that Louisa had ever seen, grand and stately, at least three levels, if the rows of windows were any indication. With his assistance, she climbed out of his coach and stared in awe at her surroundings. The gardens were immaculately kept. They circled the drive, they surrounded the house. They made everything seem grander, more beautiful, more alive.

"You've somehow managed to keep your gardener," she said.

"Denby is devoted to the grounds. After spending years cultivating them, he refuses to leave them, even though I can no longer provide him with a salary. He finds his pleasure in his work. He says it is enough."

"He is a fortunate man, then," she said. "Would that we could all find happiness as easily."

"Indeed. Come, I'll introduce you to my mother."

She tried not to be nervous, but she couldn't seem to help herself. Meeting his mother was almost as daunting as going through an interview with Mrs. Rose. "What is she like, your mother?" she asked, as she walked beside him, her hand on his arm, up the wide steps leading to the massive front door.

"Quiet and kind. Not one to find fault with others."

"She will think poorly of me when she learns the reason we are married."

"She doesn't think poorly of anyone." He pushed open the front door. "We no longer have a butler."

His voice sounded strained and she realized it couldn't be easy for him to reveal all his financial shortcomings. Before today, they'd been rumor. Now she was experiencing them as reality. She didn't want this day to be difficult on either of them.

"Before moving in with the Roses, I'd managed sometime without one myself, so I assure you that

I find doing without no hardship." She stepped past him and into the grand entry hallway.

Stairs ascended on either side. Portraits lined the walls. Beautiful crystal vases held the most gorgeous flowers.

"You have as many flowers inside as out," she said, again in awe of their magnificence.

"My mother has always found comfort in them."

"They're incredibly lovely."

"She arranges them herself."

Louisa walked over to a particularly bright and colorful arrangement. She sniffed. "What are these? Their scent isn't overpowering like some flowers."

"You'll have to ask her."

She spun around and smiled. "It will give us something to talk about, I suppose. It's always difficult to carry on a conversation when you've only just met—"

"Hawk! You're home!"

Louisa watched as a young lady in a simple blue dress and bare feet rushed across the foyer and skidded to a stop in front of Hawkhurst. With a deeply furrowed brow, she reached up and touched his face. The swelling was gone, and the bruises had faded to yellow. "What in the world happened?"

"I wasn't watching where I was going, and I collided with a door. Rather clumsy of me."

"Does it hurt?"

"Not any longer."

"We didn't know you were coming home so soon. You could at least send word so we could prepare."

"I've brought a surprise." He extended his hand toward Louisa and arched a brow. Dazed, trying to determine exactly who this young woman was, she moved toward him, felt his hand close firmly over hers.

"Allow me to introduce my beloved sister, Caroline."

Louisa was quite pleased with herself for not jerking her head around to stare at him. "It's a pleasure, Lady Car—"

"Not Lady, just Caroline," he said quietly.

Louisa cleared her throat, forced herself to smile. "Caroline."

"Caroline, I'd like you to meet my duchess."

Caroline's dark eyes widened. "Oh, then you must be Jenny Rose. Hawk told me all about you. He said you were the most beautiful—"

"No," Hawkhurst interrupted. "She is the daughter to the Earl of Ravensley. Lady Louisa, before she became my duchess."

"Oh," Caroline said, looking sheepish, pressing her fingers to her mouth. "I'm so sorry—"

"It's all right, Moppet," Hawkhurst said, immense concern woven through his voice. "I handled the introduction poorly."

That, Louisa thought, was an understatement if she'd ever heard one.

"You are married, though, if she is your duchess," Caroline said.

"Yes, we were wed this afternoon, a few hours ago."

"Oh, won't Mother be surprised?"

"I daresay she will be. Where is she?"

"Denby wanted to share with her a new variety of flower he'd discovered at the far end of the property. They should be back any moment."

"When she returns, tell her I'm in the library and wish to speak with her. Meanwhile, I shall leave you two to get acquainted."

Louisa stared in bewilderment, as he headed across the foyer and disappeared down a hallway.

"I'm frightfully sorry for mistaking who you were and saying what I did," Caroline said.

Louisa looked at her and smiled, swallowing her own pride and hurt because he'd been fascinated enough by Jenny to mention her to his sister. "Please, you have no need to apologize. Jenny Rose is indeed beautiful, and I've no doubt your brother did speak of her often."

"Only the once actually. After the first ball." She lifted her shoulders. "I'm so glad you married him. He's been frightfully lonely for so long."

"He told you that?"

"Oh, no. He never speaks of himself, but I can tell. It is the way he gazes off at nothing, and it makes me wonder what it is that occupies his thoughts. Have you a brother?"

"Yes, as a matter of fact. He and Hawkhurst are friends." Or had been friends. It was difficult

to think of them as no longer being in that regard.

"Fancy that. Would you like me to take you on
a tour of the manor?"

Louisa reached out and squeezed Caroline's
hand. "Perhaps later. Right now I desperately
want to visit your brother in the library."

"Is it because you love him so that you can't
stand to be away from him for any length of
time?"

"Something like that," Louisa said, with a bright
smile that threatened to unhinge her jaw.

Hawk was fascinated watching the varied de-
grees of anger wash over Louisa's face like an
ever-changing kaleidoscope.

He'd barely finished his first glass of brandy
before she'd stormed into the library, a woman
with a definite mission and a determination to
take him to task. He was unaccustomed to being
questioned, but she seemed to do it at every turn.

"It didn't occur to you I should be informed
you had a sister?"

She made no attempt to hide the fact that she
was seething. At least he hoped she'd made no attempt. He didn't fancy contemplating that he
might ever see her angrier than she was at that
precise moment.

"I don't see how you can claim to be unin-
formed. I introduced you shortly after she appeared."

Slapping her hands on his desk, she leaned

menacingly toward him. "A bit of advance warning would have been welcomed, so I didn't gawk."

"You didn't gawk. You handled the introduction admirably. It was Caroline who needed the advance warning. I apologize for her assumption—"

She waved her hand in front of his face, nearly hitting his nose in the process. "You can't apologize for another's action. You can only apologize for you own."

"Still, her words—"

"You are attempting to distract me from the purpose of my rant. I should have been warned."

"Would the knowledge have influenced your decision to marry me?"

"No."

"Then I fail to see what difference telling you before might have made."

"Does Alex know you have a sister?"

"No."

"But he has visited your estates."

"When company has come to call, we've always ushered Caroline off to another property. No one of any consequence knows about her."

"Why not?"

"Why not what?"

"Why haven't you told anyone about her?"

"I didn't see the need."

"Are you ashamed of her?"

His gut tightened painfully, his chest ached. "No," he ground out.

"Then why all the secrecy?"

Her voice contained true compassion and baf-
flement. How could he explain the unexplain-
able?

"We've always tried to protect her," he said.

"This would all go much easier if you would
simply state what needs to be stated."

Taken aback, he stared at her. "I have no idea
what you're talking about."

"Your sister. You're obviously hiding something."

"I don't know what it is you want," he snapped,
then reined in his own temper. He'd considered
sending word to his mother to cart Caroline off to
another estate, but he'd decided he couldn't keep
her existence a secret from his wife forever.

"I want to know about your sister without having to pry the information out of you as though
you're an old chest with a rusty lock."

He couldn't help himself. His mouth twitched.
"An old chest with a rusty lock?"

"Metaphors are not my strong suit, especially
when I'm frustrated. You give me little tidbits
about your sister, enough to pique my curiosity,
then you clam up as though you've said too much
when you've said nothing at all."

"I'm not in the habit of discussing Caroline . . .
with anyone."

"Hawkhurst—"

He held up a hand to silence her. "First of all, it
is Hawk, not Hawkhurst. You are my wife, and a
bit of informality is now appropriate."

"Do not seek to change the subject."

He knew a hundred women who were easier to deal with than she. Why was it that he'd managed always to resist all except her?

He sighed. "All right. You wish me to unlock and open the box." He swallowed hard. "You have met her. You see how innocent she is. She recently turned seventeen. She was born five years after my father's passing. I don't know who fathered her. My mother refuses to speak of him, no doubt because she knows if I knew his identity I would kill him for not standing by her, for abandoning her, for playing her falsely. Over the years I have come to despise and loathe a man who is no more than a shadow. For all I know he is dead, and if so, I hope it was a painful end."

Straightening, she folded her hands in front of her and studied him. He wondered what she was thinking, what she was contemplating.

"Is your mother's experience the reason you insisted on marrying me?"

"Seventeen years, Louisa, and she has not returned to London. For seventeen years I have made payments on an empty opera box in hopes she would return and take delight in finding it available to her. She has withdrawn into a world that is nothing more than her garden, her daughter, and on occasion her son. You think you could have withstood Society's censure? That you could go it alone? I know you have no respect for me or the life I have led, but I assure you that while I may *leave* women, I do not *abandon* them."

"Your mother is the reason you married me,"

she said quietly. "But your sister is the reason you desperately wanted to marry Jenny Rose."

"Money is a great equalizer."

He walked to the window and stared out on the garden. "When we return to London, you'll discover we have very few possessions remaining there. I have sold off what I could. In a way, Mother's not coming to the city is a blessing. She is as innocent as Caroline regarding some matters. I do not care about objects. I do not care that my estates are in need of repair. I do not care that in winter I am chilled to the bone or that my clothing is not of the latest fashion."

He faced her. "I did not want Caroline to be whispered about. I did not want her to experience a cut direct. I wanted men to court her in the hopes of marrying her. Compare your experience against that of the Rose sisters and tell me that money does not make a difference."

"I cannot."

"I'm well aware of that, Louisa. My statement was rhetorical."

She shook her head. "You shouldn't have married me."

"That choice was taken out of my hands the moment you walked into Pemburton's library."

He thought she was going to say something else, but before she could speak, he heard his mother calling him.

"Hawk!"

Turning to the doorway, he smiled. "Hello, Mother."

Her expression animated, Caroline stood beside her. He could tell she was bursting, wanting to announce his news.

"What happened to your face?" his mother asked.

"He ran into a door. Can you believe he would be so clumsy?" Caroline asked.

"No, I cannot," his mother said, reaching up to caress his face with feathery touches. "Caroline tells me you've brought us a surprise."

It was then that her gaze fell on Louisa, and she furrowed her brow even more deeply.

"I didn't tell her what it was so you'd best handle the introductions a bit better this time," Caroline said, "because I did tell her the other thing, and you don't want her to make the same mistake I did."

"What mistake was that?" his mother asked, and he could see the worry in her eyes.

"It was nothing, Your Grace," Louisa said before he had a chance to explain. She curtsied. "I'm Lady Louisa Wentworth, or at least I was before your son did me the honor of marrying me this afternoon."

His mother jerked her head around to look at him, and he could see the questions in her eyes, questions she wouldn't voice in front of his wife. She gave Louisa a tremulous smile. "Well, this *is* a surprise. Allow me the honor of welcoming you to the family."

She placed her hands on Louisa's shoulders

and pressed her cheek against Louisa's. "Welcome, my dear."

But over Louisa's shoulder his mother held his gaze, and the message of her pointed look was clear: What the hell have you done?

Chapter 16

Sometime later he found his mother in the garden, her customary wicker basket over her arm as Denby cut flowers beside her. She dismissed the gardener as Hawk neared, but the man hesitated.

"I understand congratulations are in order, Your Grace," he said.

"Yes, thank you."

"If your wife takes pleasure in any particular flower, please let me know, and I shall add it to the garden."

"Thank you. I'll inform her of your kindness. I have no doubt she will greatly appreciate your gesture."

Denby bowed slightly, and, with clippers in hand, he took his leave.

Hawk's mother rubbed a delicate petal between her fingers. "I thought to make a nice arrangement of flowers to place in the bedchamber beside yours. I assume that's where your duchess will sleep."

"Yes, she's there now, putting away her things."

His mother nodded, then held his gaze. "This marriage came about of a sudden, didn't it?"

"Yes." He cleared his throat. She deserved the truth. "Louisa and I were discovered in a rather compromising situation."

"Am I to assume the door you ran into belonged to her brother?"

"I ran into two doors actually. The other belonged to young Jeremy Rose, and his was a much sturdier wood."

She furrowed her brow. "Is he a relation to this Jenny Rose you told me about?"

He nodded. "Her brother."

"May I ask how all this came about?"

"Suffice it to say I was foolish, and Louisa is now paying the price for that foolishness."

She reached out and stroked his cheek. "You silly boy. I raised you better than that."

He sighed. "Yes, you did."

"Do you have feelings for her? For Louisa?"

"I cannot deny I'm drawn to her. I don't know if that is the same as having feelings. I'm determined to be a good husband, but I fear I have not been a good brother. Where Caroline is concerned, things will be more difficult."

"That is my worry."

"We are a family. It is my worry as well." He
gave her a wry smile. "And I suspect Louisa will
make it hers, too. She is . . ." He hardly knew how
to put his thoughts into words that would do his
wife justice.

"Yes?" his mother prodded.

"I admire her greatly. She is not one to avoid
the more difficult path, nor does she avoid facing
difficult choices. It is ironic that it was my weakness that placed me in the library and her strength
that brought her there—where we were discovered."

"Do not underestimate your own worth,
Hawk."

"What do I offer her, Mother? A title? It will not
keep her from going hungry. It will not keep her
warm in winter."

She gave him a mischievous smile unlike any
she'd ever given him. "It is your place to keep her
warm in winter."

If at all possible, he planned at least to keep her
warm tonight.

Sitting at the dining table, Louisa found herself
watching her husband with interest. She'd thought
she knew Hawkhurst. She'd deemed him entirely
unsuitable for Jenny or Kate Rose—for any
woman for that matter. Unworthy as a husband,
yet there she was married to him. And mesmerized by him, mesmerized by the kindness he
showed his mother and sister.

He was far more complex than she'd realized.

When he'd confessed to keeping the opera box for his mother in hopes of bringing her joy should she ever return to London, something within Louisa had snapped—some resentment for his past misbehaviors fell away like so much discarded rubbish.

He had been worthy of Jenny Rose, so very worthy. She knew firsthand that he could deliver the passion the young lady so desired. Now she was coming to realize he quite possibly could have delivered love as well. The potential was there in his eyes when he looked at his mother, in his lips when he smiled at his sister.

She'd done him a horrible disservice, the hint of which had first appeared when he'd insisted on marrying her, the confirmation of which was now slamming into her with resounding verification. It was her wedding day, her wedding night, and she didn't know if she'd ever been more miserable.

She wanted to take back the vows they'd exchanged that afternoon, tear up the document they'd signed. She wanted to return to London and inform Jenny she'd found the duke she should wed.

"Since you married much sooner than you anticipated, does that mean I'll get to go to London this Season?" Caroline asked, effectively slicing into Louisa's thoughts.

Hawkhurst's gaze shot to Louisa, and she thought she saw trepidation and disappointment in his eyes. He lifted his wineglass, swirled its contents as though the answer rested in the red liquid. "No, not this Season."

"But you promised when you married I would have my coming out."

"I know, Moppet, but so many things need to be arranged that it would be best to wait another Season."

"Oh." Caroline skewed her mouth. "What else needs to be arranged?"

"Caroline, darling," the dowager duchess said, "let's not press matters tonight. This is a wedding dinner to celebrate Hawk's marriage to Louisa." She lifted her wineglass toward Louisa. "May you always be as happy here as we have been."

"Thank you, Your Grace." Sipping her wine, Louisa watched as Hawk did the same. She couldn't help but wonder if he would be happy married to her, or would he look at her and always wonder how much easier life would be if she'd not opened the door to Pemburton's library? She couldn't help but think it had been equal to opening Pandora's box.

"How did you meet?" Caroline asked, shifting her attention from Hawkhurst to Louisa.

"Your brother used to visit mine at our country estate," Louisa explained.

"Did you fall in love with him immediately upon meeting him?" Caroline asked.

"No, she did not," Hawk answered before Louisa could say anything. "She thought rather badly of me, and I can hardly blame her. She caught me smoking her father's pipe and drinking his liquor. I was young, and the behavior quite inappropriate."

"You seem to have forgotten about trying to kill my nanny," she said.

"I didn't forget," he ground out, and sounded as though he might be strangling.

"Why would you try to kill her nanny?" Caroline asked.

"I didn't. It was all a misunderstanding. I was walking through the stables, and I tripped and fell on top of her. I had not yet gotten up when Louisa walked by."

Louisa gasped, pressed a hand to her mouth, and met his amused gaze. With maturity, she saw that encounter in a new light. "Oh."

"Yes. Oh," he said.

"All these years I"—she felt the heat suffuse her face as she realized exactly what she'd interrupted—"it is little wonder you avoided me."

"I'm terribly confused," Caroline said. "Why did you avoid her?"

He held Louisa's gaze. "I avoided all ladies of quality."

"Is that the sign of a gentleman, then?" Caroline asked.

"No, it is the sign of a rake. It is not a time in my life of which I am proud, but"—he held up his wineglass—"I shall drink to being reformed by marriage."

Following dinner, they sat in the parlor and listened as Caroline skillfully played the piano. The music had a haunting quality to it, was a tune with which Louisa was not familiar, but it stirred images of loneliness. She couldn't help but remember the girl's earlier comment that afternoon that her brother had been lonely, and Louisa wondered if the same could be true of Caroline. What friends did she have? Hidden away at various estates, whom could she have met or confided in? A girl needed more than her mother and her brother.

Selwyn Manor was much larger than the home in which Louisa had grown up. She tried to envision living here for the remainder of her days, but it was not a vision she could easily imagine. She tried to imagine her children growing up here. That, too, was unimaginable. Perhaps her guilt simply wouldn't allow her to find her happiness here.

A part of Louisa wished that she'd never walked into Pemburton's library, had never deterred Hawkhurst from his purpose. A part of her wondered if it was really Jenny she'd been trying to protect . . . or did Mrs. Rose truly have the right of it? Had a part of her secretly wished to marry Hawkhurst?

If that were so, she could see now that she'd been terribly unfair to him and his family. She'd deprived them of the funds needed to protect Caroline.

She also realized, as she watched him enjoying his sister's performance, that she might have done a disservice to Jenny, because she was beginning to suspect that he was a man not only capable of delivering a good deal of passion but an exceptional amount of love as well.

Hawk paced in his bedchamber, his hair still damp from his bath. On the other side of the door lay heaven and hell. The same was mirrored on this side of the door.

To know she was within reach and to deny himself the pleasure of touching her . . .

They were married, and while the circumstances were not ideal, they gave him the right to have his fill of her. She was his, body and soul. Her heart, he might never possess but by God, he could have her body.

After dinner, he'd promised her that he would come to her bedchamber to say good night. It was time he carried through on that promise.

He wore nothing except his silk dressing gown, and while he intended to have a more leisurely joining this time, he saw no need to provide himself with encumbrances. He would have her tonight and douse the fire for her that rampaged through his blood. Tonight he would truly bring the quest to a satisfactory end.

She was no different from any other woman, and once he truly had her, he could move on.

The three women of the household had one lady's maid among them. She helped Louisa with her bath, but when Louisa was finished and completely dry, with nothing except the towel wrapped around her, she'd asked the servant to leave so she could prepare herself for bed.

For her wedding night.

For her husband.

It was a strange thing suddenly to find herself too shy to take joy in someone helping her. It seemed such an intimate thing to prepare oneself for her husband's nightly arrival.

With trembling hands, Louisa put on the scandalous white gossamer gown Jenny and Kate had given her as a wedding present.

As Hawkhurst and she had come up the stairs after Caroline's recital, he'd informed Louisa he would be in after a while to say good night. They had avoided discussing the particulars of their marriage, but she was rather certain he planned to do a good deal more than speak two words. Otherwise, why not say good night at the door?

Sitting at the vanity, she dabbed a few drops of perfume behind her ears, between her breasts, and at her wrists. It was silly to go to so much trouble when lovemaking took place in such a short span of time, but she couldn't help herself. For those few minutes, while he was with her, she wanted him to want to be with her as much as she wanted to be with him. She wanted to appear desirable. She wanted him to forget the beautiful Jenny Rose, the woman he'd told Caroline about. Louisa wanted him to see only her, to smell only her.

Dear God in heaven help her, but she wanted him to want only *her*.

She was his wife by default because she'd been too weak to turn away from his touch. She knew in all likelihood the touch he gave her tonight would be cold. The touch of duty, not desire.

Yet she desperately wanted him to desire her.

She was not the one he'd pursued, but she was the one he'd captured. For the few moments he was with her this night, she wanted him to be glad it was her in his bed.

She began brushing her hair again, anything to occupy her hands, her mind. She kept her gaze on her reflection in the mirror to keep it from traveling to the door separating their bedchambers. What if he didn't come? What if he'd changed his mind about saying good night?

How long should she give him before she insisted he carry through with his husbandly duties? Should she insist?

She heard the door separating his bedchamber from hers click. She felt immense relief even as her nerves caused her to tremble. She knew what to expect, had no reason to be nervous. And hadn't he promised she would experience no discomfort this time?

She started to rise—

"No, stay as you are," he commanded.

She sat back down, wondering if she dared to look at him.

"I simply want to look at you for a moment," he said.

"Is it all right if I look at you?"

"If you like."

He stepped behind her so she could see him in the mirror. He wore a dark blue silk dressing gown. Before he was completely behind her, she'd glimpsed the sash, merely tied at his waist, not knotted. It would take little to loosen it.

Reaching down, he uncurled her fingers from around the brush she hadn't realized she was still clutching. Very slowly he dragged it through her hair.

"The night I asked you to marry me, in the Roses' garden, you said you weren't like Jenny, requiring only passion."

She nodded, wondering where he was going with this. Should they be talking? Shouldn't he already have her on her back? Did the talking mean he did not want her? That he would not take her to bed?

"Does that mean you find me capable of delivering passion?"

She nodded.

"So our time in Pemburton's library—"

"Was passionate indeed," she said hastily.

He smiled, the proud smile of a man satisfied with the answer given.

"Tonight will be nothing at all like that night," he said quietly.

Disappointment slammed into her. It would not be the same because tonight he knew who he was taking to his bed. Tonight he knew she was not Jenny. Still she refused to acknowledge the keen frustration to him. Instead, she angled her chin, determined not to let on that she knew the exact reason it would be different. Perhaps a part of her needed to pretend otherwise, needed to imagine he wanted her. "Yes, I know. You promised no discomfort the next time."

"It is a promise I shall make good on." He came around, set the brush on the vanity, wrapped his hands around her arms, and brought her to her feet. "I did not expect you to dress so provocatively."

"The gown was a gift from Jenny and Kate."

"They have excellent taste."

Before she could respond, he covered her mouth with his, his tongue imploring her lips to part. Cradling her face with his large hands, he angled her head so he could deepen the kiss.

He had told her tonight would not be as it had been in the library, and already she could sense the difference. There was no hurry, no rush. Just a slow, deep kiss that caused a yearning so intense she thought she might die from it.

When he drew back, his eyes were darkened with the passion she thought she might never know again.

"When you said tonight would be different, I thought you meant it would be without passion," she murmured.

He dipped down and lifted her into his arms. "While tonight will be different, I assure you there will be passion."

She wound her arms around his neck and

nestled her head against his shoulder. "I'm ever so glad."

He chuckled low. "Who would have thought you'd be incredibly easy to please?"

"I'm always quite agreeable."

"No, you're not, and I forbid you to change."

He laid her on the bed and stood looking down on her. "I like that you challenge me," he said. "I like that you state your mind."

He loosened his sash, and his dressing gown parted to reveal the splendor of him.

"I like that you're unafraid," he said.

She lifted her gaze to his. "I'm only afraid of disappointing you."

"You couldn't disappoint me if you tried."

He shrugged off the silk, and before it had skimmed halfway down his back, he was draped halfway over her body, his mouth covering hers in a kiss unlike any he'd given her before. This one, she knew instinctively, was to be delivered to no one except her. She was not the messenger.

She was the recipient. The one to whom he was delivering the gift. And what a gift it was. He was holding nothing back, and while she sensed his eagerness, his hunger, there was no hurry, and she was slowly coming to realize what he'd meant when he'd told her that tonight would not be as the other.

Tonight they were in no danger of being caught. Tonight they had no need to be done as quickly as possible. Tonight it quite possibly might take longer than a matter of minutes. She did wish she'd taken time to put on a bit more perfume.

Not that he seemed to find fault with anything at all. He eased one side of her nightgown off her shoulder and nibbled the newly exposed skin. She shivered as his tongue caressed what his teeth had grazed.

She adored the weight of his body on hers, the light dusting of hair over his chest. She relished his patience as he slowly revealed more of her flesh. He'd not seen the full length of her before, nor she him. She wondered if he would find her as pleasing as she found him now.

She couldn't explain why she didn't feel shy, why she didn't try to hide herself when he finally removed her nightgown. Perhaps because he was now her husband—her husband! Perhaps it was because she'd been as intimate with him as a woman could be with a man.

Perhaps it was simply because she was coming to realize that she cared for him deeply, that perhaps she had for a while and had simply not wanted to acknowledge it. That in truth, she'd not sought to stop him before because no other man intrigued her as he did. No other man caused her heart to stir or her skin to warm.

No other man made her long for a dowry as he did. Yet even without it, she'd found herself married to him.

Raised up on an elbow, he leisurely allowed his heated gaze to roam over her flushed body like a gentle caress. She wanted to pull him down, ask him not to torture her so. She'd had the courage to go out in the world and hire herself out as a social chaperone, but she lacked the bravery to ask of her husband what she so desperately desired: his hands, mouth, and body covering hers.

Suddenly he returned his mouth to hers, his eagerness more evident, his desire more apparent. With his hands and mouth, he made her feel treasured, and she sought to make him feel the same, running her palms over his broad shoulders, along his chest, down his flat stomach.

"Teach me how to pleasure you," she said at one point, and she felt his moan of approval vibrating through his body.

He taught her where to touch him—everywhere. No place was forbidden, no portion of his body did not want to be touched. She was amazed by the varying textures, amazed by his patience as he gave her leave to explore every inch of him with her hands and her mouth as he had explored her. When his breathing got so harsh, his body so tight, he groaned, "Enough!"

She found herself not on her back, but on her stomach, with his mouth trailing along her spine.

"You have dimples," he said, and she heard in his voice that he was pleased.

"Only when I smile," she murmured.

Laughing, he kissed the curve of her backside. "No, here. And here."

"I didn't know that."

"I suspect you will find I look at your body much more closely than you do."

He kissed behind her knees, kissed her ankles, kissed her toes.

Then he dropped down on his back beside her. "Straddle me."

In his demand was a request and she couldn't deny it. She was beginning to think that she couldn't deny this man anything he asked. He was an attentive lover, and she couldn't help but believe that his attentiveness would extend beyond the bedroom. Had she not already seen evidence of his caring?

He positioned her above him. "Go at your leisure, inch by inch, no hurry, no rush, no discomfort."

"As you promised."

"As I promised." He cupped the back of her head and brought her down to him for a slow, sensual kiss that demanded nothing and in so doing, demanded everything.

He filled her as slowly as dawn pushed back the night. Raised up on her arms above him, she bowed her head, allowing her hair to form a silken curtain around them. She rocked against him, feeling the pleasure mounting as his fingers caressed her breasts while his tongue and lips made love to her mouth.

Pleasure coursed through her, increasing in intensity, until suddenly it was no longer content to linger but rushed forward with purpose. He was thrusting his hips, his body tightening beneath her as she met each thrust. She writhed above him, wanting more, wanting everything—

And when it arrived, it eclipsed all that had come before.

Hawk lay with Louisa curled against his side, his body sated and still glistening with sweat. He was familiar with her now. He knew every dip, curve, and flat plane of her body, because he had pressed his lips to every inch of her flesh. He knew the sound of her moans, her cries, her gasps.

He knew what it felt like when she reached the pinnacle of pleasure and her body clutched his and pulsed around him afterward.

He knew everything. No surprises remained.

Yet he wanted her again with a fierceness that astounded him.

He'd covered them with a sheet to keep her warm, and now he wanted to cast it aside so he could gaze on all her naked glory.

He felt her eyelashes flutter against his chest. He looked down at her and found her looking up at him, a contented smile on her face.

"I thought it always happened quickly," she said.

"Not always."

She reached down and began to stroke him. His body responded immediately.

"You only have one."

He arched a brow in question. "Yes?"

"So how can you have two ladies at once?"

He did not want to get into all the details, so he simply said, "They took turns."

"I don't think I would like sharing you with another woman."

He stroked his thumb across her cheek. "You won't have to."

She rose up on her elbow, looking down on him, so serious. "You told me it is the thrill of the hunt you enjoy."

He swallowed at the reminder of how well she'd known him, before she truly knew him. "Yes."

"You conquer and move on."

"Yes."

Sadness touched her eyes. "I believe I have been well and truly conquered."

"Yet here I am, wanting you again."

"But you will grow bored with me after a time."

"I cannot imagine it, but if it comes to pass . . . I will not be unfaithful to you, Louisa."

She gave him a smile, dipped her head, and ran her tongue around his nipple. He moaned low.

"Perhaps I shall accept the challenge of keeping you from getting bored," she said.

He rolled her onto her back. "And perhaps I shall accept the challenge of pleasuring you at least once more before I go to sleep."

And he did just that.

Chapter 17

L ouisa awoke that morning to find herself still in Hawk's arms. After he made love to her once again, very, very slowly, he left her to see to his affairs.

As she stepped on to the terrace, she realized that until recently she would have thought he was talking about visiting other women, but she had no doubt he was referring to the affairs of his estates. He might not love her, he might never love her, but she did trust he'd keep his word and remain faithful.

Just as she would remain faithful to him.

She'd learned he was a man who took actions based on obligations and responsibilities, while she was a woman who made her choices based on love.

She stumbled to a stop. She'd made her decision to become a social chaperone because of her conviction that she'd never have love. She'd married Hawkhurst because of her desire to protect a child who might not even be growing within her. She'd not married Hawkhurst because of love for him, yet she couldn't deny that she'd begun to have some affection for him, a sentiment that had begun with his first atrocious attempt to discredit a lord. He was a gentleman, and he could stir passion.

Perhaps in time a fondness would develop between them. She could hope for that, pray for it. Anticipate it. Perhaps she could even instigate it. Did affection breed affection?

Passion certainly seemed to result in passion. Could passion lead to love? Was it possible she'd gain more than she'd bargained for?

She wanted a few moments alone to contemplate those intriguing thoughts before she sought out Hawkhurst's mother and asked her what duties she could see to around the house. She didn't want to usurp the dowager duchess's authority, but neither was Louisa accustomed to idle moments.

She began to walk through the lush gardens and immediately her thoughts drifted back to Hawkhurst. Strange how her opinion of him had changed so drastically in such a short time. She realized now that her entire original estimation of him had been based on Alex's drunken ramblings, the ramblings of a man she had trusted and shouldn't have. A man who had betrayed her in one of the worst ways possible, by duping her into believing his lies, by setting her up in order to destroy her. He knew full well the consequences of his actions, how she would suffer, and what it would cost her. Yet still he carried through on them. She thought she might never recover from his betrayal. If she never saw him again, it would be far too soon.

That thought brought her equal sadness because he was her brother, and she'd never expected not to have him in her life. What had his actions gained him, except a lack of respect for himself?

She spotted Caroline sitting on a bench beneath the wide boughs of a tree, a book in her lap. She looked young and as innocent as Hawk claimed her to be. Louisa was reminded of Kate, always reading. She wondered if both ladies read in order to escape into a world much more pleasant than the one in which they lived.

Louisa could hardly blame them. Of late, she'd had moments where escape had been incredibly tempting, but in the end she'd remained in reality.

Louisa contemplated returning to the manor, but she'd done this girl a disservice, whether intentional or not, and she was determined to do what she could to make it up to the girl, one way or another. But perhaps she would do it later. Talk to the girl—

Caroline looked up, smiled brightly, and waved.

There was no hope for it. Louisa would have to say something. She walked over, taking delight in the cloudless sky, hoping for Caroline's sake that some sort of meaningful conversation would come to her. She'd never before spoken as an equal to someone in Caroline's situation, and it was imperative that she do so, that she do nothing to make the girl feel less valuable because of the circumstances of her birth.

If not for Hawk's insistence they marry, Louisa might have given birth to a child who would have faced the same challenges.

"Hello," Louisa said, smiling. Perhaps, over time as they became better acquainted, Caroline would become the sister Louisa had never had. "What are you reading?"

"Something you've probably never read," Caroline said, her bright smile turning mischievous.

Louisa sat on the bench beside her. "You might be surprised. I've done quite a bit of reading."

"This is the only copy in existence," Caroline said.

"Oh, a very rare edition, then." She angled her head, studying the binding. "It doesn't look that old. What's the title?"

Once Upon a Magical Moor.

"You guessed correctly. I've never read it." She leaned closer. "Never heard of it actually. What's it about?"

"It's the tale of a faerie princess, only she doesn't know she's a faerie or a princess. She just thinks she's an ordinary girl until magical things start to happen. It's really good. Would you like to read it?"

"Perhaps when you're finished with it."

She laughed lightly. "I've read it a hundred times at least." She held it out to Louisa. "Please, I would love for you to read it."

Louisa took it from her. "Thank you. I'll be very careful with it." She turned back the thick paper cover and read the inscription:

HAPPY BIRTHDAY, MOPPET.
LOVE ALWAYS, HAWK.

"Your brother gave it to you," she murmured quietly, struck by his promise always to love her, a child born out of wedlock, a child destined to become his burden.

"He did more than that," Caroline said. "He wrote it."

Louisa snapped her head around. "Pardon?"

"Yes, it's one of three that he's given me." Suddenly Caroline was looking quite serious. "When I was child, I would get so lonely, and Hawk would write stories for me, so I would have friends. Friends whom he promised would never leave me. Although I'm almost a grown lady, I still enjoy reading them. I like to think that someday I shall have a daughter to read them to. Hawk promised me that I would marry. He always keeps his promises."

"You care for him very much, don't you?" Louisa said, stunned to realize a man she'd thought so poorly of had this girl's absolute devotion.

How she wished he'd revealed more of himself to her, that she had truly known him. She would have recommended him to Jenny without misgivings.

Caroline laughed lightly. "Of course. He's my brother. But even if he weren't, I would still care for him a great deal. I don't see how anyone cannot care for him. You married him, so you must love him. You do, don't you?"

"People marry for many reasons, Caroline."

"Or not marry," she said quietly. She looked down at her book still resting in Louisa's lap, reached over, and touched the words written with such care on the paper. Then she lifted her gaze, her eyes filled with earnestness. "My mother didn't marry my father."

"I know. We don't have to talk about it."

She smiled shyly. "You're like everyone else."

"What do you mean?"

"No one wants to talk about . . . my situation. They think if they don't talk about it, then my feelings will be spared. But sometimes what is not said hurts as much as what might be said."

At the wisdom of the girl's words, Louisa reached over and squeezed her hand. Hawk had wanted so badly to marry a lady with money so he could give to Caroline what he thought she needed. Perhaps all she needed was not to feel as though she were a secret, hidden away, not to be discussed.

"Do you know anything about your father?" Louisa asked, then held her breath, wondering if she'd been too bold. She could easily see Kate or Jenny asking such an impertinent question without any compunction. Had she picked up their brazen habits in such a short time while in their company?

"I know he loved my mother." She widened her eyes. "And me. He wanted to marry her, but she said it wouldn't be fair to Hawk, and her first obligation had to be to him."

"I'm sure she didn't mean that she loved Hawk more—"

"Oh, no, I know she loves us the same, but Hawk is a duke, and she said it wouldn't do for her to marry the man she loved. I always thought that was sad. It's the reason we never go to London, because she didn't want to bring Hawk shame or scandal before he found a wife. But now that he's married, I think we can go to London. I would like to attend a ball, more than anything."

"Do you know how to dance?"

"Oh, yes, Hawk taught me."

"Last night during dinner . . . the conversation . . . he promised you a Season after he was married."

She nodded. "He said it was best to wait, because Mother doesn't want to come to London, and so he needed a wife who could serve as my chaperone and give me an entry into Society."

A wife with money who could do a great deal more than that.

"Do you know where your brother is now?" Louisa asked.

"Looking over the estate I imagine. It's silly really, because he has only a couple of tenants left, and the income they provide us is hardly worth the effort." She leaned near. "Mama says they actually cost us, because Hawk will see that they are fed in winter. He is very generous in that regard. Looking out for those entrusted to his care."

"So I'm coming to realize," Louisa murmured.

"He does not boast of his good deeds," Caroline said.

"No, he doesn't," Louisa said.

Caroline angled her head slightly. "Sometimes you say things in such a way it makes me believe you don't know Hawk at all."

"I think it is the way of marriage that one learns new things about the other every day."

"Did he kneel when he asked for your hand in marriage?"

Tears burned the backs of her eyes as she remembered—

"Yes, he was kneeling," she admitted.

"I imagine it was frightfully romantic."

"I can honestly say that I have never been so touched in my entire life."

"I fear I shall never have the love of a gentleman," Caroline said wistfully.

Louisa sighed. Here she was a married woman with the same fear.

"You've known Hawk for years," Caroline murmured.

"Yes."

The girl held Louisa's gaze. "But you didn't know about me, did you?"

Louisa swallowed hard, wishing she'd kept their time together short. "No." She smiled. "But then you didn't know about me either, so it worked out didn't it?"

Caroline looked away. "Not really."

"I've known who your brother is, but I've not really known him well," Louisa said, feeling as though she were digging herself into a large pit from which she might never climb out.

"Yet you married him, and still he didn't tell you about me."

"I suppose he wanted to surprise me with the knowledge that I'd have such a lovely sister-in-law."

"Yes, I'm sure that's it," Caroline said.

But Louisa heard in her voice that she recognized the truth: She was a secret not to be shared until absolutely necessary.

She suddenly wished she'd not ventured out into the garden.

The rain arrived in the afternoon, darkening the sky with black clouds and a heavy downpour, flashing occasional lightning and echoing resounding thunder. It was perfect weather during which to curl up in a plush chair and read and escape thoughts of her morning blunder with Caroline. Louisa had not known how to reassure the girl of her worth. She knew so little about her, about her place in this family, and Hawkhurst was so hesitant to discuss her, to help Louisa to understand.

It was a worry she would address this evening, when he came to say good night.

For now, Louisa sat in a chair beside the window in her bedchamber, transported to a world of make-believe unlike any she'd ever before read: faeries, unicorns, knights . . . and a villainous prince who very much resembled her husband in appearance. She thought of all the times she'd told him she considered him unsuitable, and it appeared he held the same opinion of himself.

If indeed what she was reading was a self-portrait.

Was it possible for a writer not to include a small portion of himself in his chosen words? Her drawings always contained a reflection of herself. Even the rose she'd watercolored in the conservatory had been more than a flower, the dew drop representing a tear as she left behind the world she'd always known.

She'd been terrified, her bravado simply a front so no one would realize how much she feared failure, how much she longed for success. Was Hawkhurst any different?

She closed the book and stared out the window at the sheets of rain pouring down, slashing against the pane. What did she truly know of this man whom she'd married?

That he enjoyed wicked nights . . . and brandy balls. That he would compromise a wealthy woman in order to ensure marriage to her and access to her funds . . .

No, he would do anything, including compromising a woman, tarnishing his own reputation as a gentleman, in order to ensure he had the means to protect his family. And when he'd found the wrong woman in his arms, he'd become her champion.

"At what cost to his family?" she whispered to the rain. "At what cost to himself?"

What man could write so convincingly of villains, heroes, sacrifice, and love if he did not possess at least a small measure of each within his own heart?

She set the book on the table beside her, picked up her sketch pad, and began to draw what he had so beautifully described. A world where good always prevailed. A world she'd not expected him to believe in, much less care about creating. A world designed to keep a lonely girl from experiencing loneliness.

She stilled her hand, remembering Caroline's declaration that Hawkhurst had been lonely. She'd found it difficult to believe, yet his villain's life reflected a poignant loneliness. Was it based on experience?

His sister obviously adored him. For that bond to develop, he had to have spent time with her, time away from Society, away from friends because she was a secret carefully guarded.

Louisa thought of all she'd done without while Alex had bought baubles for his mistress. She thought of the rumors that had quickly circulated, rumors intended to ensure that Jenny was not available to Hawkhurst, rumors instigated by her brother.

She'd done Hawkhurst a grave disservice. It wasn't he who was the bad influence. Rather it was her brother. How was it that she'd failed to see Alex for the selfish, self-centered man he truly was?

She'd always attributed those characteristics to his friends. Yet, here she was finding evidence of a generous heart in a man whom she'd always thought heartless.

Passion was not achieved merely by caressing. Rather it required reaching deep within. She touched the book. It was putting someone else before oneself. Sacrificing love for duty, happiness for obligation and responsibilities.

She'd never considered the unfairness of Hawk's situation or the unfairness of her own, and she couldn't help but wonder, if she were with child, what stories he might weave for his son. For surely, he would give as much to his own children as he'd given to his sister.

That was an aspect to him she'd not considered: He might be a truly wonderful father.

But how long before he began to resent the woman who had given him the children? The woman who had altered his plans with her impulsiveness, shattered his dreams with her own weaknesses?

Enough recriminations. They'd both exercised

poor judgment. And while she might never possess his heart, she did believe they could take matters into their own hands, reshape their destiny.

Once again, she began sketching a faerie princess in a glade with a unicorn. When she was finished with this drawing, she thought she might give sketching the villain a go.

Once she began sketching in earnest, she became quite lost in the endeavor. Finally, she stopped only because the sky had become much darker, the shadows of evening arriving to alert her that dinner would soon be served. She wanted a few moments alone with her husband before the family gathered for the evening.

After much searching, she found him in a bedchamber in the east wing, studying the contents of the room as though he'd never before seen them, lifting a vase to the poor lighting, then making a note in the ledger before moving on to a delicate figurine—a woman sitting beneath a tree, a book set in her lap.

He wore no jacket, no waistcoat. Only his shirt, with three buttons undone, a relaxed dress, and yet he seemed anything but relaxed. She caught glimpses of dirt and dust on his sleeves. His hair contained furrows where his fingers had repeatedly plowed. As she watched, he took another swipe through the thick strands, a melancholy sigh accompanying his actions.

Turning from his examination of the figurine, he came up short at the sight of her. He had the look of someone caught doing something he shouldn't have been doing. She'd always assumed it would be a common, natural look for him—a man she'd believed was always engaged in acts he shouldn't be.

But writing stories for a lonely child, striving to ensure her happiness . . .

"I suppose it is your wish to see me into an early grave," he said. "Appearing when unexpected could very well stop my heart."

"You've never struck me as one easily frightened," she said, curling her mouth up ever so slightly, wondering at the joy she felt by simply being in his presence. It was a dangerous thing to hope this marriage of theirs could ever be anything other than punishment for misbehavior. Clutching her sketch pad, she stepped farther into the room. "What are you doing?"

"Attempting to decide which objects have the most financial value and the least sentimental value."

"So you might sell them," she stated quietly.

"I have always strived to keep my debt at a minimum. It bothers me immeasurably that someone's generosity in extending me credit might cause his family to do without. Exceptions are made for aristocrats that are not made for the common man."

"You don't see it as your right: to be held above others?"

"I don't see as I've earned it."

She dug her fingers into her sketch pad. "I wasn't aware you held those feelings."

"I suspect, dear Louisa, where my feelings are concerned, you are unaware of a good deal."

She took a step closer. "Enlighten me."

He glanced down, trailing his finger over the bonnet worn by the lady in the figurine. "It is not an easy matter to bare them, and I suspect doing so will not raise my esteem in your eyes."

"Is it important to you what I think? I'd always thought you had no care for others' opinions."

"If I did not care, I would not have married you."

The words came out sharply, biting into her tender heart. He'd swung his head around, to gauge her reaction perhaps, although she thought it more likely to apologize for his outburst, for his eyes held regret.

"My apologies. You weren't deserving of that outburst, and the words spoken did not adequately convey the sentiment."

"It is a wonder that a man who can use words to portray beautifully a story has such difficulty expressing himself in conversation."

He furrowed his brow, in confusion, but she also feared as a prelude to anger. "Pardon?"

His voice was cautious, and she suspected he wasn't going to be pleased to learn his sister has shared his stories.

"I did not come here to torment you," she said. "Rather I wanted to share something with you." Taking a deep breath for fortification, realizing she'd come too far to turn back now, she marched across the short distance separating them and presented her sketch pad. "While the rain has been falling, I've been drawing. I'd like your opinion."

Warily, he set his ledger beside the figurine on the small round table and took her sketch pad. He studied the first sketch, a muscle in his jaw jumping sporadically as though he fought to keep himself from speaking. He turned the paper back and scrutinized the next drawing. Very slowly, as though in a daze, he walked to the window where the light was better. Turned slightly, he presented little more than his profile as he looked at the third drawing. When he was finished with the fourth, he gazed out the window, as still and silent as stone.

"Do you find them displeasing?" she dared to ask.

He shook his head. "How did you come to envision this world?"

"Caroline gave me the honor of reading one of your stories this afternoon."

He closed his eyes, his jaw again ticking.

"Don't be angry with her."

"I'm not angry. It is simply that they were never meant to be shared."

"Why ever not?"

He opened his eyes, but still refused to turn around and meet her gaze. "They were merely a poor attempt to ease her loneliness."

"And perhaps a bit of your own?"

He snapped his head around. "Do not attempt to read more into these silly stories than exists."

"They are not silly. At least not the one I read,

and I can scarcely wait to read the others. Why have you never sought to get it published?"

He released a bitter laugh. "As I said, they weren't written to be shared."

"Is it because you're afraid, afraid of the rejection, afraid of failure?"

"It is not fear that prevents me from seeking publication."

"Then what is it?"

"It is not fear," he repeated. "I simply have no desire to be published."

"I don't believe that."

"Believe what you will. You do not know what it is to bare oneself and risk being turned away."

"Do I not? My hands shook when I penned my advert. My entire body quivered when I faced the dragon. I'm not brave or bold, but I'm quite decidedly determined I shall not go through life as my mother, merely an ornament on display. You have a gift for storytelling. You should not fear sharing it."

"You are making much of nothing."

"You should take those drawings and your stories to London, to a publisher—"

"Enough! I am a duke, charged with overseeing the responsibilities of my family and my estates, not with writing some fanciful stories to keep a child entertained."

"You would be paid for the stories."

"A pittance, a mere pittance."

"It is *something*, at least. But more than that, it is

sharing your vision with others. Your earnings would be secondary."

"The stories were written by a young man who was once as innocent as his sister. I'm no longer that man."

"Then I pity you."

"Because I have grown up and grown wiser?"

"Because you take no joy in life. You resent your responsibilities, and I fear each of us knows it."

"I do not resent you."

"But you will in time if your financial situation does not improve." She walked across the room and stood in front of him. "I have been thinking—"

"An admirable undertaking."

"Do not make sport of me."

Reaching out, a warm smile on his lips, he cradled her face and stroked his thumb over her cheek. "I do not know why I take such delight in doing so."

She was again reminded of Mr. Rose's assertion that teasing equaled affection. Could it be possible that affection would grow between them?

She eased a little closer to him. "As I was saying . . . I see no reason why I cannot continue to be a social chaperone."

"You are my wife."

She gave him an impish smile. "A fact that has not escaped my notice."

"God, I love that smile," he said, shifting his thumb down to her mouth, stroking it softly.

She couldn't help but experience joy because he loved the smallest thing about her.

"Do not seek to distract me from my purpose," she admonished him.

"Could I?"

"You know very well you could, but I am attempting to explain what I am envisioning here."

"I will not allow my duchess to work."

"When you asked for my hand, you assured me that you would not interfere in any ventures I wished to pursue."

She saw the anger flare in his eyes a moment before he turned away from her and strode to the center of the room. "I didn't expect those ventures to include employment as a social chaperone."

"I think we could be quite successful at it."

He spun around. "*We?* You cannot for one moment honestly believe *I* am going to serve as a chaperone."

"No." She took a step toward him. Oh, this was so difficult. "This is terribly hard for me to admit, but I have come to realize that I vastly misjudged your suitability."

"Indeed?"

"You are not the blackguard I thought you were." She sighed. "I may have misjudged others. Well, not my brother. Well, yes, I did, but I misjudged him in the opposite way; he is far worse than I realized." She held up her hand. "I digress. My point is, you have knowledge about the gentlemen to which I am not privy. If we were to pool what we know, I believe we could have a rather successful enterprise arranging introductions."

"You are talking matchmaking."

"To a degree yes, but it would involve a bit more. I don't have all the particulars worked out. We wouldn't be fabulously wealthy, but it would bring in a bit of income."

He tossed her sketch pad into a chair and came toward her with the predatory stride that she'd seen him use on more than one occasion.

"We would have to pretend to have a very successful marriage," he said.

Swallowing hard at his use of the word pretend, she nodded. Was pretense all they would ever have? Or could they, over time, have more, could pretense turn into reality? "Yes."

He cradled her face between his large hands. "Oh, my little dreamer, if it is what you wish to do, then do it. Ask of me what you will. I can no more deny you than I can deny my want of you."

Before she could curb her thrill at his use of the word *want* in association with her, he was kissing her, and she was kissing him back, wondering how it was that having tasted passion, anyone could turn it aside. Little wonder Jenny had feared wanting to consume the entire meal if she sampled but a morsel of the offerings.

Hawk was terribly skilled at making Louisa forget her surroundings—they weren't in her bedchamber—or the time of day—it wasn't yet night. He made her forget she needed to prepare for supper. He made her forget everything,

everything except the feel of his hands stroking her body, the hard press of him against her.

Her world narrowed down until it was simply he and she, and within this small cocoon he wrapped around them, no one else mattered. With his attentions so fervently delivered, she could pretend for just a few moments that he desired *her.* She could pretend he'd never made love to anyone with the enthusiasm he did her. She could pretend he was doing more than stirring passions; he was awakening hearts to the possibility of love.

She heard the light *clink* of her hairpins hitting the floor only a few seconds before her hair tumbled around her shoulders.

She dropped her head back, lost in bliss as he trailed his hot mouth along her throat. He groaned low in his chest. "I love how quickly you melt in my arms."

"I'm perhaps too easy."

"No, you are perfect, and I wish to relish every inch of your perfection."

He removed her clothes with the ease of a man accustomed to doing so. She refused to think of the other women he had bared for his pleasure, but a small part of her felt sorrow for them because he had not remained with them. She could not imagine knowing his touch, then suffering through the devastation of being without it.

She was barely aware of her own fingers working to remove his shirt.

"How quickly you learn," he murmured near

her ear, sending warm chills traveling along her skin.

Then she was falling back onto the bed, relishing his weight pressing her farther into the mattress.

It was insane, Hawk thought. How badly he wanted her. Yet from the moment she had walked into the room, he'd had to concentrate on her words to stop himself from remembering how wonderful every inch of her body felt beneath his fingers.

Her drawings had effectively distracted him, not only because they were so incredibly well done, but because she had managed so perfectly to capture the imaginary world he'd created for Caroline. He was halfway tempted to do as she suggested: bundle them up with his story and take them to a publisher, but like everything else in this house, they were a secret, belonging only to those who lived in the manor.

Secrets, so damned many secrets. And his wife had her own share that he couldn't help smiling at. Hidden places that, when he ran his tongue over them, easily unlocked passion's door. Her moans were music to his ears, her writhing was a dance he thought he would never grow tired of engaging in.

It made little sense to him. He was skilled in the bedchamber, and yet never before had he taken such delight in bringing pleasure to a woman. He'd never left a woman wanting, had always considered himself a considerate lover. But with

Louisa, bringing her pleasure was more than trying to prove his prowess. With her, it was a resounding joy to give, each touch of his fingers, each stroke of his tongue a gift, her appreciation so apparent in her sighs, her languid eyes as she looked at him.

Bedding her was unlike bedding any other woman, and at moments its intensity terrified him, the thought of not having her . . . he would not think of it.

"You are mine," he rasped, as he moved up and plunged inside her.

"I'm yours," she murmured, placing her hands on his backside and urging him deeper.

She was not a woman to take without giving. She was what he'd never had before: a true partner. She was as eager and anxious to pleasure him as he was her.

Rising above her, he held her gaze, rocking against her, relishing her cries, sensing her body tightening around him. Her calling out his name in ecstasy triggered his own release, a release so intense that for a heartbeat he thought he might die from it. Little wonder the French called it the little death.

Collapsing partially, supporting his weight on his elbows, he buried his face in the curve of her shoulder, kissed the dew at her neck, and smiled in wonder, because already he was anticipating having her again.

"Hawk! Hawk!" His mother's panicked voice carried down the hallway.

"Why is it we are continually caught?" he asked in exasperation, as he reached down for the covers and threw them over Louisa and himself to protect their modesty as his mother came barging into the room.

He'd not thought to close the door because he'd not expected anyone to disturb him in this wing of the house.

"I'm frightfully sorry," his mother said, as she staggered to a stop, clutching a piece of paper, tears dampening her cheeks.

"It doesn't matter, Mother. What is it?"

"She's gone," she sobbed.

"Who? What are you talking about?" he asked.

"Caroline. She's run away!"

Chapter 18

The rain that had brought such comfort all afternoon had transformed into a frightening storm. Sitting in the drawing room, Louisa was aware of the duchess flinching each time thunder clapped.

"I'm certain he'll find her, Your Grace," she said quietly, so as not to startle the woman further. With the hounds to guide them, Hawk and several of the male servants, including the gardener, had gone searching for Caroline.

Wringing her hands, the duchess stared into the fire. "A mother should not have to choose between her children."

"You have not favored one child over the other."

With tears welling in her eyes, she looked at

Louisa. "Oh, but I did. For the sake of my son, I denied my daughter a father. I have kept her secreted away, and now she feels unworthy, and my son is burdened with her care. Now they are both out in this dreadful weather and may return frightfully ill. I could lose them both."

"You are borrowing trouble, Your Grace, and quite honestly, I see no need to do so."

The duchess released a small laugh before looking at Louisa. "You do not look on the dark side of things, do you, my dear?"

"I prefer to believe all will be well, and if it is not, then I shall deal with it at that time."

"I can quite understand why my son married you. It has been sometime since our home has been filled with optimism."

Louisa felt her stomach tighten. "I fear it was not optimism he sought, and had circumstances been different, he would not have married me."

The duchess arched a brow. "Yes, he confessed his naughty behavior, but I know my son remarkably well, Louisa. If he married you, it was because he wished to."

Louisa saw no point in revealing he'd stated outright that he did not want to.

"Do you love my son?" the duchess asked.

Louisa shook her head slightly. "I'm not certain what I feel for him. I thought I knew the sort of man he was, but I'm no longer as certain."

"He was near to being a man when I discovered I was with child again. I know he did not approve. What man with any sort of moral compass would?

Yet he never censured me. He sought to protect me, then to protect his sister from society's ridicule and penchant to be unkind to those who do not conform. I placed a terrible burden on him."

"I do not believe he views it in that manner."

"He wouldn't admit if he did. He accepts his burdens with stoicism and buries his own unhappiness."

Louisa studied the dowager duchess, who was gazing out the window. She wondered if the woman's words applied to Louisa. If Hawkhurst saw her as a burden. If he masked his unhappiness. That afternoon he'd seemed . . . content. Was it only a performance, a kindness designed to keep doubts from plaguing her?

"I believe I see lights flickering," the duchess said, as she came to her feet. "Oh, please let them be returning, let them be returning with my daughter safe."

Louisa followed her into the entry hallway where the duchess flung open the door. The duchess gasped, and her hand flew to her mouth. Louisa's chest tightened.

Two men carried lanterns and between them walked Hawkhurst, his coat billowing out behind him with the force of his strides and the strength of the wind, his sister draped limply over his arms. He ascended the steps and walked through the doorway.

"Is she—" the duchess began.

"No," Hawkhurst assured her. "She is shivering and unwell, possibly fevered. She was awake when we found her, but only for a short while. Denby has gone to fetch a physician."

Louisa felt useless following behind, ignored, as Hawkhurst swept up the stairs. She'd seen the sorrow and despair etched in his face. She watched as though observing a play as he laid his sister tenderly on her bed.

"I'll see to getting her out of her wet clothes," his mother said, as she moved in to replace him at his sister's side.

Hawkhurst stepped back, reluctantly, as though dazed. His sister moaned, he stepped forward. Louisa's heart tightened. Had she thought this man incapable of love?

She touched his arm. He looked down as though only just realizing she existed.

"Come," she said softly. "We must get you out of these clothes before you catch your death."

"Yes, go," his mother admonished. "Caroline is much too grown-up now for you to remain in this room while I undress her."

"She is still a child," he murmured, but he didn't resist when Louisa guided him out of the bedchamber and down the hallway to his own room.

It was the first time she'd been in his chamber. It was stark, bare, with no ornamentation at all. A bed. A wardrobe. A dresser. Two chairs before the fire. A lamp on the table beside the bed. She had no doubt he'd already disposed of his possessions, sacrificing whatever small things might have brought him joy.

He stood in the room as though he hardly recognized it. She could hear his teeth chattering. She went to the fireplace, knelt, and lit the kindling someone had prepared in advance so a fire could be easily started. She wished she'd thought to start it sooner so his room would already be warm and welcoming.

She returned to his side. "Here, let me help you." Although in truth, she was doing much more than helping. She was doing everything as he stood there as though in a trance. She worked his coat off his shoulders, letting the sodden garment fall to the floor.

He moved away from her, shrugging out of his jacket, letting it drop to the floor. He began unbuttoning his shirt. Stopped. "She ran away because she thinks we do not want her, that we are ashamed of her. She wouldn't listen when I tried to explain that it was out of a desire to protect her that we kept her secret."

He hardly seemed to notice as she tugged his shirt free of his trousers and helped him pull it over his head. "She is simply adjusting to the change of having a sister-in-law and the disappointment of not having a Season," Louisa said.

"She is adjusting to my breaking my promise." He began unbuttoning his trousers, and while she'd seen him without clothing, she still turned away, fearful that he would see the yearning in her eyes. Hurrying into the changing room and gathering up some towels, she wondered what sort of immoral creature she was to be so fasci-

nated by her husband's body, especially at a time
such as this.

When she returned to the room, he was standing before the fire, his back to the room, his arms
outstretched as he gripped the mantel, the muscles in his arms taut and bulging.

"I've brought towels," she said.

"Leave them."

She set the towels on the chair, walked over to
him, and placed her hand on his back. He stiffened beneath her touch.

"I'm certain she'll be all right."

"No, I cannot keep my promise to her, I cannot protect her." She saw his knuckles turning
white as his grip on the mantel tightened. "If only
you'd not walked into Pemburton's library." He
bowed his head. "If only I'd not taken you into
my arms."

His voice was ravaged with regrets, regrets so
sharp and deep that they threatened any happiness Louisa may have hoped for. She felt ill with
the realization that his love of his sister would always come before her. That he blamed her for
their present circumstance, and she couldn't deny
her culpability. She had walked into the library,
and while he had taken her into his arms, he'd
not known it was her. It was Jenny he'd been expecting. Jenny he'd thought . . .

He was so incredibly magnificent standing
there . . . and defeated. Because of her actions.
She'd had the strength to go out into the world,
but no power to resist him.

She took a step back. "I should look in on your mother."

He moved not a muscle. With tears clogging her throat, she left him alone to fight his own demons of disappointment.

Stepping into the hallway, closing the door behind her, she was astonished to see the duchess and Denby standing so near to each other. So near that her eyes had deceived her into thinking she'd seen the gardener holding the duchess's hand.

The duchess smiled softly at Louisa. "I was thanking Denby for fetching the physician so quickly. I believe the dear man put his own neck at risk."

"You instill much loyalty in your servants, Your Grace," Louisa said, wishing she knew how to instill as much loyalty in her husband, because for her, passion would not suffice. With startling clarity she suddenly realized that she desperately wanted love. Not love of her eyes, or her smile, or her body, but love of herself, of her soul, of that which was not visible. "It is a tradition I hope to emulate."

"I do nothing special except appreciate them."

"I should be going," Denby said. "I hope your daughter will recover quickly from her ordeal."

The duchess reached out and squeezed his hand, an entirely unheard of gesture for a lady to give a servant. "I have faith that she will. Thank you again, Denby. I'm not certain what we'd do without you."

"Send word if I may be of any further assistance."

"I shall without hesitation."

It looked as though he wanted to say more. Instead, he nodded toward Louisa before turning on his heel and heading down the stairs.

Louisa approached cautiously, with a sense that perhaps she'd interrupted something very important, for the duchess continued to look where the gardener had disappeared.

With a sigh, she eventually faced the door of her daughter's bedchamber. "The physician is examining her now."

"Has she awoken?"

"Not yet. I fear her ordeal, as Denby referred to it, has taken a decidedly unfavorable toll on her."

"It was very good of him to console you while you waited," Louisa said.

"He is a good man."

Louisa couldn't help but notice the duchess had referred to him as a man rather than a servant, and she couldn't help but wonder if the slip held significance.

Caroline would recover if the chill did not settle in her lungs. The physician had offered the words of reassurance before he departed. Yet Hawk was not reassured.

He sat beside Caroline's bed, watching her sleep, fearful if he turned away for even a heartbeat, death would slip in. It was well into the late hours of the night, the flame in the lamp, the fire on the hearth, providing the light.

He'd succeeded in convincing his mother to retire, so she would be refreshed and could take over the vigil at dawn, as though their mere presence was enough. It took all within his power to remain seated when he dearly wished to depart. If his wife weren't sitting on the other side of the bed, he would not have remained as stoic; he would instead be pacing and cursing and giving physical release to his worries.

He didn't want Louisa here. She served as a reminder of his failings, and while he recognized that it was unfair to her to release his frustrations at her, he was also acutely aware that if not for her, he might even now be on the cusp of marrying Jenny Rose and be in a position to keep his promises to Caroline.

"I'm certain she'll be fine," Louisa said quietly, repeating the statement she'd issued earlier in the evening as though all that was required was faith.

"I see no reason you must be here," he said. If she attempted to mask how his words had injured her, she did a poor job of it.

"I care for your sister, and I know how difficult it is to stand vigil alone. When my mother took ill, I would have given anything for Alex to have kept me company, especially in the darkest hours of the night, when all is so quiet you can almost hear death creeping near."

"To think you once told me you had no talent for metaphors."

"I had many a lonely night to ponder melancholy thoughts."

"He never sat with you?"

"No; he was otherwise occupied."

He recognized the censure in her voice and gave her a self-deprecating smile. "Enjoying drink, women, and gaming with me no doubt. Little wonder you found such fault with me. I didn't realize your mother was ill until she died."

"You're not to blame because he refused to face his responsibilities."

"I provided him with the means to escape them."

She gave him a gamin smile. "If you insist, then I shall allow you to take responsibility for his wayward ways."

"I fear I'm more responsible than you realize. My father suffered a lengthy illness. I know rumors abound that he died of the French disease, but it was cancer. A horrendous cancer. He did not wish my mother to witness his suffering, and she did not wish him to die alone."

"So it fell to you," she said quietly.

He felt his chest tighten with the memories as he nodded.

"But you were a child."

"All of twelve. A boy who with his father's passing would become a man." He felt the tears sting his eyes, fought them under control. "Yet, still he died alone, because I cowered in the corner when death came. He called my name and still I wouldn't come." Abruptly, he came to his feet, the chair scraping back with the force of his movement. "I know not why I confessed that failure on my part."

Perhaps because it seems to be a night for recognizing failures.

He walked to the window, jerked the drapery aside, and gazed out on the darkness, so much easier to look at midnight shadows than his sister's pale face or his wife's disappointed expression.

Louisa studied her husband as he gazed out, her heart pounding with his confession. She couldn't imagine how difficult it had been for him to hear his father's plea, his last rasping breath . . . to know he had carried this guilt for more than twenty years. She did not take pleasure in his suffering, and yet she couldn't deny she was deeply touched he had shared with her a secret he'd shared with no other.

How could he curse their marriage only hours before and now speak to her of such private sufferings? What did he want of her? What did he want of them?

As quietly as possible, wanting not to disturb the intimacy his revelation had created, she rose from her chair and joined him at the window, placing her hand on his back, covered only by his linen shirt. She felt his muscles bunch and stiffen beneath her touch, a touch that seemed to repel him now when only earlier that evening he'd welcomed it. She dropped her hand to her side, determined to make the best of their situation.

"As I said, you were only a child. Placing such a burden on you was unfair."

"He was my father; I should not have abandoned him in his final moments."

She couldn't help but wonder how his guilt over his perceived abandonment of his father had contributed to his insistence that they marry. Had he determined he'd never again abandon another: not his mother, his sister, or a woman he'd compromised?

"My mother asked me to leave," she said quietly. "She didn't want me to witness her passing. I was twenty-three, mature enough to stay, and yet I honored her request. Perhaps if you'd gone to your father's side, he'd have asked the same of you."

"I'll never know because I didn't have the courage to answer his call." He sighed. "Ravensley should have been with you all those long nights. I apologize for my part in keeping him from you."

He seemed determined to change the subject, and she decided any further discourse would only add to his guilt. Sometimes it was easier for others to forgive our failings than for us to forgive ourselves.

"I quite resented you and your influence over him," she confessed.

He turned slightly, pressing his shoulder to the paned glass. "As well you should have."

"Do you believe in love?" she found herself asking, wondering if he'd ever expected more from his marriage than passion.

"No."

"Yet the characters in your story discover love. How can you write so convincingly about something in which you do not believe?"

"I also write about faeries. Surely you don't think for a single moment I believe tiny creatures flitter across the grass at night."

"I thought perhaps that was what you were doing now. Looking for them."

A corner of his mouth quirked up. "No, I was attempting to distance myself from a conversation that was serving to highlight my failure as a son and a brother."

"I don't see how you can see yourself as a failure as a brother. You've yet to leave Caroline's side, and I suspect come morning, when your mother returns, still you will not leave."

"I have failed adequately to protect Caroline. She ran away because she feared we were ashamed of her. When it is not her I am ashamed of, but Society, a society that will torment her for the unfortunate circumstances of her birth."

"So you have strived to protect her from them."

"Yes."

"Going so far as to pursue a wealthy American heiress."

"Which I subsequently botched."

"I have found too much protection is not necessarily a good thing. My father protected my mother—"

"From what? She was not illegitimate. Her circumstances are hardly the same."

She sighed with frustration. "No, her circumstances weren't the same, but his treatment of her very much mirrored yours."

He visibly straightened as though she'd delivered a blow. "I do all within my power and reason to shield Caroline—"

"Exactly. As my father did with my mother. He never told her our financial situation was burdened by her excessive spending—"

"Caroline is not a burden."

"Damnation, Hawk, will you stop interrupting and allow me the courtesy of finishing my explanation?"

She didn't think it possible, but he straightened even further, his eyes rounding slightly, no doubt at her use of profanity. Why was it with men that in order to have their undivided attention, a woman needed to either remove her clothing or resort to using vulgar language? While disrobing guaranteed their attention, it did not ensure their minds stayed focused on the conversation. Without a doubt their minds would wander in other directions.

After a moment, he tilted his head slightly. "Continue."

"Thank you. As I was saying, he sought to protect her from the reality of our financial situation.

She was quite unaware our coffers were empty or that her spending put a weight on his shoulders that caused him grief. As much as I regret saying it, I've often wondered if his worrying over our situation, exacerbated by her spending led to his heart giving out as it did."

"I assure you my heart is not in danger of giving out."

She glared at him. He pressed his finger to his mouth as though to silence himself, but she thought she detected some of the worry lifted from his eyes.

"In protecting my mother, my father failed to prepare her for the time when he would not be there to oversee her life. She was lost, so terribly lost. He had been her crutch, and, without him, she tumbled."

His mouth twitched, and she couldn't help but say, "Perhaps I should cease with metaphors. My point in all this is: I believe she succumbed to illness because it was easier than facing the world without him.

"You have expended a great deal of effort in protecting Caroline from the ridicule of society, and I find that remarkably admirable." His eyes widened slightly as though he were as astonished by her words as she was. She was surprised he didn't choose this moment to interrupt and comment on her statement. Perhaps she'd left him speechless as well. "I don't find fault with your actions, but I am left to wonder if perhaps you have misjudged how she'll be treated. What is the worst that can happen if you introduce her into Society?"

"She will be ignored, her heart bruised, her hopes shattered."

"All of which, I can attest, are painful experiences, but they are survivable. I fear you do her a disservice by not giving her the chance, at least, to survive."

Reaching out, he touched her cheek with the tenderness she was coming to expect of him, the tenderness she'd feared his outburst in his bedchamber would be denied to her as the consequences of their actions became more difficult for him to live with. "Not everyone is as strong as you, Louisa. Not everyone has your fortitude or determination. It would break my heart, my mother's heart to see Caroline wounded."

And he claimed not to love?

"She is the sister of a duke. That is a currency, Your Grace, I fear you have not taken into account."

"You give my title too much credit."

"You give yourself too little."

Again, he looked taken aback by the boldness of her words.

"And if you are wrong?"

"Then at least we will know where Society will place her."

"She is not ready for London."

"I agree. To take her there would give her an unfortunate start, for she would not be comfortable in the strange surroundings. But here . . . here she could experience her first ball within the bosom of all with which she is comfortable. We are a mere two hours from London. We could have a successful ball right here. I daresay our own scandalous beginnings will guarantee we have a large attendance as the curious seek to discover how we fare."

"You are asking me to risk bringing sorrow to the two most important women in my life."

She felt the sting to her heart because she was not one of them, and she realized she would probably never be. She'd known from the beginning he didn't love her; it was pointless to mourn that fact now.

"It is a risk you must take at some point if you ever hope to secure a suitable husband for Caroline."

"Please, Hawk."

Louisa and Hawk jerked their heads around at the softly delivered plea. Caroline was sitting up in bed, clutching the covers to her chest.

"How long have you been eavesdropping, Moppet?" he asked.

"Long enough. If you fear I will bring you shame—"

"You could never bring me shame," he stated emphatically.

"Or embarrass you—"

"You could never embarrass me more than I have already embarrassed myself."

Caroline looked past him to Louisa and gave

her an impish smile. "I've never noticed before he has the nasty habit of not letting ladies finish their sentences."

"Because he doesn't like the direction in which they are going, and so he seeks to head them off."

Caroline shifted her attention back to Hawk. "If I have but one dance, and it is with you, my dear brother, I shall be happy."

"You do not know how cruel some people can be."

"To the sister of the Duke of Hawkhurst? I daresay they would be fools to slight me and face your wrath in our home. I suspect they'd not fancy facing Louisa's wrath either. Please, can we have a ball?"

"We could have a Cinderella ball," Louisa said.

"Does that mean I'd turn into a pumpkin at midnight?" Caroline asked.

"No, it is a less formal affair, beginning at eight, rather than ten, and ending at midnight, rather than three."

"It sounds perfect. Please, Hawk?"

Louisa watched as he closed his eyes, and she could see the burden her suggestion had placed on him.

"It will be a much smaller gathering, and I will be most selective in whom I invite," Louisa said solemnly.

He opened his eyes and met her gaze. "Now that the idea has been put forth, it seems I have no choice for my options are to make Caroline sad now and perhaps hinder her recovery or risk her unhappiness later. So have your ball, and we shall pray I have in fact misjudged the situation."

She'd never known a man who wished to be proven wrong, but she could see in his eyes that if he were proven right, he'd never forgive her for leading his sister into societal hell.

Chapter 19

⟨⟨∽∽⟩⟩

"You can't be serious," Hawk's mother said. "Whatever are you thinking even to consider hosting a ball here?"

She paced in front of the window, clutching the flower she'd been on the verge of tucking safely into the vase before he'd made his announcement.

"That I promised Caroline a ball, and it is time I made good on that promise."

"How do you intend to introduce her?"

"As I introduced her to Louisa: as my beloved sister, Miss Caroline Selwyn."

His mother stopped pacing, tears in her eyes.

"You need not attend if you're not feeling quite up to it," he said. God knew he didn't want to attend.

"Society will judge me."

"What does their judgment matter?"

"Fine words from a gentleman who married a lady to protect her from society's censure."

"My reasons for marrying Louisa are mine and mine alone, and have no bearing on my attempt to introduce Caroline into Society except that she has served to open my eyes to the unfairness of the life I've given my sister. Is this truly what you wish for her? To be always hidden away, to be fearful of others' opinions, her only joy to be found in plucking flowers?"

"It is not my only joy. My children are my joy, except for this very moment when you cause me such heartache."

He took a step toward her. "It has been more than eighteen years since you've been to London. Our society is evolving. There are those among us who have no titles. Where once they would have been shunned, now they are welcomed. There was a day when a lady would never venture out alone, and yet Louisa has strolled the streets and parks without the benefit of a chaperone. She is as courageous a woman as I've ever known. She does not sit in the shadows and wait for life. Caroline can learn much from her: that sometimes we must take a chance, we must step forward bravely if we are to step forward at all."

"I'm afraid, Hawk, afraid for all of us, for the pain that might be caused."

"I believe I would rather risk a life of occasional pain than live one of quiet complacency."

She brought the blossom to her nose, inhaling the fragrance as though to gain strength from it. "It has been a good many years since I have hosted a ball."

"Louisa will see to the particulars. It will, after all, be hosted by the Duke and Duchess of Hawkhurst, and she is my duchess."

"I suspect she is a bit more than that."

It terrified him to think his mother might have hit upon the truth: where Louisa was concerned, he often felt as lost as Caroline. He couldn't deny that everything would be much simpler, much easier, and guaranteed of success if Jenny were his wife. Yet, neither could he deny that he couldn't imagine his life without Louisa in it.

His trepidation increased with each passing hour that evening as he sat in the library and watched Caroline's enthusiasm grow. She sat on the couch beside Louisa, listening intently as Louisa outlined everything that needed to be arranged.

He glanced over at his mother and saw her worries intensifying. He wanted to have faith that all would be well, and he'd spoken with such bravado that afternoon, but as the reality began to take shape—

"I'm not convinced we shouldn't delay this endeavor," Hawk announced, and he saw the relief wash over his mother's face.

"For what exactly?" Louisa asked.

"For our situation to improve."

"My situation is never going to change, Hawk. It is as it is," Caroline said, uncharacteristically making a stand, a demand. Was that Louisa's irritating influence?

"A ball is costly," he said.

"It is going to be a small ball," Louisa said. "No more than fifty couples."

"With an orchestra," he reminded her, having overheard her plans.

"A six-piece string orchestra will not be too costly. You have enough flowers in the garden that we shan't incur that expense if your mother is willing to arrange them."

"Will you, Mama?" Caroline asked, and he could see that his mother despised taking part in what she was certain would eventually break Caroline's heart.

Why had he agreed to this madness?

"If you like," his mother said quietly.

Hawk shoved his chair back—the sound startling all three women—came to his feet, and strode to the window. He'd always known his mother was far too timid. Suddenly he found himself quite irritated by it.

"I have a gown the Rose sisters gave me that I can alter to fit Caroline, so we'll not have that expense," Louisa said.

"Food," he snapped.

"A Cinderella ball doesn't require a dinner. Refreshments for our arriving guests, of course, but again that can be minimal."

"And who is going to see to taking care of all these guests as they arrive?"

"We can hire a few servants from the village. I can train them."

He spun around. "In two weeks? You are planning this event to take place in two weeks."

"They will do little more than take wraps and hats and serve refreshments."

"But still we must pay them. We must purchase the food and invitations and pay the orchestra. How do you propose we do that?"

She came to her feet. "Why are you being so disagreeable?"

"I'm not being disagreeable, but as I listen to all your plans, the absurdity of attempting to host a ball when we have no funds—"

"We have funds. The money the Roses gave me—"

"I will not use your money."

"It became yours when we married."

He shook his head. "I will not pay for this ball with money you earned."

"Yet you'd have had no qualms at all about using Jenny's money."

"Because she had an abundance. She did not work for it!"

Louisa looked as though he'd struck her.

"I was not issuing an insult," he said hastily.

"You think your life would be easier if you'd married Jenny."

"That goes without saying, but she's not the one who walked into the damned library!"

"How often do you plan to throw that into my face? You were being unscrupulous, and it was my duty to protect her at any cost, and I will remind you that it has cost me dearly. I didn't want to marry you any more than you wanted to marry me, but here we are. You said we'd make the best of it. Well, obviously you are unclear as to the meaning of *best*!"

He spun around because his mother and sister had both widened their eyes and dropped their jaws. And his wife, dear God, she challenged him at every turn, and he was in danger of crossing over to her and taking her in his arms. She would never be as his mother was. She would never be timid; she would never not stand her ground.

"Caroline, darling, perhaps we should leave," his mother said.

"There is no need," Hawk said. "I have said all I have to say."

"I'm sorry, Hawk," Caroline said. "We don't have to have a ball. It was selfish of me to want one so badly."

Fisting his hands, he dropped his head back, anguish piercing his heart. How many times must he swallow his pride? *Once more, just once more. Take the money Louisa offered.*

"Take your father's portrait off the wall," his mother said.

He glanced over his shoulder. "Pardon?"

"Take your father's portrait off the wall."

"Why?"

She shook her head. "Just do as I ask."

He crossed the room to the far wall, where his father's portrait hung. Below it was one of three sitting areas in the room. The painting was his father as a young man. When he was younger, he'd spent hours staring at his father's face, trying to see himself reflected in his father's features. He didn't think they looked much alike.

He took hold of the frame, lifted the painting, stepped back, lowered it to the floor, and stared at the small door with the lock housed in the wall.

He stared at his mother as she slipped a key into the lock, turned it, and opened the door. She reached inside and removed an oblong, leather box. "Take this to a jeweler. I'm certain it'll fetch a pretty penny, more than enough for Caroline's ball."

Hawk took the box, opened it, and studied the glittering emeralds and diamonds. He lifted his questioning gaze to his mother.

"Your father gave it to me on the day he married me," she said softly.

"You would barter his gift in order to have a ball for your daughter?"

"I would barter it to relieve the burden I have placed on his son. It will not fetch a great deal, but it will fetch enough, enough for the ball, enough perhaps to see us through the winter."

He shook his head.

"Sacrifices must be made," she said. " 'Tis time I made them."

"But Father gave you this—"

"I regret to say it holds no sentimental value for

me. It was a loveless marriage. That is the way of it when one marries for duty."

* * *

My dear Mr. Jeremy Rose:

I hope my letter finds you and your sisters well. You were so incredibly kind during a most difficult time in my life, and I shall always be grateful that you served as my champion. I wish to ask another favor of you, and I have little to offer in exchange except the promise to find you a suitable wife, one deserving of such a fine gentleman as yourself.

As you will see this letter is accompanied by an invitation to an upcoming Cinderella ball to be hosted by the duke and me. During the evening, he will introduce his lovely sister, Caroline, into Society. I ask that you merely dance the second dance with her.

If you will do me the courtesy of honoring this request, you will have my undying gratitude, and at your leisure, I shall help you find a wife.

Yours most gratefully,
The Duchess of Hawkhurst

The plans for the ball were coming along nicely. Louisa had sent the invitations, along with her letter to Jeremy. She was certain he would honor her request for a favor.

She'd finished altering the dress for Caroline. She'd just spent an hour walking through the gardens with the duchess and gardener, discussing the flowers they'd like to have at the ball. When she returned to the manor, she discovered she had a visitor.

"Mrs. Rose! What an unexpected . . . surprise!"

"Is not every surprise unexpected? That's what makes it a surprise is it not?"

Louisa forced herself to smile at the unpleasant woman who had come to call. She assumed one of the maids had escorted her into the foyer. Hawk had gone riding to look over his land. Caroline was probably in her room reading. Which left Louisa to face the dragon alone. Probably not a bad situation. "Forgive me for my poor choice of wording. I meant an unexpected pleasure."

Mrs. Rose glanced around. "So this is where my daughter would be living if you'd not deceived us. You have not done too shabbily for yourself."

Louisa thought about trying to explain that Alex was the one who had deceived them, deceived them all, but she saw no point. The woman would believe what she would.

"So what brings you to Selwyn Manor?" Louisa asked.

"I would have a word with you. In private."

It did not get much more private than the two of them, but they were in the entry hallway.

"Let's go into the parlor," Louisa said. "Would you like me to fetch us some tea?"

"No, I will be brief. This is not a social call."

Somehow Louisa was not surprised. She escorted Mrs. Rose into the parlor.

The woman walked to the window and gazed out. "I have never seen such exquisite gardens."

"We are very fortunate that our gardener gives them the care that he does. Although I'm certain you did not come to discuss our gardens."

"No, I most certainly did not." She turned to face Louisa. "Do you know yet if this marriage was necessary?"

"Yes, it was necessary," Louisa said, refusing to think otherwise.

"Then you know you are with child?"

"I do not see that my knowledge of my condition is your concern."

"I'm well aware, my dear, that you have no soft spot in your heart for me. That you consider me brash and perhaps vulgar when compared with your refinement, but I promise you that you will never find a mother who loves her daughters more and wishes only the best for them."

"If I may be so bold, then I suggest you let them find their own husbands."

"No, that will not do. Correct me if I'm wrong, but only three dukes remain available for marriage: Whitson, Pemburton, and Stonehaven."

"Surely you are not considering Whitson. He is at least sixty."

"Are they the only three?"

Louisa sighed. "Yes."

Mrs. Rose released a large gust of air. "No, I am not considering Whitson, but I may be left with no choice. Stonehaven has refused to consider my daughters. The man is obviously an imbecile, and

I will not give James stupid grandchildren. That leaves one duke, and I have two daughters." She threw back her shoulders. "Unless you are not with child, in which case your duke could become available again."

Louisa shook her head. "Without even asking him, I know my husband would not go through the scandal of divorce."

"I'm not talking divorce. I'm talking annulment."

Louisa felt the heat scald her face. "It is too late for that."

"Not necessarily. When you have a good deal of money, it is seldom too late for anything.

"Once I knew a young lady who became involved with a gentleman who was undeserving of her. They married, much to her family's disappointment. We were very close to this young lady, and Jeremy was able to convince her that it was not in her best interest to remain married. With James's help, we were able to obtain an annulment for her, even though she had been married for several months.

"I do not know your feelings for Hawkhurst, but if you determine that you do not wish to remain married to him, and if you are in fact, not with child, you need but let me know and I will see that your marriage is annulled."

"An annulment—"

"Is not as scandalous as a divorce. If Hawkhurst is no longer married to you, he will be available to Jenny."

"Are you implying that Jenny would marry him?"

"I would see to it."

"And if she doesn't want to marry him?"

"Leave convincing her to me."

Louisa could no longer imagine it: Jenny and Hawkhurst.

"Do not pin your hopes on our getting our annulment."

Mrs. Rose arched a brow. "Even if it meant Jeremy would marry you?"

"You would have him marry me, with all that has happened?"

"He told me of the letter you wrote him, of your offer to find him a wife. I see no reason why that wife cannot be you. The scandal created here would not follow you to America."

"Does he know you're proposing this?"

"Of course not. But he is fond of you, and it would be no hardship for him to marry you."

Louisa thought she'd never met a more socially ambitious woman.

"What of Kate?" Louisa asked.

"My plan will leave Pemburton for her. Do you not see how everyone will benefit?"

"You are manipulating lives."

"Are you denying that you manipulated Hawkhurst when you allowed him to seduce you?"

Louisa came to her feet. "Mrs. Rose, I believe it is time for you to take your leave."

"At least think on what I'm proposing."

"I see no point in wasting my time considering it for even a moment."

"Well, as my husband always says, there is never any harm in asking. Good day to you, Louisa."

"Your Grace."

The woman jerked her head back. "Pardon?"

"You will address me as Your Grace or Duchess. Marriage to my husband has earned me that respect."

To Louisa's immense surprise, Mrs. Rose tipped her head slightly. "Of course, Your Grace. Have a pleasant afternoon."

Louisa was still shaking long after the woman left. The audacity of her to come here and propose such a thing. She wouldn't dare tell Hawk about the woman's visit. She could only imagine how angry he would get.

Or perhaps she didn't want to tell him because she feared that he would welcome the annulment and the opportunity to marry Jenny. Marriage to Jenny would offer financial security. And how many times had he cursed her walking into the library?

Their Cinderella ball would be held in less than a week, a thousand things remained to be done in order for all to be readied, and Louisa suddenly had no energy to see to any of them. Instead she sat curled in the chair in her sitting area, staring at the bed where only last night her husband had made passionate love to her. For a man who claimed to lose interest after the thrill of the hunt had passed, he still displayed an inordinate amount of enthusiasm when he took her in his arms.

But that enthusiasm was certain to wane from that day forward. For their marriage had done little more than preserve her reputation. There was no child to protect.

The evidence of that truth had arrived only an hour earlier and it seemed to have sapped all her strength. The knowledge made her brother's betrayal somehow seem so much worse. If he'd kept the incident to himself, she'd have known in a little over a fortnight that marriage was not required.

Instead, his betrayal had not only been to her and Hawk, but now she knew it was also a betrayal to Caroline because it left Hawk without the means adequately to protect her. Money was indeed a great equalizer. The small Cinderella ball that Louisa had planned for Caroline's coming out paled in comparison to the one that Hawk would have been able to give her if he'd been married to Jenny. It could have been so grand, so elaborate it would have been the talk of London, eclipsing any gossip about Caroline herself.

It was not often that Louisa was plagued with doubts regarding her plans, but she was plagued now, and it seemed more important than ever that she ensure Caroline not have a moment's heartache the night of her first ball.

A brisk knock sounded on the door a second before Hawk opened it and stepped into her room. Her heart tightened. She'd come to care for him so terribly much, wanted nothing more than she wanted him to be happy.

"Your list of things that needed to be accomplished today included arranging the ballroom. I thought you were going to come tell us"—he stepped farther into the room, his brow furrowing deeply—"Louisa, are you all right?"

She forced herself to smile, to nod. "We shall arrange the ballroom tomorrow. I just realized I must go to London to see to some things."

He came farther into the room and sat in the chair opposite her. Reaching out, he took her hand. "Darling, what's wrong?"

She was struck by two things. The endearments that he used without seeming to think about them and the fact that he was becoming adept at reading her moods. It was simply the familiarity of their being together so much of the time, not because of any great feelings he held for her.

She sighed, swallowed, squeezed his hand. "I just discovered I'm not . . . carrying your heir. I'm sorry."

He gave her a tender smile. "That is a condition that we can easily rectify."

She released a small laugh. "You are attempting to make me feel better, but do you not see? We had no reason to marry."

"We had every reason to marry. This does not change the damage I did to your reputation."

"Still, I'm more aware now of the sacrifice you made in marrying me." She thought of his mother's words about marrying for duty. Had they not done exactly that?

"Marriage to you is no great hardship," he said brusquely.

His words were hardly a declaration of love. The sad reality was that they never would be. He'd told her they'd make the best of it, and the best was viewing it as no great hardship. If they were ever in a position to give each other gifts, would they hold no sentimental value?

"Yes, well." She cleared her throat. "As I said, I need to take care of some matters in London regarding the ball. I'd like to go today."

"We can leave as soon as the coach is readied."

"No," she said hastily. "I have a lot of small errands to run that will simply test the limits of your patience."

"I don't want you going alone."

"I'll be fine. I'm a married woman. I don't require an escort. Don't argue with me over this, and I'll bring you back some brandy balls."

"Why do I have a sense that you're not being forthright?"

"I'm a bit melancholy. I'd not realized how much I'd hoped to be with child. Now I simply need some time alone, and the journey to London will provide me with that."

He studied her for a moment, and she wondered if her lie was written across her face.

"I'll return before nightfall," she promised.

Releasing her hand, he came to his feet. "If it is your wish to journey alone . . ." He shook his head. "It does not feel right."

"Please, Hawk, I so enjoyed being a woman of independent means, able to shop when and where I wished. I don't wish to feel the shackles of marriage."

He stiffened, and she could see her words had hurt him. She wanted to take them back, to apologize, but she needed to go to London alone, with no encumbrances to the plan that had begun forming in her mind as soon as she'd realized she wasn't with child, a plan of which she was certain he wouldn't approve, but she was determined to set it into motion. Hawk and Caroline would benefit immensely if she were successful.

"Very well. I will see you this evening for dinner."

With that, he spun on his heel and walked from the room, leaving her bereft and knowing that during the next few days, for her, matters would only worsen.

As she journeyed in the coach to London, she mentally checked off all the things that remained to be done: the arranging of the arrival of the orchestra, the ordering of special meats and pastries.

A little over two hours later, she stood in the

Rose drawing room, having given her card to the butler, surprised she was not trembling as she had been that first morning when she'd awaited an audience with Mr. and Mrs. Rose.

Hearing the loud footsteps, she slowly took a deep breath as Mrs. Rose entered the room and did little more than arch a brow.

Louisa swallowed hard. "I've come to discuss your proposition."

Chapter 20

"**W**hat if no one comes?" Caroline asked, fidgeting on the chair as Louisa sought to arrange her hair.

"Oh, they'll come," Louisa assured her, "for curiosity's sake if nothing else."

"Curiosity about me?"

"They don't know about you, darling," her mother said, as she stood off to the side watching the preparations. "I suspect they are interested in knowing how the old duchess is faring and the new duchess is weathering her sudden marriage."

"I'm so glad you decided to attend, Mama," Caroline said.

Louisa caught the duchess's gaze in the mirror. She could see the worry in her eyes, knew she was tempted to say she'd not let her daughter walk into the lions' den alone. Instead, she smiled brightly. "I have not attended a ball in years. I would be a silly woman indeed to miss one held within my own home." She cleared her throat. "Or my son's home, as it were."

"I don't take offense at you referring to it as your home," Louisa said. "The flower arrangements in the ballroom are absolutely beautiful."

"Denby had great success at forcing some of the flowers to bloom early. He is a miracle worker, that one."

Louisa stepped back. "I think that's it for the hair."

Caroline twisted her head one way, then the other. "It's so lovely."

"Come, I'll help you get into your gown."

Sometime later, Caroline was staring at her reflection, with tears in her eyes. "I think I look like a faerie princess." She spun around. "What do you think, Mother?"

Louisa was disappointed, watching as the duchess gave her daughter a disapproving look. *Please don't ruin this night for her*, she thought. *Please don't*.

The duchess shook her head. "I think something is missing. Turn back around. Perhaps I can determine what it is."

Caroline looked so incredibly worried, Louisa's heart went out to her.

"I can see nothing amiss," Caroline said.

"I see the problem," the duchess said. She slipped her hands around in front of Caroline's throat and when she drew them back, she clasped a pearl necklace into place. "There. Every lady of quality should have pearls. Those were my mother's, and now they are yours."

Louisa did not even bother to hold back her tears as she watched the mother and daughter embrace. All she could do was hope that tonight would be as wonderful as she'd envisioned, because in the end it was going to cost her everything she held dear.

Standing by the window in the library, Hawk downed the brandy in one swallow. It was only a damned ball, and his nervousness was unprecedented. He didn't know whether to pray no one arrived or to pray everyone came. Why had he agreed to this madness? His sister was still so young, so innocent.

He would dance with her. Falconridge would dance with her. Then who? He did not expect Ravensley to show his treacherous face. He could probably entice someone with a lesser title to dance with her. A second son. A fifth son.

But even the thought of someone dancing with her brought him unease. What if the man sought to seduce her, to get her alone, to take advantage?

Dear God in heaven, what if a man such as he asked her to dance?

He prayed he'd have no daughters of his own to watch over. It was not an easy thing to give a young, innocent girl into another's keeping. Much better to have sons who could stand up for themselves. Although he suspected Louisa's daughters would not do too shabbily in that regard. She could stand up to him. If only she'd not come to the library at Pemburton's to do so.

"Hawk?"

He glanced over his shoulder and felt as though the breath had been knocked out of him.

Caroline took a step toward him. She smiled shyly. "What do you think?"

She was a vision of loveliness, dressed in white, her shoulders bared, her throat exposed.

"The ball is canceled," he snapped. "You are to return to your room straightaway. Louisa!"

She appeared immediately, from where he knew not, and she, too, was a vision of loveliness, but he had no time to fully appreciate her beauty.

"We are not having a ball," he said. "You and I shall stand on the steps and inform anyone who arrives there is a contagion in the house, and they must leave immediately."

"Have you gone stark, raving mad?" Louisa asked.

"I thought there would be nothing worse than her being ignored, but now I see it will be far worse if she catches a young man's fancy, and I have no doubt she shall successfully do that. And what if he is a blackguard such as I?"

"He shan't be, because there is no one such as you."

"You seek to appease me."

"I seek to calm you down. I shall watch her closely all night. No one will take advantage."

"She is too lovely by half. Gentlemen cannot be trusted."

Caroline laughed. "Louisa has already explained that to me." She held up a gloved finger. "I am never to go anywhere without a chaperone." She extended another finger. "I am to dance no more than two dances with the same man." Another finger. "I am to view all men as after only one thing."

His gut clenched as he glared at his wife. "And what thing would that be?"

"A kiss," Caroline said, in all her innocence. "And I'm not to allow any gentleman to bestow a kiss upon my person this evening." She held up another finger. "I'm never to leave the ballroom." Her pinky finger popped up. "And I'm to stay within view of you at all times."

"And you think that will protect her?" he asked Louisa.

"No, I suspect your scowl will accomplish that. I thought you wanted her to have attention."

"I want her to be happy."

Caroline skipped across the room and took his gloved hands in hers. "I will be. I promise."

He gazed into her dark eyes. "If at any time, you wish the ball to cease, you have but to ask. I'll send everyone away without qualm."

She rose up on her toes and kissed his cheek. "I could not ask for a better brother."

She might not ask for a better brother, but he felt certain she deserved one. Just as his wife deserved a better husband. There had been moments in his life when he'd felt unworthy of the dukedom. Glancing past his sister to his wife, who seemed so confident the evening would have a successful outcome, he could not help but be impressed.

He considered telling her she was lovely beyond measure, but he held the words in check because tonight belonged to Caroline.

He shifted his gaze over to his mother, who did not possess Louisa's confidence. She appeared terrified, and he wanted nothing more than to spare her whatever discomforts she was feeling. "Mother, truly, Louisa and I can handle the greeting if you are not feeling well."

"I brought this upon us. I shall not shirk my duties."

He saw the pain flash across Caroline's face. He took her gloved hand, brought it to his lips. "She does not consider you a duty, Moppet. None of us do. You are a treasured gift."

Tears welled in her eyes, his words not having the expected outcome of bringing her joy. "I shall bring you no shame this evening."

"You never have, Caroline."

Caroline pressed a hand to her chest. "I'm having such a difficult time breathing, I fear I shall swoon."

"You must wait to swoon until you have a gentleman to catch you," her mother said.

"That's the first time you've indicated that perhaps there will be a gentleman for me."

"There will be, my darling, I'm sure of it," his mother said.

Louisa clapped her hands. "Come, come, I hear the carriages arriving. I daresay tonight will be one that none of us shall ever forget."

Hawk stood beside his wife in the ballroom, dread tightening his stomach. He'd not been this nervous when he'd attended his first ball. Come to think of it, he hadn't been nervous at all that night. Nor any other.

But that was before he knew what it was to lift his trembling sister into his arms, to cradle her as he trudged across the moor, to know her death would be upon his shoulders.

"I pray it does not rain this evening," he murmured.

"It shan't," Louisa said, as though she oversaw the weather with the ease she did their ball. "It's going to be a lovely evening."

"You are quite the continual optimist."

She jerked her head around at his tartly delivered words. "Would you rather I be sour? I can manage that quite well if you prefer."

He offered her a small smile. "Forgive me. I . . ."

"You're nervous," she said, and he heard the disbelief in her voice.

"I'm concerned." He leaned near, inhaling her familiar fragrance, wanting to nuzzle his nose against her neck and breathe more deeply. In a low voice so as not to be heard by the sister standing beside him, he said, "As you are well aware, Caroline does not handle disappointment well."

"She won't be disappointed. Trust me."

"How can you be so sure?"

He saw guilt flicker across her face, thought she was on the verge of explaining how she could possess such confidence, but the first of their guests walked in through doors leading from the tea room. Arranging for the ball had not been as costly as he'd feared, but neither had it been cheap. Still, he prayed that it would cost them only coins and not hearts.

He'd instructed Louisa to spare no expense, and she'd apparently taken him at his word. He didn't know where she'd managed to find the servants who were escorting their guests to the rooms she'd designated to be used as cloakrooms, so their guests could shed their coats and shawls and see to straightening themselves before entering the tea room, where light refreshments awaited them. Only then, once they were refreshed from their journey, did they dare enter the ballroom, where their host and hostess were waiting to greet them. Along with Caroline and his mother.

It broke his heart to see the anticipation clearly etched on Caroline's face, the worry visible in his mother's eyes. If only he'd not been distracted from his purpose in marrying Jenny Rose then this evening would be ensured of success. As it was, he feared it was doomed to failure, for Caroline came with no dowry, no father . . . and as guests continued to parade in, no dance partner.

"Please cease your scowling," Louisa whispered after a time.

"This is not going well."

"Be patient. I assure you all will be well," she said with her eyes fixed on the doorway. Then she smiled, a jubilant smile of welcome.

He looked to the doorway and felt as though he'd taken a punch to the gut. The very last people he'd expected to see this evening were approaching: Jenny and Jeremy Rose.

"I believe you are as beautiful as my brother claimed," Caroline said to Jenny after introductions were made.

"Caroline," Hawk muttered.

"Oh, I'm sorry, that was probably the wrong thing to say. I've never met an American."

"We're not that different," Jenny said.

"You're fabulously wealthy."

"Caroline," Hawk murmured.

"Oh, that was wrong to say, too. I'm so sorry. I'm terribly nervous."

"I think you're delightful," Jeremy Rose said. "May I have the pleasure of the first waltz?"

Hawk wasn't certain who stared harder: himself or Caroline.

"Oh, yes, yes, Mr. Rose. I would be honored."

"If I may have your dance card so you don't forget . . ."

"Oh, I shan't forget, but it would be nice to have your name upon my card." She slipped it off her wrist and watched, enthralled, as he penned his name on her dance card, then his engagement card before handing her card back to her. He slipped his card and the dance list into his jacket pocket.

"I'll have a word with you before the dance," Hawk said quietly.

Jeremy smiled at him, the smile of a gentleman accustomed to having his way. "I don't believe so."

"If you so much—"

"Hawk." He heard the chastisement in his wife's voice, felt her small hand biting into his arm. "Don't ruin everything."

He glanced back at her.

"Trust me," she'd said.

Nodding, he turned back to the new arrivals. "Thank you for coming," he forced himself to say.

"I'm sorry Kate's not here this evening," Jenny said, her voice low. "She began reading a new novel and simply couldn't tear herself away from it."

"She so loves her books," Louisa said.

"A bit too much I'm beginning to think."

He did not see Louisa signal, but she must have because the strains of the music indicating the first dance, a quadrille, began to play.

"You should honor your sister with the first dance," Louisa said. "I can see to greeting our guests."

He was more than ready to leave this obligation behind. He turned to his sister. "Miss Caroline, may I have the pleasure of this dance?"

Her face lit up as though by a thousand electric lights, and while he had yet to have electricity installed in his homes, he'd seen the electric lights becoming more and more accessible throughout London, but their brilliance paled when compared with the glow in Caroline's eyes.

"I would be honored, Your Grace."

He offered her his arm and thought perhaps, for a moment at least, all would be well.

Chapter 21

❧◦◦◦❧

"Will you please stop glaring?" Louisa demanded. "You will frighten away any other would-be dance partners with your fiercesome stare."

Hawk looked down on her, and Louisa fought not to cower under his harsh demeanor. He'd approached her as soon as he'd finished dancing with Caroline, right before the second dance—the first waltz of the evening—began and insisted she put aside her hostess duties and honor him with a dance.

And she had been honored, thinking he truly wanted to dance with her. Now, she realized she was an expedient partner and gave him an excuse to stay near Caroline's side as Jeremy Rose swept her over the dance floor. Hawk's steps were dictated not so much by the music as by Jeremy's ability to direct Caroline around the room.

"I don't trust him," he said.

"Why ever not?"

"You cannot deny he served as your champion."

"Much more so than my brother, I will admit, but in my eyes his actions make him admirable and increase his trustworthiness."

"For you, yes, but if he wishes to take revenge against me, there would be no better way than to hurt Caroline."

"You can't possibly think his nature is to wound an innocent woman."

He shook his head, and she could see the worry etched so clearly in his face. Would that he would give one ounce of that worry toward her. "He will not hurt her," she assured him.

"But still she will be hurt, when he returns her to Mother's side, and no other gentleman asks her to dance."

"When he returns her to your mother's side, I daresay Caroline's dance card will fill up very quickly."

"It will not happen."

"Would you care to make a wager?"

He narrowed his eyes. "What would we wager?"

"An hour of pleasure given to the winner, an hour of pleasure denied to the loser."

"That is a rather bold proposal. Are you in a position to make good on that wager?"

She knew what he was asking. Her courses had ended a few days ago, but she'd not said anything, because it was imperative to her plan nothing happen that might cause her to get pregnant. Yet she wanted one more night in his arms, one more night of passion, and he'd taught her ways to have pleasure without the peril of pregnancy.

"I am," she said quietly.

"So if Caroline's dance card does not fill, you will pleasure me and take none for yourself?"

She nodded, her stomach quivering.

He smiled confidently, the conqueror certain of conquering. "I accept the terms of the wager."

"You'll pleasure me as I ask and take none for yourself?" she repeated.

"Should I lose, which, unfortunately, I shall not."

"Oh, you shall lose, without a doubt. If you will recall, I'm the one who determined the guest list."

He cocked his head to the side as though thinking. "And what clever plan did you put into place?"

"Look around, Your Grace. You will see several mothers talking to their sons. Those mothers have daughters who are in attendance. Or you will see sisters speaking to their brothers, and I daresay those brothers care for their sisters' happiness as much as you care for yours. The daughters and sisters have one thing in common: They want no competition for Jeremy Rose. They cannot insist he ask them to dance, but they can encourage their sons and brothers to keep the lady who so quickly gained his attention otherwise occupied, so he might not have another opportunity to dance with her."

"You believe a man in line for a dukedom or an earldom will give attention to a lady who doesn't have a proper lineage?"

"I seriously doubt they will ask for her hand in marriage, but they will ask her to dance. Otherwise, they'll hear an earful on the way home, and it is, after all, a two-hour journey back to London."

She saw appreciation light his eyes, and for the first time since she'd suggested they have a ball, she saw the worry lift.

"You little minx."

Then he laughed joyously loud, and she felt her own jaw begin to ache with the strain of her smile. His laughter died, and he was no longer watching Jeremy's every step. He was watching her.

"You are diabolically clever," he said quietly, "manipulating our guests with such ease."

She feared he was going to reference her manipulation of him in the library, and she didn't want the conversation to turn to the night that had ruined both their dreams.

"I have known your sister but a short time, but I have come to care for her deeply, and I did not wish her first ball to be as disappointing for her as mine was for me."

"Your first ball was disappointing?"

She nodded. "I didn't have near the attention I had hoped."

"Does any woman?"

"Hopefully tonight Caroline shall."

"Are you certain everything is all right with Kate?" Louisa asked Jenny as they strolled through the garden. Upon her arrival, Jenny had instructed Louisa to keep her sixth dance free so they could take a turn about the garden and catch up on the latest news. It did not escape her notice that Jenny chose the very dance number that had led to Louisa's ruin.

Keeping a dance open was much more of a challenge for Jenny than for her. And more of a challenge for Caroline. Louisa could not have been more pleased to see Hawk's sister dancing every dance, radiant and happy. Even Hawk's mother had taken a turn about the dance floor with the Duke of Whitson.

"Kate is becoming more and more withdrawn of late. I don't understand her. Pass up an evening of dancing in order to read a book? It's not as though the book wouldn't be there once she returned home."

"She doesn't seem to embrace any of this as enthusiastically as you."

"She never has."

They walked in silence for several moments, before Jenny said, "Do you ever hear from your brother?"

"No, no, and at present I have no desire to. Perhaps in time I will forgive him, but for now the wounds are still too raw."

"I refuse to see him as well," Jenny said.

"Has he tried to call on you?" Louisa asked, surprised by his audacity.

Jenny stepped off the walk and brought Louisa into the shadows with her. "I had been meeting him in secret."

Louisa stared at her. "When was this?"

"During several of our outings . . . when you trusted I was going to straighten my hair."

"I can't believe you deceived me like that."

"I know. I feel absolutely awful about it. I enjoyed slipping away and being naughty. And he delivered passion so expertly. I miss it sometimes. But I feel in betraying you, he betrayed my confidence."

Louisa studied her in the shadows. "Your mother told you about our arrangement?"

"Yes, she did, and I'm all for it."

"Because you're feeling guilty?"

"Because it's what I want." She squeezed Louisa's hand. "Just be sure it's what you want."

"I have no doubts."

"You haven't told Hawkhurst, have you?"

"No, I planned to tell him tomorrow. He has enough to worry about this evening."

Besides, she feared he might not take the news well, and she wanted one last night, before she told him everything.

Louisa and Jenny were on their way back to

the manor when Louisa caught sight of the man standing outside a distant window, gazing into the ballroom. The pale light from the gaslit chandeliers and flickering candles she'd set on various tables around the room washed over him for only a second as he neared the window, then stepped back as though fearful of being discovered.

"I believe I'm going to take another turn about the garden," she said, as they neared the terrace.

"But the next dance will begin soon," Jenny said.

"My dance card is blank."

"Your husband might wish to dance with you."

He hadn't indicated he favored another dance, but she supposed there was always hope for it. "I won't be but a few more moments. Go on, now. I know your dance card isn't blank."

She waited until Jenny disappeared inside before cautiously making her way across the lawn, making certain none of the others out strolling took notice of her. Invisible, always invisible.

Even the man gazing into the ballroom didn't notice her, but she could see his face clearly now that she was closer. He'd not moved completely beyond the light, and she experienced such an ache in her heart watching him.

"Hello, Denby," she said softly.

He jerked back and spun around, guiltily, the look of a man caught pilfering the silver.

"Your Grace, I apologize for my spying. I simply

wanted to look at my flowers, ensure they did the dowager duchess proud."

She moved closer to the window, peered through pane. "I suspect two blossoms in particular caught your fancy."

"I assure you I give equal care to all my flowers."

She turned from the window. "If I may be so bold, Denby, I am well acquainted with the look in a father's eyes when he is watching his daughter with love."

"I assure you I have no idea what you're talking about. If I look upon Miss Caroline as though she were my daughter, it is only because of my long-standing association with this family."

"Of course, forgive me. I was presumptuous to think otherwise. Still, I do think Miss Caroline looks beautiful tonight."

"Yes, she does," he said quietly.

"And the duchess as well."

"She has always looked beautiful to me."

He took a step farther back into the shadows. "I would appreciate it if you would keep my rudeness at staring through the window between us. As I said, it was only my flowers I wished to check on."

"I shan't tell a soul." Reaching out, she squeezed his arm. "Enjoy the music, Denby, and the beauty of your flowers."

She left him there, not turning back to see if he did indeed leave or if he inched closer to the

window to watch for a fleeting moment what he
could only observe but never join.

She'd almost reached the terrace doorway when
Jeremy stepped outside. "Avoiding me?"

She smiled at him. "Of course not. As hostess,
I've been rather busy."

"You found time for my sister."

"Now I shall find time for you. Shall we go inside and dance?"

"I don't think I could survive another blistering
glare from your husband. Let's take a turn about
the garden."

She thought it silly suddenly to be nervous.
What would Hawk think if he should spy them
walking together? She could convince him it was
harmless. She was certain of it.

She and Jeremy walked along the lighted path.

"You haven't told him of your plans, have you?"
he asked.

"No."

"My mother is quite good at bullying people
into doing her bidding. Are you certain this is
what you want?"

"Yes."

"Has he been unkind to you then?"

"He has not treated me poorly, but I know he
regrets it was me who walked into the library
and not Jenny."

"And you? Do you regret that it was you who
walked into the library?"

Rather than answer his question with a lie in

order to appease him, she said, "You don't have to marry me if you don't want to."

"Too late. My mother has already bullied me into it. Marrying the daughter of an earl will make me the envy of New York, don't you know."

"And it will make your mother very happy."

"Indeed. And I do want her to be happy." They walked on in silence for several moments.

"She's dying," he said quietly.

Louisa touched his arm, stopping him. "Who?"

"Mother. Jenny and Kate don't know, but it's the reason she's so desperate to see them married."

"And you as well."

"Me as well."

"How long does she have?"

He shook his head. "A year or so. I only told you because I don't want you to judge her harshly. Her intentions are good—"

"But she could be paving roads to hell."

"Let's hope not, shall we."

She shook her head. Hell would be staying with Hawkhurst always knowing she was with him by default. Hawkhurst had not wanted her, but he'd settled for her out of obligation. If she'd learned one thing about him while being married to him, it was that he took his obligations seriously.

"I'm truly sorry about your mother," she said quietly.

"Thank you. Now, enough melancholy. I have decided to risk waltzing with you."

She laughed. He was kind and sweet. She would be happy with him.

Once she got over the heartbreak of leaving Hawkhurst.

"Oh, Hawk!" Caroline cried, rushing up to him the moment he and Louisa walked into the library after seeing the last of their guests' carriages rolling off into the night. She wound her arms around his neck and hugged him tightly. "Thank you! Thank you for giving me the most wonderful night of my life!"

Holding her close, he looked past her to his wife, who stood nearby, a soft smile on her face. "I believe it is Louisa who deserves all the credit."

Caroline released her hold on him, spun around to face Louisa, and hugged her as well. "Thank you."

"I took great delight in arranging everything."

"If I never attend another ball, I shall be forever content."

"I suspect you will be attending a good many other balls."

"I can't believe how well it went," his mother said, moving away from the fireplace.

"I noticed you dancing with Whitson," Hawk said, as he walked to the table and poured claret into four glasses.

"Yes, I'd forgotten what a charmer he is," his mother said.

And Hawk wondered if the man's charms would be enough to entice his mother into returning to London. He handed a glass to each of the ladies and lifted his. "I would like to make a toast. To Caroline and her successful introduction into Society, and to my lovely wife, who made it all come about so splendidly."

He took pleasure in watching Louisa blush as she sipped on her wine.

As far as balls went, theirs had been relatively small, with only fifty couples, but Louisa had kept true to her word, being extremely select in whom she invited. Those in attendance weren't easily scandalized, because most had experienced scandals in their own family. Except for the Roses, but then they weren't British, and that by default made them scandalous. He had a very clever wife: introduce his sister into Society by first presenting her to those who could not cast stones.

Little wonder she'd managed to acquire the position of chaperone. She was not easily intimidated. She was well acquainted with those of influence. She had a laugh that was music to his ears and a smile that dazzled. She'd made a wicked wager he couldn't wait to make good on.

Was it any wonder he adored her?

Dear God. That thought had his wine catching in his throat. He covered his mouth, choked, coughed, cleared his throat, coughed again, all the while his mother pounded his back.

"Are you all right?" his mother asked.

"Yes, I believe I'll switch to brandy." He returned to the table and poured himself a generous helping.

Caroline yawned. "I'm so tired, and yet I'm sure I shall be unable to sleep."

"Come along," his mother said. "I'll help you get ready for bed."

Caroline walked to the door, stopped, and turned back. "Midnight came and went, and I didn't turn into a pumpkin."

"I promised you wouldn't," Louisa said.

"Indeed you did. Again, thank you."

She walked out of the room, but his mother lingered a moment longer. "Yes, my dear, thank you, thank you for everything you've done for all of us."

He watched tears fill his wife's eyes. "You're welcome, Your Grace."

His mother finally left the room.

Hawk walked over to Louisa and lifted her into his arms. She released a small squeal as she wound her arms around his neck.

"I thought they would never leave," he said. "I have a wager to pay."

He would not allow her to touch him. Louisa had not counted on that.

"The wager was to pleasure me, and I take pleasure in touching you," she told him.

"The wager was also that I be denied pleasure. I take pleasure in your touching me, so therefore, you cannot."

"Hawk—"

"Perhaps later," he said in a low provocative voice.

He did remove his clothes after removing all

of hers, and simply gazing on his magnificent, sculpted form brought her pleasure, but he managed for a good bit of the time to remain beyond her reach, giving an inordinate amount of attention to her ankles, her calves, the dimples on her backside, her back. He used some sort of fragrant oil—he wouldn't reveal where he'd obtained it— that made his large hands slick and when he ran them over her skin, her body melted further with each caress.

Sometimes she'd hear him groan low in his throat as though running his hands along her back brought him as much pleasure as it brought her. Perhaps, indeed, it was impossible to give pleasure absolutely without receiving at least a small bit in return.

What a silly wager she'd made, because it was pure torture to have him touching her when she couldn't touch him. And once his hands had their way with her, his mouth skillfully followed. Slowly, no rush, no hurry. His teeth nipping gently at her delicate skin, then his tongue slowly caressing as though in apology.

When he rolled her onto her back and did move up her body to bestow a long, lingering kiss, he held her wrists in one large hand above her head, while his other hand stroked and caressed her intimately. She writhed beneath him, desperate to be freed, desperate to be held, wanting release, but wanting to remain on the cusp forever. Anything to hold his attention, to keep him near. Forever and a day. Forever and a night.

He released his hold on her wrists. She went to touch him, desperate to feel his skin beneath her hands. He quickly grabbed them and gave her a pointed look. "Not yet."

"When? You were supposed to pleasure me, not torture me."

He gave her a knowing smile. "It is a fine line between pleasure and torture."

"But you were supposed to do as I instructed."

"And I will. As soon as I'm finished doing as I please."

Slowly, so slowly, as though he were memorizing the feel of every muscle, every bone from her fingers to her toes, he worked the scented oil into her flesh until she didn't know if she'd have the strength to lift her arms if she had to. She was lethargic, so terribly lethargic that when he placed his hands between her thighs and parted them, she did not object. And when he used his tongue to stroke her with an incredible intimacy, she could do little more than gasp.

"Now," he rasped, "now, you may touch me."

But all she could reach was his head, his shoulders as he worked his magic, until she was no longer relaxed, until her body was thrumming with desire, tightening with passion reborn.

"Oh, my word," she croaked. "Oh, Hawk!"

Her back came off the bed as she clutched him to her and quite simply shattered into a thousand bits of pleasure.

* * *

Stretched out on his side, raised on his elbow, Hawk continued to stroke his wife, trailing his finger beneath her breasts. He was certain he'd never seen a woman who looked more gloriously pleasured.

"I should do that to you," she said, languidly.

"Perhaps later. You should sleep well now. You've been such a busy girl of late."

A corner of her mouth quirked up. "You have no idea. I feel almost drunk. I can hardly move."

He leaned down and kissed her temple. "Go to sleep."

With a contented sigh, she rolled on to her side, nestled her head against his shoulder, and draped her arm over his stomach. He lay there for a long while, staring at the canopy and listening to her soft, gentle breathing, knowing he would never grow tired of her.

"I'll pleasure you when I wake up," she murmured.

He said nothing as she drifted off to sleep. But he wouldn't be there when she awoke.

She deserved a man far better than he.

For too many years he'd been angry at his mother, living in her isolated world, her pleasure her garden. He'd thought he was so different, living in the exciting and bustling city of London. But he was no different. He was still a recluse; his haven wine and women.

Louisa had courageously carved a place for herself in the world. She had defied tradition, had not settled for living a life of quiet desperation.

She deserved a husband who had the courage to go forth as she had. In a few hours, he would leave for London and take his first step toward becoming that man.

Chapter 22

As the coach journeyed back to Selwyn Manor, Hawk knew a sense of satisfaction he'd never before realized. Even if nothing came of his actions, he would take gratification in knowing he'd done *something*.

This afternoon he'd include Louisa in other plans, and he'd work with her to help bring to fruition her desire again to serve as a social chaperone. Together they could work to get their estates back into order, could get Caroline to London and find her a suitable husband.

He suddenly felt quite invincible. The future held promise, and he could hardly wait to share with Louisa what he'd done.

As the coach neared the manor, he spotted a black coach in the drive. Nothing ornamental

353

about it told him to whom it belonged. It was a bit early for a gentleman caller for Caroline, but it was the only logical explanation. She'd obviously caught someone's eye the evening before.

He descended from his own coach. The breeze brought Caroline's laughter to him. He walked around to the side of the house. She did indeed have a gentleman caller: Jeremy Rose.

They were on the tennis lawn, volleying the ball back and forth. He watched as Jeremy missed the serve, then laughed.

"I believe you have soundly beat me yet again, Miss Selwyn!" he called.

"You are far too easy," she said, walking toward the net. She must have spotted Hawk, because she waved her hand. "Hawk. Look who's come to call."

He headed toward them, only to have his mother approach. Obviously she'd been watching them. He wondered where Louisa was. She'd promised never to let Caroline out of her sight when gentlemen were near. He hadn't planned his first words to her this day to be a chastisement for not properly overseeing the situation.

"I'm going to take Caroline farther into the garden," his mother said.

"A splendid idea," Hawk said.

He waited until Caroline had said good-bye to Rose before approaching the young man, who was hitting his racket against the palm of his hand. Hawk decided pleasantries were not in order, that he needed to get straight to the crux of the matter.

"My sister . . . she is not the daughter of my father."

Rose's eyes widened. "I went to Yale, Your Grace. I'm very good at ciphering and deducing."

"Your mother will not approve of your interest in her. She would no doubt cut you off if this relationship led to anything of a permanent nature."

"And that would concern me because . . ."

"I have not the means to support you in the manner to which you are accustomed to living. You would, of course, be welcome to live on one of my estates—"

Rose laughed. The man actually had the audacity to laugh.

"I do not see the humor in this situation," Hawk said.

"No, I suppose you don't. You mistake my purpose in being here. I was playing tennis with your delightful sister to keep from getting bored. I did not actually come to visit her. I came to take your wife back to London."

The door to the bedchamber opened with a crash, the knob banging into the wall.

Louisa jumped back from the trunk she'd been packing and stared at her husband. He was fearsome in his fury. It fairly shimmered through the room.

"Rose says he's come to take you back to London. Care to explain?" he ground out.

Louisa swallowed hard. "I'd planned to explain this morning, but you weren't here when I awoke."

"I'm here now."

"So I see."

"Why is he taking you to London, and why are you packing?"

She closed the lid on her trunk. "I don't want you to be cross."

"It's a bit late for that."

"Yes, I see that as well." She wrung her hands. "I haven't been entirely honest of late."

"For God's sake, Louisa, don't be an old chest with a rusty lock. This would all go much easier if you would simply state what needs to be stated."

At any other time she might have smiled at his using her poor metaphor, but all she felt like doing at this moment was weeping. She took a deep breath. "After I'd sent out invitations to the ball, Mrs. Rose came to visit. It was too late to cancel the ball, but the more I knew I could make it a success, I wanted to make it a success, because I felt so responsible for your present situation, and I thought a successful ball would make it up somehow, a bit at least."

"I've yet to hear the key turning the lock and have no clue as to what you're rambling about."

"Mrs. Rose told me that if I discovered I was not with child, she would help me acquire an annulment, and would allow Jenny to marry you."

She watched his jaw tighten, a muscle in his cheek jump.

"Does Jenny know?" he asked pointedly.

"Yes."

"So I'm the last to know?"

"Yes."

"And what of your reputation?"

"Jeremy has offered to marry me and take me to America. My reputation will not follow me there."

"And this is what you want?"

"Yes." *Only because I know it is what you secretly want.*

She thought of the times he'd reminded her that if only she'd not come into the library, his life would be so very different. He would have the funds he needed to repair his estates, the funds he needed to protect Caroline and his mother, the two most important women in his life.

Each second he glared at her in silence was a slice from her heart.

"Then go with my blessing," he finally said, and stormed from the room.

Louisa dropped down onto the trunk, shaking uncontrollably. Saying yes to his final question had nearly destroyed her. But she was right to leave. She knew that now. It was Jenny he wanted. It had always been Jenny.

Hawk filled the glass to the brim with brandy, downed it with one long swallow, and filled it again.

Pragmatic, practical Louisa was right. As always she was damned right. There was little reason for them to remain married. She was not with child; they had done nothing of late to put her at risk of being with child. An annulment would raise fewer eyebrows than a divorce. In America, no one would care about the scandal she'd created here.

He downed the brandy and poured more.

He would finally acquire the woman he'd set his sights on originally: Jenny Rose.

A lucrative settlement would make life easier for them all. Caroline would have many suitors.

He tossed back the brandy and poured more.

He could quickly rebuild his estates. He could make life easier for his heir.

So why in God's name did he feel so bloody awful? Why did he feel as though his heart had been ripped from his chest? Why did he feel bereft, with a need to weep, a need to howl like a wounded animal?

He heard the rapid footsteps. He turned with hope beginning to unfold like the petals on a rose. She'd changed her mind.

But it was his mother who entered the library. "Louisa asked Denby to help cart her trunks to Jeremy Rose's coach."

He turned back to the bottle, refilled his glass, and drank its contents. "We're having the marriage annulled. She's leaving."

"Is this what you want?"

"It does not matter what I want. Her happiness comes above all else."

"And why should her happiness be so damned important?"

He swung around. "Because I love her above all else!" He shook his head, fighting back the bitter tears. Turning from her, he downed more brandy.

"Then go after her," his mother said.

He glared over her shoulder. "What would you have me do? Hoist her over my shoulder? Lock her in a tower?"

His mother shook her head. "I would have you not be so proud. I would have you find the courage to go after what you want. I know what it is to live every day regretting that I had far too much pride and too little courage to say yes when Caroline's father asked me eighteen years ago to marry him. But I was a duchess, my son was a duke, and he was but a gardener."

Hawk stared at her, stunned. "Denby is her father?"

Tears filled her eyes. "I let my daughter be born out of wedlock, born in shame, I placed a terrible burden upon my son, because I refused to marry a man whom I feared Society would consider to be beneath me, to be unworthy when it was I who was unworthy. I am faced with that bitter truth every day as his love and loyalty have never waned."

He took a step toward her, his greatest fear on the tip of tongue. "Is he my father as well?"

Her eyes widened with shock. "No, no, your father was the fourth Duke of Hawkhurst. I swear to you. I remained faithful to him until the end."

He bowed his head with the weight of doubt lifted from his shoulders.

He felt her fingers in his hair. "Oh, my dear son, all these years—"

"I was afraid I was not the true duke. That I was tainted."

Tears washed down her face. "I have done so poorly by my children. Forgive me. I beg of you, forgive me." She touched his cheek. "Do not let her go if you truly love her."

Louisa sat in the carriage, staring at the manor house. She was no good with good-byes, hadn't been since she'd said good-bye to her mother. She could hardly do them without a flood of tears, and so she'd simply left a letter in the duchess's bedchamber, as well as in Caroline's.

"We'll leave when you're ready," Jeremy said.

"I've grown rather fond of the drafty old place."

"I'll purchase you a drafty old place if that will make you happy."

She looked at him. "Money makes everything so much easier, doesn't it?"

Slowly, he shook his head. "No, not really. Do you love him, Louisa?"

"I'm not what he needs. What if I'm not what you need?"

Before he could answer, she heard the rush of heavy footsteps on the drive, looked out the window, and saw Hawk running toward her. "Something must be terribly wrong." She moved to open the door. "Let me see what's amiss. I won't be but a moment."

Not waiting for his response, in a most unlady-like manner, she scrambled out of the carriage as Hawk, breathing harshly, stumbled to a stop be-fore her.

"Denby is Caroline's father," he said.

She nodded, wondering at his urgency to tell her something that was no longer her concern. "I thought as much."

She watched as he swallowed. "I feared he was mine as well. I knew my mother's marriage was not a love match, and I feared she might have been unfaithful to my father. That I was not the true heir, but she assures me that is not the case. She didn't marry Denby because she considered him beneath her. I cannot imagine the torment of marrying a woman who doesn't love you enough, who doesn't believe in you."

He bowed his head, his breathing becoming less harsh. "I wasn't in bed when you awoke this morning because I went to London." He lifted his dark gaze to hers, a gaze she thought she would forever see whenever she closed her eyes. "I had decided a woman as courageous as you should have a husband who did not live in the shadows."

"But you don't—"

"I do, Louisa. I'm no different from my mother. What have I truly accomplished with my life? The only thing of any value I have truly done was to marry you. You have inspired me. This morning I took my manuscript to a publisher."

Her heart expanded to such a degree that she

could almost feel it pressed against her ribs. "What did they say?"

He shook his head. "I dropped it over the transom. I'd heard once Dickens simply did that, and so I thought to give it a try. I don't know if anything will come of it, but I decided you were right. Just as you were right about Caroline's introduction into Society: It is better to know than to spend one's life always wondering."

She squeezed his hand. "I'm so glad you did it. If it is published, I shall purchase the first copy."

"If it is purchased I shall gift you with a copy."

"Even if you give me a copy, I shall want the joy of purchasing one."

He held her gaze, and she watched as he swallowed. "Do you love him?" he asked in a low voice. "Do you love Jeremy Rose?"

"I'm quite fond of him."

He nodded as though uncertain what to say next.

"I shall not marry Jenny," he finally said.

She stared at him, stupefied. "But it is arranged—"

"It was not arranged by me, and it is not what I want."

"Not what you want? It was Jenny you thought was in the library, Jenny whom you schemed to obtain."

"I swear to you that from the moment you agreed to become my wife, I have never regretted a moment I have had with you.

"If you truly love Jeremy Rose and wish to be his wife, then I have done you a disservice more terrible than I realized, and you may leave with no guilt or regrets and know I will not object to an annulment. I shall wish you the best and pray for your fervent happiness.

"But if you do not love him, or if you only suspect you might love him and are not entirely sure, then I beg of you not to leave, I beg of you to stay and to give me the opportunity to entice you into falling in love with me.

"If the only affection you can ever hold for me is no larger than the tip of your pinky, it shall be more enough."

"And if it is my entire heart?"

"Then I beg you, do not go."

She felt the tears burning her eyes. "I want only what is best for you."

"That settles it then. You're staying."

Before she could respond, he'd lifted her into his arms and swung around. "Rose, she's staying with me."

Jeremy was gazing out the carriage window.

"I thought she might be."

"Oh, Jeremy, I'm so frightfully sorry," Louisa said.

"Don't be. I wasn't really keen on living in an old drafty manor. I'll break the news to Mother."

"She'll be furious, but tell her not to worry. Assure her I'll find suitable husbands for Kate and Jenny. I shall find a wife for you as well.

And I shan't charge you a fee!" she called out, as Hawk began striding toward the manor.

"He's been so kind it's rude of us to simply walk away. I should say a bit more to him."

"You've said more than enough, I assure you," Hawk said. "Denby!"

Louisa saw the gardener moving away from the roses he'd been pruning.

"Yes, Your Grace?"

"My duchess is staying. Please assist with getting her trunks back into the house. And when you're finished, ask my mother for her hand in marriage and keep asking until she gives it."

"Yes, Your Grace."

"Do you think she'll say yes this time?" Louisa asked.

"She damned well better. There is no greater pleasure in life than having at your side the one you love."

"I thought you didn't believe in love."

"*That*, darling, was before I came to know you."

Sated and content, languid, and barely able to move from the thorough loving she'd just received—and given—Louisa lay nestled against her husband's side. He'd carried her straightaway to his bedchamber and proceeded to prove, once again, that when it came to passion, he was exceptionally skilled.

"Dear God, but you are so beautiful."

"Not like Jenny," she murmured.

He lifted his head, looked down on her, and she did wish she'd kept her thoughts to herself.

"To me you are beautiful. Ask me the color of Jenny's eyes or the shape of her mouth, and I could not tell you. But your eyes I see in all things blue."

Reaching up, she combed her fingers through his hair. "You took my advice and began reading poetry."

"No. You deserve words that have been uttered to no other."

She felt tears sting her eyes. "For so long, I have vastly misjudged you."

"Considering your original opinion of me, I could not ask for a kinder compliment."

He lay back down, drawing her up against his side. "You said something earlier that is only just now becoming clear in my mind," he murmured, as he pressed his lips to the top of her head where it was nestled in the crook of his shoulder. "You said it was Jenny I thought was in the library."

She tilted her head back. He was looking down on her, his eyes dark as they met her gaze. "Well, yes. Hawk, I am fully aware you thought you were compromising Jenny, and you married me to spare my reputation—"

She released a small squeak as he rolled them both over until she was lying beneath him, his body raised up above her, his dark eyes searching, the knuckles of one hand grazing her cheek tenderly.

"Louisa, do you honestly believe I did not know who was in the library with me?"

"You were expecting her, and it was dark—"

He lowered his head, and she heard him inhale deeply. "I would know your scent anywhere."

He pressed a kiss to the sensitive spot below her ear. "I would know the softness of your cheek against my fingers, the press of your small body against mine.

"You think I didn't realize I had to dip my head a quarter of an inch more in order to press my lips to yours?"

Her heart was pounding so hard she barely heard what he said.

"You think I didn't recognize your voice when you spoke my name?"

"It was but a whisper."

"That's all I needed. A whisper." He kissed the column of her throat.

"A scent." He kissed behind her ear again.

"A kiss." He covered her mouth with his, his tongue imploring her lips to part. Cradling her face with his large hands, he angled her head so he could deepen the kiss.

He lifted his gaze to hers. "I knew full well who was in that room with me. I was well aware of the risk I was taking. But I could no more resist you then than I could cease to breathe.

" 'I shall take her once,' I thought, 'and be done with her.' And each time I have you I only want you more. When I wake up, I watch you sleep, and a fierce possessiveness I have never experienced with any other woman takes hold of me. You are mine.

"Do I wish I had the financial settlement that would have followed Jenny Rose to the altar? I cannot deny it would have made various aspects of life easier. Do I wish she were in my bed? Do I wish she were the one I wake up next to in the morning, the one whose breathing lulls me into slumber at night? Do I wish it were she who pricks my temper and challenges me at every turn? I absolutely do not.

"Never doubt, for one second, that I knew full well who was with me in the library."

"I don't understand. If you knew, then why—"

He pressed his thumb against her lips, silencing her words. "Because you were the one woman with whom I knew I would never grow bored. I do not know when I first realized that I loved you—"

"You love me?"

"With everything I have." He smiled sadly. "As little as that is."

Smiling wickedly, she reached down and wrapped her hand around him. "My dear husband, I think you are unaware of exactly how much you have to offer."

Sometime later, after he'd again given her everything, she lay snuggled against his side.

"Hawk?"

"Mmm?"

"Jenny and Kate are always arguing about which comes first, passion or love."

"And?"

"So which do you think comes first?"

"In our case, sweetheart, I suspect they arrived at the same time."

Epilogue

"I can't believe you kept the box all these years," the dowager duchess said, as they—she, Hawk, Caroline, and Louisa—sat in the drawing room of the London residence. They'd just returned from an evening at the opera.

"I wanted it available to you in case you ever did return to London," Hawk said, his hand stretched out along the back of the couch, his fingers toying with strands of Louisa's hair.

Although she always wore her hair up, she also always left strands dangling down, because it ensured that he constantly touched her.

"It was so frightfully exciting," Caroline said, sitting on a smaller sofa beside her mother. "I daresay there is not a thing about London that I have yet to love." She looked at Louisa. "You are

369

going to have a party to celebrate the book coming out, aren't you?"

"Of course," Louisa said. "But that won't be for a while yet."

Three of Hawk's faerie stories were going to be published. They would include pictures Louisa had drawn. Hawk had been correct when he said they'd never become rich from his writings, but it was a start.

And Louisa was certain once she finished her obligations to the Rose family—Mrs. Rose was insisting the new duchess find suitable husbands for her daughters and a wife for her son—she would be able to secure other positions. As she'd once told Hawk, his title was currency. It seemed so was hers.

Louisa couldn't be happier, although on occasion thoughts of Denby would sadden her. She didn't understand Hawk's mother's refusal to marry the gardener, but the man seemed to accept without rancor that he'd never take her to wife.

Sometime later, she stood out on the terrace, looking off into the night. She heard her husband come up behind her. He slipped his arms around her and pressed a kiss to the nape of her neck.

"Come to bed," he whispered in a voice that promised pleasure.

"In a moment."

He drew her closer against him. "Are you thinking of your brother?"

She nodded.

"One day he'll come ask for your forgiveness, but not until he's finished fighting his own demons."

"I will forgive him in a heartbeat." She turned around and wound her arms around his neck. "Because in a strange way, he is responsible for my happiness. His actions ensured that I marry you."

"Are you happy?"

"Incredibly."

"At the opera I noticed you took the Duke of Blackburn aside."

"Yes, I was making an inquiry regarding his oldest son."

"For Jenny?"

"Yes."

"Mmm."

She narrowed her eyes at him. "And what, pray tell, is wrong with the son who will one day become a duke?"

"An addiction to garlic."

She laughed. "I don't believe you."

" 'Tis true. I spoke with him at the club just last week. His breath was overpowering."

"Keep finding fault with every man I consider for Jenny, and I'll begin to think you have an interest in her."

"Never. But it is my responsibility in this chaperone endeavor of yours to ensure you make no errors in judgment."

"Then tell me what you know about the Duke of Hawkhurst."

He lifted her into his arms. "The man is perfection—"

She giggled.

"Passionate."

She couldn't deny the truth of those words. With a sigh she snuggled her head against his shoulder as he carried her into the house.

"And they say he is madly in love with his wife," Hawk finished.

"Do they also say she is madly in love with him?"

He started up the stairs. "Indeed they do."

Author's Note

~~⁓◯◯⁓~~

Dear Readers: As a writer, I know most have an uncanny ability to weave fact and fiction so that it is often difficult to distinguish between the two. As a reader myself, when I read a story, I wonder what is truly fact, what is fiction.

Social chaperones did indeed exist, and while they were to keep a watchful eye, their main purpose was to evaluate the rank and character of the gentlemen who were giving attention to the ladies under their supervision.

Titled ladies chaperoning wealthy American heiresses during the last twenty years of the nineteenth century is a fact. Many discreetly advertised their services in *The Times* or in ladies' magazines.

By the 1880s young ladies were insisting on

more freedom, and chaperones were seldom required when they participated in outdoor events.

The Rational Dress Society, begun by Viscountess Haberton and Mrs. King, did indeed exist and put forth the notion that the weight of women's clothing should be limited to no more than seven pounds.

Smaller, more intimate balls that did not include dinner and ended at midnight were referred to as Cinderella dances or balls.

I hope you enjoyed Louisa and Hawk's story. I'm looking forward to bringing you Kate and Falconridge's story next.

Sources:
Not Without a Chaperone by Cecil Porter
Daily Life in Victorian England by Sally Mitchell

DISCOVER CONTEMPORARY ROMANCES *at their*
SIZZLING HOT BEST FROM AVON BOOKS